HIS LAST

HIS LAST BOW

by SIR ARTHUR CONAN DOYLE

Sir Arthur Conan Doyle

HIS LAST BOW

Some Reminiscences of Sherlock Holmes

With an Introduction by
JULIAN SYMONS

LEOPARD

This edition published in 1996 by
Leopard, a division of Random House UK Ltd,
20 Vauxhall Bridge Road, London SW1V 2SA

His Last Bow first published
in 1917 by John Murray

ISBN 0 7529 0388 8

Printed and bound in Great Britain by
Mackays of Chatham PLC, Chatham, Kent

Contents

Introduction

When, at the end of *The Memoirs*, Conan Doyle had sent Sherlock Holmes to his death over the Reichenbach Falls, he wrote of his relief and pleasure to a friend. 'I have had such an overdose of him that I feel towards him as I do towards *pâté de foie gras*, of which I once ate too much, so that the name of it gives me a sickly feeling to this day.' Holmes returned, as we know, but one is bound to agree with the view that he was never quite the same man afterwards. Almost every pre-Reichenbach story is of the finest vintage, to be savoured again and again; post-Reichenbach is more variable. But each Holmes collection contains its particular felicities, and *His Last Bow*, which was first published as a book in 1917, is no exception.

In it, for instance, there is the only official detective positively praised by Holmes, a man who seems to be almost his equal in deductive capacity. Inspector Baynes, of the Surrey Constabulary, appears only in 'The Adventure of Wisteria Lodge', but Holmes immediately appreciates his calibre. 'Your powers, if I may say so without offence, seem superior to your opportunities', he says, and although Baynes modestly agrees that he stagnates in the provinces, it turns out that he was approaching the same conclusion about the case as Holmes. At the end of the story Baynes is awarded the accolade of Holmes's hand upon his shoulder, and the words: 'You will rise high in your profession.' It is a pity that we have no record of his later career.

Holmes was exceeded in mental acuity only by his brother Mycroft, and in 'The Bruce-Partington Plans' Mycroft makes one of his two appearances in the saga, actually moving out of a customary daily circuit between his Pall Mall lodgings, the Diogenes Club opposite and Whitehall, to visit Baker Street. ('It is as if you met a tram-car coming down a country lane.') He is not quite in the sparkling form he showed in 'The Greek Interpreter', but it is a pleasure to meet him again. It is always a pleasure, too, to find Watson playing detective, as he does in one of these stories, immensely pleased with his own deductions, not bothering to answer Holmes's apparently facetious telegram asking for a description of Dr Shlessinger's left ear, and being finally put down by his friend's scornful rebuke. 'Well, Watson, a very pretty hash you have made of it.'

It is on the relationship of Holmes and Watson that the stories rest, for their first Victorian public and for us. Their fascination springs from the fact that they represent two parts of Doyle's own personality. In appearance Doyle resembled Watson, and many of his views were Watson's too. Watson-Doyle was a bluff Imperialist extrovert, whose opinions on art, politics and the proper ordering of society were conventional to the verge of philistinism. But Holmes-Doyle occupied the same skin as Watson-Doyle, and was a very different person. It was Holmes-Doyle who drew up the petition for Roger Casement's reprieve. Many liberals refused to sign it on moral grounds, but Holmes-Doyle did not flinch when shown the Black Diaries revealing Casement's homosexuality. It was Holmes-Doyle also who fought for years to prove the innocence of Oscar Slater, even though he detested the man he helped to free from prison.

Watson and Holmes together made up a double image of the conventional and the eccentric, the law-keeper and the law-breaker. The instant attraction held by the short stories for their Victorian audience from their appearance in 1891 was that they offered the chance of virtuous but outrageous excitement to readers whose lives were generally stodgy. The vast majority of Victorians and Edwardians were law-keepers. They respected the law because it was a powerful buttress for the support of bourgeois English society, which, at the end of the nineteenth century and the beginning of the twentieth, was thought to be threatened by the activities of the anarchists who assassinated McKinley in America and Carnot in France. Anarchism held a fascination for the respectable British, reflected in the way that the Siege of Sidney Street was instantly taken into the national folklore. Holmes was not an anarchist but he was a law-breaker, and such a figure could be admired if he was himself congenial. Hence the immense success of Raffles, the gentleman cracksman invented by Conan Doyle's brother-in-law E. W. Hornung. Raffles made his living by burglary, but his audience excused and loved him because he remained a gentleman.

Doyle did not approve of Raffles, saying severely to Hornung, 'You must not make the criminal into a hero.' Holmes of course is not a criminal, but he often engages in illegal activities, and he is a man outside ordinary society, a misanthrope, an emotionless reasoning and observing machine, and, when we first meet him, a drug-addict. The difference between the Victorian attitude to drug-taking and our own is shown by the casualness with which we are introduced to a Holmes who has been on three cocaine injections a day for months. Watson-Doyle regards this as regrettable rather than morally reprehensible. This early Holmes also showed a deep distaste, verging on contempt, for many human beings, and was immune to the charms of women. 'He never spoke of the softer passions, save with a gibe and a sneer ... For the trained reasoner to admit such intrusions into his own delicate and finely adjusted temperament was to introduce a distracting factor which might throw a doubt upon all his mental results.' Holmes was not exactly a Nietzschean Superman (Watson-Doyle thought that Nietzsche's philosophy was founded upon lunacy), but he was emphatically a Superior Man. It was comforting to have a man like that on the side of the right people, and he could be forgiven for breaking the law occasionally.

That quotation about the softer passions is from the very first

short story, 'A Scandal in Bohemia', and as time went on, the
portrait of Holmes was made much less harsh. It proved that he
had turned to cocaine as a protest against the monotony of
existence, and with Watson beside him and a case to work on,
he was satisfied by pipe tobacco. The ignorance about the Solar
System that he displayed early on does not seem to have lasted,
and Watson was obviously wrong in putting 'nil' against
Holmes's knowledge of literature, philosophy and astronomy in
the chart he drew up soon after their first meeting in *A Study
in Scarlet*. The man then totally ignorant of literature was able
later to quote Goethe, and to compare Richter and Carlyle. It
would have been impossible for the Superior Man to have
married, and Irene Adler of that first short story remained *the*
woman, but the later Holmes often talks tenderly about the
softer passions, particularly about a mother's love for her child.
And in spite of occasional acerbities, Holmes's affection for
Watson is so great that it embraces even his occasional stupidity
and literalness. Watson is, as Holmes says on the last page of this
book after a moment of Watsonic literalness, the one fixed
point in a changing age. In one of the stories here, 'The Devil's
Foot', Holmes apologizes to his friend for having risked his
life, and Watson answers with some emotion, because 'I had
never seen so much of Holmes's heart before'. The affection is
always apparent, even though Holmes was never able to bring
himself to call his friend by anything but a surname. Watson
reciprocated. It would hardly have done, after all, for a Superior
Man to have been on Christian name terms with anybody.

In spite of Holmes's apology to Watson about leading him
into danger, he was always prepared to ask his friend to engage
in some joint illegal activity. 'My dear fellow, you shall keep
watch in the street. I'll do the criminal part,' he says in 'The
Bruce-Partington Plans'. He is not always so considerate, and
indeed in this very story he has already given Watson the job
of bringing round to him a jemmy, a dark lantern, a chisel and
a revolver. A brisk little breaking and entering in 'Wisteria

Lodge' is justified by Holmes on the ground that a woman may be in danger of her life. 'If the law can do nothing we must take the risk ourselves.' Asked to produce his warrant in the affair of Lady Frances Carfax, Holmes responds by half drawing a revolver and cheerfully remarking, in the face of Holy Peters's description of him as a common burglar, that his companion also is a dangerous ruffian. It is plain that Watson thoroughly enjoys these excursions into illegal territory, strong in the knowledge that the law is being broken for the sake of virtue. He can never have felt this more fervently than when, in the title story, he helps to walk Von Bork down the garden walk of his long, low house by the sea, after Holmes has tricked the German spy. Useless for Von Bork to protest that 'the whole proceeding is absolutely illegal and outrageous': Watson, like Holmes, knows that he is acting for a higher good.

Any idea that *His Last Bow* is exceptional in showing Holmes's disregard for the law would be wrong. There are a dozen cases in which Holmes dispenses his personal idea of justice, most notably in 'Charles Augustus Milverton', when the friends calmly decide not to reveal the identity of the woman who fires 'barrel after barrel' of her revolver into the body of the blackmailer, and then grinds her heel into his face. Before Holmes, detectives in fiction had generally stayed within the law, but almost every Superior Man or Great Detective since then has bent the law a little or broken it outright. Few went so far as Philo Vance, who murdered a murderer by switching the poisoned drink meant for himself, but from Father Brown to Lord Peter Wimsey, Great Detectives acted as a final court of appeal, administering justice when the law faltered. Perhaps it is a good thing that there are fewer Great Detectives about nowadays.

Of course, the identification of readers with Holmes as Superior Man and law-giver is unconscious. It was for other reasons that my son and daughter read and loved the stories when they were teenagers. They include the masterly evocation of a sinister London, and an even more sinister smiling country-side, which in modern teenage eyes was the harmless suburban-ized Surrey or Kent; the strong romantic feeling present in many stories; and the stories themselves, not every one mech-anically perfect in its plotting, but almost all of them interesting as tales, in a way that few short detective stories are interesting. It is Doyle's skill as a story-teller, combined with the ability to bring those two strands of his own character so memorably to life in Holmes and Watson, that makes successive generations go on reading.

JULIAN SYMONS

1974

Preface

The friends of Mr Sherlock Holmes will be glad to learn that he is still alive and well, though somewhat crippled by occasional attacks of rheumatism. He has, for many years, lived in a small farm upon the Downs five miles from Eastbourne, where his time is divided between philosophy and agriculture. During this period of rest he has refused the most princely offers to take up various cases, having determined that his retirement was a permanent one. The approach of the German war caused him, however, to lay his remarkable combination of intellectual and practical activity at the disposal of the Government, with historical results which are recounted in *His Last Bow*. Several previous experiences which have lain long in my portfolio, have been added to *His Last Bow* so as to complete the volume.

JOHN H. WATSON, M.D.

The Adventure of Wisteria Lodge

I – *The Singular Experience of Mr John Scott Eccles*

I find it recorded in my notebook that it was a bleak and windy day towards the end of March in the year 1892. Holmes had received a telegram whilst we sat at our lunch, and he had scribbled a reply. He made no remark, but the matter remained in his thoughts, for he stood in front of the fire afterwards with a thoughtful face, smoking his pipe, and casting an occasional glance at the message. Suddenly he turned upon me with a mischievous twinkle in his eyes.

'I suppose, Watson, we must look upon you as a man of letters,' said he. 'How do you define the word "grotesque"?'

'Strange – remarkable,' I suggested.

He shook his head at my definition.

'There is surely something more than that,' said he; 'some underlying suggestion of the tragic and the terrible. If you cast your mind back to some of those narratives with which you have afflicted a long-suffering public, you will recognize how often the grotesque has deepened into the criminal. Think of that little affair of the red-headed men. That was grotesque enough in the outset, and yet it ended in a desperate attempt at robbery. Or, again, there was that most grotesque affair of the five orange pips, which led straight to a murderous conspiracy. The word puts me on the alert.'

'Have you it there?' I asked.

He read the telegram aloud.

'"Have just had most incredible and grotesque experience. May I consult you? – Scott Eccles, Post Office, Charing Cross."'

'Man or woman?' I asked.

'Oh, man, of course. No woman would ever send a reply-paid telegram. She would have come.'

'Will you see him?'

'My dear Watson, you know how bored I have been since we locked up Colonel Carruthers. My mind is like a racing engine, tearing itself to pieces because it is not connected up with the work for which it was built. Life is commonplace, the papers are sterile; audacity and romance seem to have passed for ever from the criminal world. Can you ask me, then, whether I am ready to look into any new problem, however trivial it may prove? But here, unless I am mistaken, is our client.'

A measured step was heard upon the stairs, and a moment later a stout, tall, grey-whiskered and solemnly respectable person was ushered into the room. His life history was written in his heavy features and pompous manner. From his spats to his gold-rimmed spectacles he was a Conservative, a Churchman, a good citizen, orthodox and conventional to the last degree. But some amazing experience had disturbed his native composure and left its traces in his bristling hair, his flushed, angry cheeks, and his flurried, excited manner. He plunged instantly into his business.

'I have had a most singular and unpleasant experience, Mr Holmes,' said he. 'Never in my life have I been placed in such a situation. It is most improper – most outrageous. I must insist upon some explanation.' He swelled and puffed in his anger.

'Pray sit down, Mr Scott Eccles,' said Holmes, in a soothing voice. 'May I ask, in the first place, why you came to me at all?'

'Well, sir, it did not appear to be a matter which concerned the police, and yet, when you have heard the facts, you must admit that I could not leave it where it was. Private detectives are a class with whom I have absolutely no sympathy, but none the less, having heard your name——'

'Quite so. But, in the second place, why did you not come at once?'

'What do you mean?'

Holmes glanced at his watch.

'It is a quarter past two,' he said. 'Your telegram was dispatched about one. But no one can glance at your toilet and attire without seeing that your disturbance dates from the moment of your waking.'

Our client smoothed down his unbrushed hair and felt his unshaven chin.

'You are right, Mr Holmes. I never gave a thought to my toilet. I was only too glad to get out of such a house. But I have been running round making inquiries before I came to you. I went to the house agents, you know, and they said that Mr Garcia's rent was paid up all right and that everything was in order at Wisteria Lodge.'

'Come, come, sir,' said Holmes, laughing. 'You are like my friend Dr Watson, who has a bad habit of telling his stories wrong end foremost. Please arrange your thoughts and let me know, in their due sequence, exactly what those events are which have sent you out unbrushed and unkempt, with dress boots and waistcoat buttoned awry, in search of advice and assistance.'

Our client looked down with a rueful face at his own unconventional appearance.

'I'm sure it must look very bad, Mr Holmes, and I am not aware that in my whole life such a thing has ever happened before. But I will tell you the whole queer business, and when I have done so you will admit, I am sure, that there has been enough to excuse me.'

But his narrative was nipped in the bud. There was a bustle outside, and Mrs Hudson opened the door to usher in two robust and official-looking individuals, one of whom was well known to us as Inspector Gregson of Scotland Yard, an energetic, gallant, and, within his limitations, a capable officer. He shook

hands with Holmes, and introduced his comrade as Inspector
Baynes of the Surrey Constabulary.

'We are hunting together, Mr Holmes, and our trail lay in this
direction.' He turned his bulldog eyes upon our visitor. 'Are
you Mr John Scott Eccles, of Popham House, Lee?'

'I am.'

'We have been following you about all the morning.'

'You traced him through the telegram, no doubt,' said
Holmes.

'Exactly, Mr Holmes. We picked up the scent at Charing
Cross Post Office and came on here.'

'But why do you follow me? What do you want?'

'We wish a statement, Mr Scott Eccles, as to the events which
led up to the death last night of Mr Aloysius Garcia, of Wisteria
Lodge, near Esher.'

Our client had sat up with staring eyes and every tinge of
colour struck from his astonished face.

'Dead? Did you say he was dead?'

'Yes, sir, he is dead.'

'But how? An accident?'

'Murder, if ever there was one upon earth.'

'Good God! This is awful! You don't mean – you don't
mean that I am suspected?'

'A letter of yours was found in the dead man's pocket, and
we know by it that you had planned to pass last night at his
house.'

'So I did.'

'Oh, you did, did you?'

Out came the official notebook.

'Wait a bit, Gregson,' said Sherlock Holmes. 'All you desire
is a plain statement, is it not?'

'And it is my duty to warn Mr Scott Eccles that it may be
used against him.'

'Mr Eccles was going to tell us about it when you entered the
room. I think, Watson, a brandy and soda would do him no

harm. Now, sir, I suggest that you take no notice of this addition to your audience, and that you proceed with your narrative exactly as you would have done had you never been interrupted.'

Our visitor had gulped off the brandy and the colour had returned to his face. With a dubious glance at the inspector's notebook, he plunged at once into his extraordinary statement.

'I am a bachelor,' said he, 'and, being of a sociable turn, I cultivate a large number of friends. Among these are the family of a retired brewer called Melville, living at Albemarle Mansion, Kensington. It was at his table that I met some weeks ago a young fellow named Garcia. He was, I understood, of Spanish descent and connected in some way with the Embassy. He spoke perfect English, was pleasing in his manners, and as good-looking a man as ever I saw in my life.

'In some way we struck up quite a friendship, this young fellow and I. He seemed to take a fancy to me from the first, and within two days of our meeting he came to see me at Lee. One thing led to another, and it ended in his inviting me out to spend a few days at his house, Wisteria Lodge, between Esher and Oxshott. Yesterday evening I went to Esher to fulfil this engagement.

'He had described his household to me before I went there. He lived with a faithful servant, a countryman of his own, who looked after all his needs. This fellow could speak English and did his housekeeping for him. Then there was a wonderful cook, he said, a half-breed whom he had picked up in his travels, who could serve an excellent dinner. I remember that he remarked what a queer household it was to find in the heart of Surrey, and that I agreed with him, though it has proved a good deal queerer than I thought.

'I drove to the place – about two miles on the south side of Esher. The house was a fair-sized one, standing back from the road, with a curving drive which was banked with high evergreen shrubs. It was an old, tumbledown building in a crazy state of disrepair. When the trap pulled up on the grass-grown drive in front of the blotched and weather-stained door, I had doubts as to my wisdom in visiting a man whom I knew so slightly. He opened the door himself, however, and greeted me with a great show of cordiality. I was handed over to the man-servant, a melancholy, swarthy individual, who led the way, my bag in his hand, to my bedroom. The whole place was depressing. Our dinner was *tête à tête*, and though my host did his best to be entertaining, his thoughts seemed to continually wander, and he talked so vaguely and wildly that I could hardly understand him. He continually drummed his fingers on the table, gnawed his nails, and gave other signs of nervous impatience. The dinner itself was neither well served nor well cooked, and the gloomy presence of the taciturn servant did not help to enliven us. I can assure you that many times in the course of the evening I wished that I could invent some excuse which would take me back to Lee.

'One thing comes back to my memory which may have a bearing upon the business that you two gentlemen are investigating. I thought nothing of it at the time. Near the end of dinner a note was handed in by the servant. I noticed that after my host had read it he seemed even more distrait and strange than before. He gave up all pretence at conversation and sat, smoking endless cigarettes, lost in his own thoughts, but he made no remark as to the contents. About eleven I was glad to go to bed. Some time later Garcia looked in at my door – the room was dark at the time – and asked me if I had rung. I said that I had not. He apologized for having disturbed me so late, saying that it was nearly one o'clock. I dropped off after this and slept soundly all night.

'And now I come to the amazing part of my tale. When I woke it was broad daylight. I glanced at my watch, and the time was nearly nine. I had particularly asked to be called at eight, so I was very much astonished at this forgetfulness. I sprang up and rang for the servant. There was no response. I rang again and again, with the same result. Then I came to the conclusion that the bell was out of order. I huddled on my clothes and hurried downstairs in an exceedingly bad temper to order some hot water. You can imagine my surprise when I found that there was no one there. I shouted in the hall. There was no answer. Then I ran from room to room. All were deserted. My host had shown me which was his bedroom the night before, so I knocked at the door. No reply. I turned the handle and walked in. The room was empty, and the bed had never been slept in. He had gone with the rest. The foreign host, the foreign footman, the foreign cook, all had vanished in the night! That was the end of my visit to Wisteria Lodge.'

Sherlock Holmes was rubbing his hands and chuckling as he added this bizarre incident to his collection of strange episodes.

'Your experience is, so far as I know, perfectly unique,' said he. 'May I ask, sir, what you did then?'

'I was furious. My first idea was that I had been the victim of some absurd practical joke. I packed my things, banged the hall door behind me, and set off for Esher, with my bag in my hand. I called at Allan Brothers', the chief land agents in the village, and found that it was from this firm that the villa had been rented. It struck me that the whole proceeding could hardly be for the purpose of making a fool of me, and that the main object must be to get out of the rent. It is late in March, so quarter-day is at hand. But this theory would not work. The agent was obliged to me for my warning, but told me that the rent had been paid in advance. Then I made my way to town and called at the Spanish Embassy. The man was unknown there. After this I went to see Melville, at whose house I had first met Garcia, but I found that he really knew rather less about him than I did. Finally, when I got your reply to my wire I came out to you, since I understand that you are a person who gives advice in difficult cases. But now, Mr Inspector, I gather, from what you said when you entered the room, that you can carry the story on, and that some tragedy has occurred. I can assure you that every word I have said is the truth, and that, outside of what I have told you, I know absolutely nothing about the fate of this man. My only desire is to help the law in every possible way.'

'I am sure of it, Mr Scott Eccles – I am sure of it,' said Inspector Gregson, in a very amiable tone. 'I am bound to say that everything which you have said agrees very closely with the facts as they have come to our notice. For example, there was that note which arrived during dinner. Did you chance to observe what became of it?'

'Yes, I did. Garcia rolled it up and threw it into the fire.'

'What do you say to that, Mr Baynes?'

The country detective was a stout, puffy, red man, whose face was only redeemed from grossness by two extraordinarily bright eyes, almost hidden behind the heavy creases of cheek and brow. With a slow smile he drew a folded and discoloured scrap of paper from his pocket.

'It was a dog-grate, Mr Holmes, and he overpitched it. I picked this out unburned from the back of it.'

Holmes smiled his appreciation.

'You must have examined the house very carefully, to find a single pellet of paper.'

'I did, Mr Holmes. It's my way. Shall I read it, Mr Gregson?'

The Londoner nodded.

'The note is written upon ordinary cream-laid paper without watermark. It is a quarter-sheet. The paper is cut off in two snips with a short-bladed scissors. It has been folded over three times and sealed with purple wax, put on hurriedly and pressed down with some flat, oval object. It is addressed to Mr Garcia, Wisteria Lodge. It says: "Our own colours, green and white. Green open, white shut. Main stair, first corridor, seventh right, green baize. God speed. D." It is a woman's writing, done with a sharp-pointed pen, but the address is either done with another pen or by someone else. It is thicker and bolder, as you see.'

'A very remarkable note,' said Holmes, glancing it over. 'I must compliment you, Mr Baynes, upon your attention to detail in your examination of it. A few trifling points might perhaps be added. The oval seal is undoubtedly a plain sleeve-link – what else is of such a shape? The scissors were bent nail-scissors. Short as the two snips are, you can distinctly see the same slight curve in each.'

The country detective chuckled.

'I thought I had squeezed all the juice out of it, but I see there was a little over,' he said. 'I'm bound to say that I make nothing of the note except that there was something on hand, and that a woman, as usual, was at the bottom of it.'

Mr Scott Eccles had fidgeted in his seat during this conversation.

'I am glad you found the note, since it corroborates my story,' said he. 'But I beg to point out that I have not yet heard what has happened to Mr Garcia, nor what has become of his household.'

'As to Garcia,' said Gregson, 'that is easily answered. He was found dead this morning upon Oxshott Common, nearly a mile from his home. His head had been smashed to pulp by heavy blows of a sand-bag or some such instrument, which had crushed rather than wounded. It is a lonely corner, and there is no house within a quarter of a mile of the spot. He had apparently been struck down first from behind, but his assailant had gone on beating him long after he was dead. It was a most furious assault. There are no footsteps nor any clue to the criminals.'

'Robbed?'

'No, there was no attempt at robbery.'

'This is very painful – very painful and terrible,' said Mr Scott Eccles, in a querulous voice; 'but it is really uncommonly hard upon me. I had nothing to do with my host going off upon a nocturnal excursion and meeting so sad an end. How do I come to be mixed up with the case?'

'Very simply, sir,' Inspector Baynes answered. 'The only document found in the pocket of the deceased was a letter from you saying that you would be with him on the night of his death. It was the envelope of this letter which gave us the dead man's name and address. It was after nine this morning when we reached his house and found neither you nor anyone else inside it. I wired to Mr Gregson to run you down in London while I examined Wisteria Lodge. Then I came into town, joined Mr Gregson, and here we are.'

'I think now,' said Gregson, rising, 'we had best put this matter into an official shape. You will come round with us to the station, Mr Scott Eccles, and let us have your statement in writing.'

'Certainly, I will come at once. But I retain your services, Mr Holmes. I desire you to spare no expense and no pains to get at the truth.'

My friend turned to the country inspector.

'I suppose that you have no objection to my collaborating with you, Mr Baynes?'

'Highly honoured, sir, I am sure.'

'You appear to have been very prompt and businesslike in all that you have done. Was there any clue, may I ask, as to the exact hour that the man met his death?'

'He had been there since one o'clock. There was rain about that time, and his death had certainly been before the rain.'

'But that is perfectly impossible, Mr Baynes,' cried our client. 'His voice is unmistakable. I could swear to it that it was he who addressed me in my bedroom at that very hour.'

'Remarkable, but by no means impossible,' said Holmes, smiling.

'You have a clue?' asked Gregson.

'On the face of it the case is not a very complex one, though it certainly presents some novel and interesting features. A further knowledge of facts is necessary before I would venture to give a final and definite opinion. By the way, Mr Baynes, did you find anything remarkable besides this note in your examination of the house?'

The detective looked at my friend in a singular way.

'There were', said he, 'one or two *very* remarkable things. Perhaps when I have finished at the police-station you would care to come out and give me your opinion of them.'

'I am entirely at your service,' said Sherlock Holmes, ringing the bell. 'You will show these gentlemen out, Mrs Hudson, and kindly send the boy with this telegram. He is to pay a five-shilling reply.'

We sat for some time in silence after our visitors had left. Holmes smoked hard, with his brows drawn down over his keen eyes, and his head thrust forward in the eager way characteristic of the man.

'Well, Watson,' he asked, turning suddenly upon me, 'what do you make of it?'

'I can make nothing of this mystification of Scott Eccles.'

'But the crime?'

'Well, taken with the disappearance of the man's companions, I should say that they were in some way concerned in the murder and had fled from justice.'

'That is certainly a possible point of view. On the face of it you must admit, however, that it is very strange that his two servants should have been in a conspiracy against him and should have attacked him on the one night when he had a guest. They had him alone at their mercy every other night in the week.'

'Then why did they fly?'

'Quite so. Why did they fly? There is a big fact. Another big fact is the remarkable experience of our client, Scott Eccles. Now, my dear Watson, is it beyond the limits of human ingenuity to furnish an explanation which would cover both these big facts? If it were one which would also admit of the mysterious note with its very curious phraseology, why, then it would be worth accepting as a temporary hypothesis. If the fresh

facts which come to our knowledge all fit themselves into the
scheme, then our hypothesis may gradually become a solution.'

'But what is our hypothesis?'

Holmes leaned back in his chair with half-closed eyes.

'You must admit, my dear Watson, that the idea of a joke
is impossible. There were grave events afoot, as the sequel
showed, and the coaxing of Scott Eccles to Wisteria Lodge had
some connection with them.'

'But what possible connection?'

'Let us take it link by link. There is, on the face of it, something unnatural about this strange and sudden friendship
between the young Spaniard and Scott Eccles. It was the
former who forced the pace. He called upon Eccles at the other
end of London on the very day after he first met him, and he
kept in close touch with him until he got him down to Esher.
Now, what did he want with Eccles? What could Eccles supply?
I see no charm in the man. He is not particularly intelligent –
not a man likely to be congenial to a quick-witted Latin. Why,
then, was he picked out from all the other people whom Garcia
met as particularly suited to his purpose? Has he any one
outstanding quality? I say that he has. He is the very type of
conventional British respectability, and the very man as a
witness to impress another Briton. You saw yourself how neither
of the inspectors dreamed of questioning his statement, extraordinary as it was.'

'But what was he to witness?'

'Nothing, as things turned out, but everything had they gone
another way. That is how I read the matter.'

'I see, he might have proved an alibi.'

'Exactly, my dear Watson; he might have proved an alibi.
We will suppose, for argument's sake, that the household of
Wisteria Lodge are confederates in some design. The attempt,
whatever it may be, is to come off, we will say, before one
o'clock. By some juggling of the clocks it is quite possible that
they may have got Scott Eccles to bed earlier than he thought,

but in any case it is likely that when Garcia went out of his way to tell him that it was one it was really not more than twelve. If Garcia could do whatever he had to do and be back by the hour mentioned he had evidently a powerful reply to any accusation. Here was this irreproachable Englishman ready to swear in any court of law that the accused was in his house all the time. It was an insurance against the worst.'

'Yes, yes, I see that. But how about the disappearance of the others?'

'I have not all my facts yet, but I do not think there are any insuperable difficulties. Still, it is an error to argue in front of your data. You find yourself insensibly twisting them round to fit your theories.'

'And the message?'

'How did it run? "Our own colours, green and white." Sounds like racing. "Green open, white shut." That is clearly a signal. "Main stair, first corridor, seventh right, green baize." This is an assignation. We may find a jealous husband at the bottom of it all. It was clearly a dangerous quest. She would not have said "God speed" had it not been so. "D" – that should be a guide.'

'The man was a Spaniard. I suggest that "D" stands for Dolores, a common female name in Spain.'

'Good, Watson, very good – but quite inadmissible. A Spaniard would write to a Spaniard in Spanish. The writer of this note is certainly English. Well, we can only possess our souls in patience, until this excellent inspector comes back for us. Meanwhile we can thank our lucky fate which has rescued us for a few short hours from the insufferable fatigues of idleness.'

An answer had arrived to Holmes's telegram before our Surrey officer had returned. Holmes read it, and was about to place it in his notebook when he caught a glimpse of my expectant face. He tossed it across with a laugh.

'We are moving in exalted circles,' said he.

The telegram was a list of names and addresses: 'Lord Harringby, The Dingle; Sir George Ffolliott, Oxshott Towers; Mr Hynes Hynes, J.P., Purdey Place; Mr James Baker Williams, Forton Old Hall; Mr Henderson, High Gable; Rev. Joshua Stone, Nether Walsling.'

'This is a very obvious way of limiting our field of operations,' said Holmes. 'No doubt Baynes, with his methodical mind, has already adopted some similar plan.'

'I don't quite understand.'

'Well, my dear fellow, we have already arrived at the conclusion that the message received by Garcia at dinner was an appointment or an assignation. Now, if the obvious reading of it is correct, and in order to keep this tryst one has to ascend a main stair and seek the seventh door in a corridor, it is perfectly clear that the house is a very large one. It is equally certain that this house cannot be more than a mile or two from Oxshott, since Garcia was walking in that direction, and hoped, according to my reading of the facts, to be back in Wisteria Lodge in time to avail himself of an alibi, which would only be valid up to one o'clock. As the number of large houses close to Oxshott must be limited, I adopted the obvious method of sending to the agents mentioned by Scott Eccles and obtaining a list of them. Here they are in this telegram, and the other end of our tangled skein must lie among them.'

It was nearly six o'clock before we found ourselves in the pretty Surrey village of Esher, with Inspector Baynes as our companion.

Holmes and I had taken things for the night, and found comfortable quarters at the Bull. Finally we set out in the company of the detective on our visit to Wisteria Lodge. It was a cold, dark March evening, with a sharp wind and a fine rain beating upon our faces, a fit setting for the wild common over which our road passed and the tragic goal to which it led us.

II – *The Tiger of San Pedro*

A cold and melancholy walk of a couple of miles brought us to a high wooden gate, which opened into a gloomy avenue of chestnuts. The curved and shadowed drive led us to a low, dark house, pitch-black against a slate-coloured sky. From the front window upon the left of the door there peeped a glimmer of a feeble light.

'There's a constable in possession,' said Baynes. 'I'll knock at the window.' He stepped across the grass plot and tapped with his hand on the pane. Through the fogged glass I dimly saw a man spring up from a chair beside the fire, and heard a sharp cry from within the room. An instant later a white-faced, hard-breathing policeman had opened the door, the candle wavering in his trembling hand.

'What's the matter, Walters?' asked Baynes, sharply.

The man mopped his forehead with his handkerchief and gave a long sigh of relief.

'I am glad you have come, sir. It has been a long evening and I don't think my nerve is as good as it was.'

'Your nerve, Walters? I should not have thought you had a nerve in your body.'

'Well, sir, it's this lonely, silent house and the queer thing in the kitchen. Then when you tapped at the window I thought it had come again.'

'That what had come again?'

'The devil, sir, for all I know. It was at the window.'

'What was at the window, and when?'

'It was just about two hours ago. The light was just fading. I was sitting reading in the chair. I don't know what made me look up, but there was a face looking in at me through the lower pane. Lord, sir, what a face it was! I'll see it in my dreams.'

'Tut, tut, Walters! This is not talk for a police-constable.'

'I know, sir, I know; but it shook me, sir, and there's no use to deny it. It wasn't black, sir, nor was it white, nor any colour that I know, but a kind of queer shade like clay with a splash of milk in it. Then there was the size of it – it was twice yours, sir. And the look of it – the great staring goggle eyes, and the line of white teeth like a hungry beast. I tell you, sir, I couldn't move a finger, nor get my breath, till it whisked away and was gone. Out I ran and through the shrubbery, but thank God there was no one there.'

'If I didn't know you were a good man, Walters, I should put a black mark against you for this. If it were the devil himself, a constable on duty should never thank God that he could not lay his hands upon him. I suppose the whole thing is not a vision and a touch of nerves?'

'That, at least, is very easily settled,' said Holmes, lighting his little pocket lantern. 'Yes,' he reported, after a short examination of the grass bed, 'a number twelve shoe, I should say. If he was all on the same scale as his foot he must certainly have been a giant.'

'What became of him?'

'He seems to have broken through the shrubbery and made for the road.'

'Well,' said the inspector, with a grave and thoughtful face, 'whoever he may have been, and whatever he may have wanted, he's gone for the present, and we have more immediate things to attend to. Now, Mr Holmes, with your permission, I will show you round the house.'

The various bedrooms and sitting-rooms had yielded nothing to a careful search. Apparently the tenants had brought little or nothing with them, and all the furniture down to the smallest details had been taken over with the house. A good deal of clothing with the stamp of Marx and Co., High Holborn, had been left behind. Telegraphic inquiries had been already made which showed that Marx knew nothing of his customer save that he was a good payer. Odds and ends, some pipes, a few novels, two of them in Spanish, an old-fashioned pinfire revolver, and a guitar were amongst the personal property.

'Nothing in all this,' said Baynes, stalking, candle in hand from room to room. 'But now, Mr Holmes, I invite your attention to the kitchen.'

It was a gloomy, high-ceilinged room at the back of the house, with a straw litter in one corner, which served apparently as a bed for the cook. The table was piled with half-eaten dishes and dirty plates, the debris of last night's dinner.

'Look at this,' said Baynes. 'What do you make of it?'

He held up his candle before an extraordinary object which stood at the back of the dresser. It was so wrinkled and shrunken and withered that it was difficult to say what it might have been. One could but say that it was black and leathery and that it bore some resemblance to a dwarfish, human figure. At first, as I examined it, I thought that it was a mummified negro baby, and then it seemed a very twisted and ancient monkey. Finally I was left in doubt as to whether it was animal or human. A double band of white shells was strung round the centre of it.

'Very interesting – very interesting, indeed!' said Holmes, peering at this sinister relic. 'Anything more?'

In silence Baynes led the way to the sink and held forward his candle. The limbs and body of some large, white bird, torn savagely to pieces with the feathers still on, were littered all over it. Holmes pointed to the wattles on the severed head.

'A white cock,' said he; 'most interesting! It is really a very curious case.'

But Mr Baynes had kept his most sinister exhibit to the last. From under the sink he drew a zinc pail which contained a quantity of blood. Then from the table he took a platter heaped with small pieces of charred bone.

'Something has been killed and something has been burned. We raked all these out of the fire. We had a doctor in this morning. He says that they are not human.'

Holmes smiled and rubbed his hands.

'I must congratulate you, inspector, on handling so

distinctive and instructive a case. Your powers, if I may say so without offence, seem superior to your opportunities.'

Inspector Baynes's small eyes twinkled with pleasure.

'You're right, Mr Holmes. We stagnate in the provinces. A case of this sort gives a man a chance, and I hope that I shall take it. What do you make of these bones?'

'A lamb, I should say, or a kid.'

'And the white cock?'

'Curious, Mr Baynes, very curious. I should say almost unique.'

'Yes, sir, there must have been some very strange people with some very strange ways in this house. One of them is dead. Did his companions follow him and kill him? If they did we should have them, for every port is watched. But my own views are different. Yes, sir, my own views are very different.'

'You have a theory then?'

'And I'll work it myself, Mr Holmes. It's only due to my own credit to do so. Your name is made, but I have still to make mine. I should be glad to be able to say afterwards that I had solved it without your help.'

Holmes laughed good-humouredly.

'Well, well, inspector,' said he. 'Do you follow your path and I will follow mine. My results are always very much at your service if you care to apply to me for them. I think that I have seen all that I wish in this house, and that my time may be more profitably employed elsewhere. *Au revoir* and good luck!'

I could tell by numerous subtle signs, which might have been lost upon anyone but myself, that Holmes was on a hot scent. As impassive as ever to the casual observer, there were none the less a subdued eagerness and suggestion of tension in his brightened eyes and brisker manner which assured me that the game was afoot. After his habit he said nothing, and after mine I asked no questions. Sufficient for me to share the sport and lend my humble help to the capture without distracting that intent brain with needless interruption. All would come round to me in due time.

I waited, therefore – but, to my ever-deepening disappointment I waited in vain. Day succeeded day, and my friend took no step forward. One morning he spent in town, and I learned from a casual reference that he had visited the British Museum. Save for this one excursion, he spent his days in long and often solitary walks, or in chatting with a number of village gossips whose acquaintance he had cultivated.

'I'm sure, Watson, a week in the country will be invaluable to you,' he remarked. 'It is very pleasant to see the first green shoots upon the hedges and the catkins on the hazels once again. With a spud, a tin box, and an elementary book on botany, there are instructive days to be spent.' He prowled about with this equipment himself, but it was a poor show of plants which he would bring back of an evening.

Occasionally in our rambles we came across Inspector Baynes. His fat, red face wreathed itself in smiles and his small eyes glittered as he greeted my companion. He said little about the case, but from that little we gathered that he also was not dissatisfied at the course of events. I must admit, however, that I was somewhat surprised when, some five days after the crime, I opened my morning paper to find in large letters:

THE OXSHOTT MYSTERY
A SOLUTION
ARREST OF SUPPOSED ASSASSIN

Holmes sprang in his chair as if he had been stung when I read the headlines.

'By Jove!' he cried. 'You don't mean that Baynes has got him?'

'Apparently,' said I, as I read the following report:

Great excitement was caused in Esher and the neighbouring district when it was learned late last night that an arrest had been effected in connection with the Oxshott murder. It will be remembered that Mr Garcia, of Wisteria Lodge, was found dead on Oxshott Common, his body showing signs of extreme violence, and that on the same night his servant and his cook fled, which appeared to show their participation in the crime. It was suggested, but never proved, that the deceased gentleman may have had valuables in the house, and that their abstraction was the motive of the crime. Every effort was made by Inspector Baynes, who has the case in hand, to ascertain the hiding place of the fugitives, and he had good reason to believe that they had not gone far, but were lurking in some retreat which had been already prepared. It was certain from the first, however, that they would eventually be detected, as the cook, from the evidence of one or two tradespeople who have caught a glimpse of him through the window, was a man of most remarkable appearance – being a huge and hideous mulatto, with yellowish features of a pronounced negroid type. This man has been seen since the crime, for he was detected and pursued by Constable Walters on the same evening, when he had the audacity to revisit Wisteria Lodge. Inspector Baynes, considering that such a visit must have some purpose in view, and was likely, therefore, to be repeated, abandoned the house, but left an ambuscade in the shrubbery. The man walked into the trap, and was captured last night after a struggle, in which Constable Downing was badly bitten by the savage. We understand that when the prisoner is brought before the magistrates a remand will be applied for by the police, and that great developments are hoped from his capture.

'Really we must see Baynes at once,' cried Holmes, picking up his hat. 'We will just catch him before he starts.' We hurried down the village street and found, as we had expected, that the inspector was just leaving his lodgings.

'You've seen the paper, Mr Holmes?' he asked, holding one out to us.

'Yes, Baynes, I've seen it. Pray don't think it a liberty if I give you a word of friendly warning.'

'Of warning, Mr Holmes?'

'I have looked into this case with some care, and I am not convinced that you are on the right lines. I don't want you to commit yourself too far, unless you are sure.'

'You're very kind, Mr Holmes.'

'I assure you I speak for your good.'

It seemed to me that something like a wink quivered for an instant over one of Mr Baynes's tiny eyes.

'We agreed to work on our own lines, Mr Holmes. That's what I am doing.'

'Oh, very good,' said Holmes. 'Don't blame me.'

'No, sir; I believe you mean well by me. But we all have our own systems, Mr Holmes. You have yours, and maybe I have mine.'

'Let us say no more about it.'

'You're welcome always to my news. This fellow is a perfect savage, as strong as a carthorse and as fierce as the devil. He chewed Downing's thumb nearly off before they could master him. He hardly speaks a word of English, and we can get nothing out of him but grunts.'

'And you think you have evidence that he murdered his late master?'

'I didn't say so, Mr Holmes; I didn't say so. We all have our little ways. You try yours and I will try mine. That's the agreement.'

Holmes shrugged his shoulders as we walked away together. 'I can't make the man out. He seems to be riding for a fall. Well, as he says, we must each try our own way and see what comes of it. But there's something in Inspector Baynes which I can't quite understand.'

'Just sit down in that chair, Watson,' said Sherlock Holmes, when we had returned to our apartment at the Bull. 'I want to put you in touch with the situation, as I may need your help tonight. Let me show you the evolution of this case, so far as I have been able to follow it. Simple as it has been in its leading features, it has none the less presented surprising difficulties in the way of an arrest. There are gaps in that direction which we have still to fill.

'We will go back to the note which was handed in to Garcia upon the evening of his death. We may put aside this idea of Baynes's that Garcia's servants were concerned in the matter. The proof of this lies in the fact that it was *he* who had arranged for the presence of Scott Eccles, which could only have been done for the purpose of an alibi. It was Garcia, then, who had an enterprise, and apparently a criminal enterprise, in hand that night, in the course of which he met his death. I say criminal because only a man with a criminal enterprise desires to establish an alibi. Who, then, is most likely to have taken his life? Surely the person against whom the criminal enterprise was directed. So far it seems to me that we are on safe ground.

'We can now see a reason for the disappearance of Garcia's household. They were *all* confederates in the same unknown crime. If it came off, then Garcia returned, any possible suspicion would be warded off by the Englishman's evidence, and all would be well. But the attempt was a dangerous one, and if Garcia did *not* return by a certain hour it was probable that his own life had been sacrificed. It had been arranged, therefore, that in such a case his two subordinates were to make for some prearranged spot, where they could escape investigation and be in a position afterwards to renew their attempt. That would fully explain the facts, would it not?'

The whole inexplicable tangle seemed to straighten out before me. I wondered, as I always did, how it had not been obvious to me before.

'But why should one servant return?'

'We can imagine that, in the confusion of flight, something

precious, something which he could not bear to part with, had been left behind. That would explain his persistence, would it not?'

'Well, what is the next step?'

'The next step is the note received by Garcia at the dinner. It indicates a confederate at the other end. Now, where was the other end? I have already shown you that it could only lie in some large house, and that the number of large houses is limited. My first days in this village were devoted to a series of walks, in which in the intervals of my botanical researches I made a reconnaissance of all the large houses and an examination of the family history of the occupants. One house, and only one, riveted my attention. It is the famous old Jacobean grange of High Gable, one mile on the farther side of Oxshott, and less than half a mile from the scene of the tragedy. The other mansions belonged to prosaic and respectable people who live far aloof from romance. But Mr Henderson, of High Gable, was by all accounts a curious man, to whom curious adventures might befall. I concentrated my attention, therefore, upon him and his household.

'A singular set of people, Watson – the man himself the most singular of them all. I managed to see him on a plausible pretext, but I seemed to read in his dark, deep-set, brooding eyes that he was perfectly aware of my true business. He is a man of fifty, strong, active, with iron-grey hair, great bunched black eyebrows, the step of a deer, and the air of an emperor – a fierce, masterful man, with a red-hot spirit behind his parchment face. He is either a foreigner or has lived long in the Tropics for he is yellow and sapless but tough as whipcord. His friend and secretary, Mr Lucas, is undoubtedly a foreigner, chocolate brown, wily, suave and cat-like, with a poisonous gentleness of speech. You see, Watson, we have come already upon two sets of foreigners – one at Wisteria Lodge and one at High Gable – so our gaps are beginning to close.

'These two men, close and confidential friends, are the centre of the household; but there is one other person, who for our immediate purpose may be even more important. Henderson has two children – girls of eleven and thirteen. Their governess is a Miss Burnet, an Englishwoman of forty or thereabouts. There is also one confidential manservant. This little group forms the real family, for they travel about together, and Henderson is a great traveller, always on the move. It is only within the last few weeks that he has returned, after a year's absence, to High Gable. I may add that he is enormously rich, and whatever his whims may be he can very easily satisfy them. For the rest, his house is full of butlers, footmen, maidservants, and the usual overfed, underworked staff of a large English country-house.

'So much I learned partly from village gossip and partly from my own observation. There are no better instruments than discharged servants with a grievance, and I was lucky enough to find one. I call it luck, but it would not have come my way had I not been looking out for it. As Baynes remarks, we all have our systems. It was my system which enabled me to find John Warner, late gardener of High Gable, sacked in a moment of temper by his imperious employer. He in turn had friends among the indoor servants, who unite in their fear and dislike of their master. So I had my key to the secrets of the establishment.

'Curious people, Watson! I don't pretend to understand it all yet, but very curious people anyway. It's a double-winged house, and the servants live on one side, the family on the other. There's no link between the two save for Henderson's own servant, who serves the family's meals. Everything is carried to a certain door, which forms the one connection. Governess and children hardly go out at all, except into the garden. Henderson never by any chance walks alone. His dark secretary is like his shadow. The gossip among the servants is that their master is terribly afraid of something. "Sold his soul to the devil in exchange for money," says Warner, "and expects his creditor to come up and claim his own." Where they came from, or who they are, nobody has an idea. They are very violent. Twice Henderson has lashed at folk with his dog-whip, and only his long purse and heavy compensation have kept him out of the courts.

'Well, now, Watson, let us judge the situation by this new information. We may take it that the letter came out of this strange household, and was an invitation to Garcia to carry out some attempt which had already been planned. Who wrote the note? It was someone within the citadel, and it was a woman. Who then, but Miss Burnet, the governess? All our reasoning seems to point that way. At any rate, we may take it as a hypothesis, and see what consequences it would entail. I may add that Miss Burnet's age and character make it certain that my first idea that there might be a love interest in our story is out of the question.

'If she wrote the note she was presumably the friend and confederate of Garcia. What, then, might she be expected to do if she heard of his death? If he met it in some nefarious enterprise her lips might be sealed. Still, in her heart she must retain bitterness and hatred against those who had killed him, and would presumably help so far as she could to have revenge upon them. Could we see her, then, and try to use her? That was my first thought. But now we come to a sinister fact. Miss Burnet has not been seen by any human eye since the night of the murder. From that evening she has utterly vanished. Is she alive? Has she perhaps met her end on the same night as the friend whom she had summoned? Or is she merely a prisoner? There is the point which we still have to decide.

'You will appreciate the difficulty of the situation, Watson. There is nothing upon which we can apply for a warrant. Our whole scheme might seem fantastic if laid before a magistrate. The woman's disappearance counts for nothing, since in that extraordinary household any member of it might be invisible for a week. And yet she may at the present moment be in danger of her life. All I can do is to watch the house and leave my agent, Warner, on guard at the gates. We can't let such a situation

continue. If the law can do nothing we must take the risk
ourselves.'

'What do you suggest?'

'I know which is her room. It is accessible from the top of an
outhouse. My suggestion is that you and I go tonight and see
if we can strike at the very heart of the mystery.'

It was not, I must confess, a very alluring prospect. The old
house with its atmosphere of murder, the singular and formidable inhabitants, the unknown dangers of the approach, and the
fact that we were putting ourselves legally in a false position,
all combined to damp my ardour. But there was something in
the ice-cold reasoning of Holmes which made it impossible to
shrink from any adventure which he might recommend. One
knew that thus, and only thus, could a solution be found. I
clasped his hand in silence, and the die was cast.

But it was not destined that our investigation should have
so adventurous an ending. It was about five o'clock, and the
shadows of the March evening were beginning to fall, when an
excited rustic rushed into our room.

'They've gone, Mr Holmes. They went by the last train. The
lady broke away, and I've got her in a cab downstairs.'

'Excellent, Warner!' cried Holmes, springing to his feet.
'Watson, the gaps are closing rapidly.'

In the cab was a woman, half-collapsed from nervous
exhaustion. She bore upon her aquiline and emaciated face the
traces of some recent tragedy. Her head hung listlessly upon
her breast, but as she raised it and turned her dull eyes upon us,
I saw that her pupils were dark dots in the centre of the broad
grey iris. She was drugged with opium.

'I watched at the gate, same as you advised, Mr Holmes,'
said our emissary, the discharged gardener. 'When the carriage
came out I followed it to the station. She was like one walking
in her sleep; but when they tried to get her into the train she
came to life and struggled. They pushed her into the carriage.
She fought her way out again. I took her part, got her into a cab,

and here we are. I shan't forget the face at the carriage window as I led her away. I'd have a short life if he had his way – the black-eyed, scowling, yellow devil.'

We carried her upstairs, laid her on the sofa, and a couple of cups of the strongest coffee soon cleared her brain from the mists of the drug. Baynes had been summoned by Holmes, and the situation rapidly explained to him.

'Why, sir, you've got me the very evidence I want,' said the inspector, warmly, shaking my friend by the hand. 'I was on the same scent as you from the first.'

'What! You were after Henderson?'

'Why, Mr Holmes, when you were crawling in the shrubbery at High Gable I was up one of the trees in the plantation and saw you down below. It was just who would get his evidence first.'

'Then why did you arrest the mulatto?'

Baynes chuckled.

'I was sure Henderson, as he calls himself, felt that he was suspected, and that he would lie low and make no move so long as he thought he was in any danger. I arrested the wrong man to make him believe that our eyes were off him. I knew he would be likely to clear off then and give us a chance of getting at Miss Burnet.'

Holmes laid his hand upon the inspector's shoulder.

'You will rise high in your profession. You have instinct and intuition,' said he.

Baynes flushed with pleasure.

'I've had a plain-clothes man waiting at the station all the week. Wherever the High Gable folk go he will keep them in sight. But he must have been hard put to it when Miss Burnet broke away. However, your man picked her up, and it all ends well. We can't arrest without her evidence, that is clear, so the sooner we get a statement the better.'

'Every minute she gets stronger,' said Holmes, glancing at the governess. 'But tell me, Baynes, who is this man Henderson?'

'Henderson', the inspector answered, 'is Don Murillo, once called the Tiger of San Pedro.'

The Tiger of San Pedro! The whole history of the man came back to me in a flash. He had made his name as the most lewd and bloodthirsty tyrant that had ever governed any country with a pretence to civilization. Strong, fearless, and energetic, he had sufficient virtue to enable him to impose his odious vices upon a cowering people for ten or twelve years. His name was a terror through all Central America. At the end of that time there was a universal rising against him. But he was as cunning as he was cruel, and at the first whisper of coming trouble he had secretly conveyed his treasures aboard a ship which was manned by devoted adherents. It was an empty palace which was stormed by the insurgents next day. The Dictator, his two children, his secretary, and his wealth had all escaped them. From that moment he had vanished from the world, and his identity had been a frequent subject for comment in the European Press.

'Yes, sir; Don Murillo, the Tiger of San Pedro,' said Baynes. 'If you look it up you will find that the San Pedro colours are green and white, same as in the note, Mr Holmes. Henderson he called himself, but I traced him back, Paris and Rome and Madrid to Barcelona, where his ship came in in '86. They've been looking for him all the time for their revenge, but it is only now that they have begun to find him out.'

'They discovered him a year ago,' said Miss Burnet, who had sat up and was now intently following the conversation. 'Once already his life has been attempted; but some evil spirit shielded him. Now, again, it is the noble, chivalrous Garcia who has fallen, while the monster goes safe. But another will come, and yet another, until some day justice will be done; that is as certain as the rise of tomorrow's sun.' Her thin hands clenched, and her worn face blanched with the passion of her hatred.

'But how come you into this matter, Miss Burnet?' asked

Holmes. 'How can an English lady join in such a murderous affair?'

'I join in it because there is no other way in the world by which justice can be gained. What does the law of England care for the rivers of blood shed years ago in San Pedro, or for the ship-load of treasure which this man has stolen? To you they are like crimes committed in some other planet. But *we* know. We have learned the truth in sorrow and in suffering. To us there is no fiend in hell like Juan Murillo, and no peace in life while his victims still cry for vengeance.'

'No doubt,' said Holmes, 'he was as you say. I have heard that he was atrocious. But how are you affected?'

'I will tell you it all. This villain's policy was to murder, on one pretext or another, every man who showed such promise that he might in time come to be a dangerous rival. My husband – yes, my real name is Signora Victor Durando – was the San Pedro Minister in London. He met me and married me there. A nobler man never lived upon earth. Unhappily, Murillo heard of his excellence, recalled him on some pretext, and had him shot. With a premonition of his fate he had refused to take me with him. His estates were confiscated, and I was left with a pittance and a broken heart.

'Then came the downfall of the tyrant. He escaped as you have just described. But the many whose lives he had ruined, whose nearest and dearest had suffered torture and death at his hands, would not let the matter rest. They banded themselves into a society which should never be dissolved until the work was done. It was my part after we had discovered in the transformed Henderson the fallen despot, to attach myself to his household and keep the others in touch with his movements. This I was able to do by securing the position of governess in his family. He little knew that the woman who faced him at every meal was the woman whose husband he had hurried at an hour's notice into eternity. I smiled on him, did my duty to his children, and bided my time. An attempt was made in Paris, and failed. We zigzagged swiftly here and there over Europe, to throw off the pursuers, and finally returned to this house, which he had taken upon his first arrival in England.

'But here also the ministers of justice were waiting. Knowing that he would return there, Garcia, who is the son of the former highest dignitary in San Pedro, was waiting with two trusty companions of humble station, all three fired with the same reasons for revenge. He could do little during the day, for Murillo took every precaution, and never went out save with his satellite Lucas, or Lopez as he was known in the days of his greatness. At night, however, he slept alone, and the avenger might find him. On a certain evening, which had been prearranged, I sent my friend final instructions, for the man was for ever on the alert, and continually changed his room. I was to see that the doors were open and the signal of a green or white light in a window which faced the drive was to give notice if all was safe, or if the attempt had better be postponed.

'But everything went wrong with us. In some way I had excited the suspicion of Lopez, the secretary. He crept up behind me, and sprang upon me just as I had finished the note. He and his master dragged me to my room, and held judgment upon me as a convicted traitress. Then and there they would have plunged their knives into me, could they have seen how to escape the consequence of the deed. Finally, after much debate, they concluded that my murder was too dangerous. But they determined to get rid for ever of Garcia. They had gagged me, and Murillo twisted my arm round until I gave him the address. I swear that he might have twisted it off had I understood what it would mean to Garcia. Lopez addressed the note which I had written, sealed it with his sleeve-link, and sent it by the hand of the servant, José. How they murdered him I do not know, save that it was Murillo's hand who struck him down, for Lopez had remained to guard me. I believe he must have waited among the gorse bushes through which the path winds and struck him down as he passed. At first they were of a mind to let him enter the house and to kill him as a detected burglar; but they argued that if they were mixed up in an inquiry their own identity would at once be publicly disclosed and they would be open to further attacks. With the death of Garcia the pursuit might cease, since such a death might frighten others from the task.

'All would now have been well for them had it not been for my knowledge of what they had done. I have no doubt that there were times when my life hung in the balance. I was confined to my room, terrorized by the most horrible threats, cruelly ill-used to break my spirit – see this stab on my shoulder and the bruises from end to end of my arms – and a gag was thrust into my mouth on the one occasion when I tried to call from the window. For five days this cruel imprisonment continued, with hardly enough food to hold body and soul together. This afternoon a good lunch was brought me, but the moment after I took it I knew that I had been drugged. In a sort of dream I remember being half led, half carried to the carriage; in the same state I was conveyed to the train. Only then, when the wheels were almost moving did I suddenly realize that my liberty lay in my own hands. I sprang out, they tried to drag me back, and had it not been for the help of this good man, who led me to the cab, I should never have broken away. Now, thank God, I am beyond their power for ever.'

We had all listened intently to this remarkable statement. It was Holmes who broke the silence.

'Our difficulties are not over,' he remarked, shaking his head. 'Our police work ends, but our legal work begins.'

'Exactly,' said I. 'A plausible lawyer could make it out as an act of self-defence. There may be a hundred crimes in the background, but it is only on this one that they can be tried.'

'Come, come,' said Baynes, cheerily; 'I think better of the law than that. Self-defence is one thing. To entice a man in cold blood with the object of murdering him is another, whatever danger you may fear from him. No, no; we shall all be justified when we see the tenants of High Gable at the next Guildford Assizes.'

It is a matter of history, however, that a little time was still to elapse before the Tiger of San Pedro should meet with his deserts. Wily and bold, he and his companion threw their pursuer off their track by entering a lodging-house in Edmonton Street and leaving by the back-gate into Curzon Square. From that day they were seen no more in England. Some six months afterwards the Marquess of Montalva and Signor Rulli, his secretary, were both murdered in their rooms at the Hotel Escurial at Madrid. The crime was ascribed to Nihilism, and the murderers were never arrested. Inspector Baynes visited us at Baker Street with a printed description of the dark face of the secretary, and of the masterful features, the magnetic black eyes, and the tufted brows of his master. We could not doubt that justice, if belated, had come at last.

'A chaotic case, my dear Watson,' said Holmes, over an evening pipe. 'It will not be possible for you to present it in that compact form which is dear to your heart. It covers two continents, concerns two groups of mysterious persons, and is further complicated by the highly respectable presence of our friend Scott Eccles, whose inclusion shows me that the deceased Garcia had a scheming mind and a well-developed instinct of self-preservation. It is remarkable only for the fact that amid a perfect jungle of possibilities we, with our worthy collaborator the inspector, have kept our close hold on the essentials and so been guided along the crooked and winding path. Is there any point which is not quite clear to you?'

'The object of the mulatto cook's return?'

'I think that the strange creature in the kitchen may account for it. The man was a primitive savage from the backwoods of San Pedro, and this was his fetish. When his companion and he had fled to some prearranged retreat – already occupied, no doubt by a confederate – the companion had persuaded him to leave so compromising an article of furniture. But the mulatto's heart was with it, and he was driven back to it next day, when, on reconnoitring through the window, he found policeman Walters in possession. He waited three days longer, and then his piety or his superstition drove him to try once more. Inspector Baynes, who, with his usual astuteness, had minimized the incident before me, had really recognized its importance, and had left a trap into which the creature walked. Any other point, Watson?'

'The torn bird, the pail of blood, the charred bones, all the mystery of that weird kitchen?'

Holmes smiled as he turned up an entry in his notebook.

'I spent a morning in the British Museum reading up that and other points. Here is a quotation from Eckermann's *Voodooism and the Negroid Religions*:

The true Voodoo-worshipper attempts nothing of importance without certain sacrifices which are intended to propitiate his unclean gods. In extreme cases these rites take the form of human sacrifices followed by cannibalism. The more usual victims are a white cock, which is plucked in pieces alive, or a black goat, whose throat is cut and body burned.

'So you see our savage friend was very orthodox in his ritual. It is grotesque, Watson,' Holmes added, as he slowly fastened his notebook; 'but, as I have had occasion to remark, there is but one step from the grotesque to the horrible.'

The Adventure of the Cardboard Box

In choosing a few typical cases which illustrate the remarkable mental qualities of my friend, Sherlock Holmes, I have endeavoured, so far as possible, to select those which presented the minimum of sensationalism, while offering a fair field for his talents. It is, however, unfortunately, impossible entirely to separate the sensational from the criminal, and a chronicler is left in the dilemma that he must either sacrifice details which are essential to his statement, and so give a false impression of the problem, or he must use matter which chance, and not choice, has provided him with. With this short preface I shall turn to my notes of what proved to be a strange, though a peculiarly terrible, chain of events.

It was a blazing hot day in August. Baker Street was like an oven, and the glare of the sunlight upon the yellow brickwork of the house across the road was painful to the eye. It was hard to believe that these were the same walls which loomed so gloomily through the fogs of winter. Our blinds were half-drawn, and Holmes lay curled upon the sofa, reading and re-reading a letter which he had received by the morning post. For myself, my term of service in India had trained me to stand heat better than cold, and a thermometer at 90 was no hardship. But the morning paper was uninteresting. Parliament had risen. Everybody was out of town, and I yearned for the glades of the New Forest or the shingle of Southsea. A depleted bank account had caused me to postpone my holiday, and as to my companion, neither the country nor the sea presented the slightest attraction to him. He loved to lie in the very centre of five millions of people, with his filaments stretching out and running through them, responsive to every little rumour or suspicion of unsolved crime. Appreciation of nature found no place among his many gifts, and his only change was when he turned his mind from the evil-doer of the town to track down his brother of the country.

Finding that Holmes was too absorbed for conversation I had tossed aside the barren paper and, leaning back in my chair, I fell into a brown study. Suddenly my companion's voice broke in upon my thoughts.

'You are right, Watson,' said he. 'It does seem a most preposterous way of settling a dispute.'

'Most preposterous!' I exclaimed, and then suddenly realizing how he had echoed the inmost thought of my soul, I sat up in my chair and stared at him in blank amazement.

'What is this, Holmes?' I cried. 'This is beyond anything which I could have imagined.'

He laughed heartily at my perplexity.

'You remember,' said he, 'that some little time ago when I read you the passage in one of Poe's sketches in which a close reasoner follows the unspoken thoughts of his companion, you were inclined to treat the matter as a mere *tour de force* of the author. On my remarking that I was constantly in the habit of doing the same thing you expressed incredulity.'

'Oh, no!'

'Perhaps not with your tongue, my dear Watson, but certainly with your eyebrows. So when I saw you throw down your paper and enter upon a train of thought, I was very happy to have the opportunity of reading it off, and eventually of breaking into it, as a proof that I had been in rapport with you.'

But I was still far from satisfied. 'In the example which you read to me,' said I, 'the reasoner drew his conclusions from the actions of the man whom he observed. If I remember right, he stumbled over a heap of stones, looked up at the stars, and so on. But I have been seated quietly in my chair, and what clues can I have given you?'

'You do yourself an injustice. The features are given to man as the means by which he shall express his emotions, and yours are faithful servants.'

'Do you mean to say that you read my train of thoughts from my features?'

'Your features, and especially your eyes. Perhaps you cannot yourself recall how your reverie commenced?'

'No, I cannot.'

'Then I will tell you. After throwing down your paper, which was the action which drew my attention to you, you sat for half a minute with a vacant expression. Then your eyes fixed themselves upon your newly-framed picture of General Gordon, and I saw by the alteration in your face that a train of thought had been started. But it did not lead very far. Your eyes flashed across to the unframed portrait of Henry Ward Beecher which stands upon the top of your books. Then you glanced up at the wall, and of course your meaning was obvious. You were thinking that if the portrait were framed, it would just cover that bare space and correspond with Gordon's picture over there.'

'You have followed me wonderfully!' I exclaimed.

'So far I could hardly have gone astray. But now your thoughts went back to Beecher, and you looked hard across as if you were studying the character in his features. Then your eyes ceased to pucker, but you continued to look across, and your face was thoughtful. You were recalling the incidents of Beecher's career. I was well aware that you could not do this without thinking of the mission which he undertook on behalf of the North at the time of the Civil War, for I remember your expressing your passionate indignation at the way in which he was received by the more turbulent of our people. You felt so strongly about it, that I knew you could not think of Beecher without thinking of that also. When a moment later I saw your eyes wander away from the picture, I suspected that your mind had now turned to the Civil War, and when I observed that your lips set, your eyes sparkled, and your hands clenched, I was positive that you were indeed thinking of the gallantry which was shown by both sides in that desperate struggle. But then, again, your face grew sadder; you shook your head. You were dwelling upon the sadness and horror and useless waste of life. Your hand stole towards your own old wound and a smile quivered on your lips, which showed me that the ridiculous side of this method of settling international questions had forced itself upon your mind. At this point I agreed with you that it was pre-posterous, and was glad to find that all my deductions had been correct.'

'Absolutely!' said I. 'And now that you have explained it, I confess that I am as amazed as before.'

'It was very superficial, my dear Watson, I assure you. I should not have intruded it upon your attention had you not shown some incredulity the other day. But I have in my hands here a little problem which may prove to be more difficult of solution than my small essay in thought reading. Have you observed in the paper a short paragraph referring to the remark-able contents of a packet sent through the post to Miss Cushing, of Cross Street, Croydon?'

'No, I saw nothing.'

'Ah! then you must have overlooked it. Just toss it over to me. Here it is, under the financial column. Perhaps you would be good enough to read it aloud.'

I picked up the paper which he had thrown back to me, and read the paragraph indicated. It was headed, 'A Gruesome Packet.'

Miss Susan Cushing, living at Cross Street, Croydon, has been made the victim of what must be regarded as a peculiarly revolting practical joke, unless some more sinister meaning should prove to be attached to the incident. At two o'clock yesterday afternoon a small packet, wrapped in brown paper, was handed in by the postman.

A cardboard box was inside, which was filled with coarse salt. On emptying this, Miss Cushing was horrified to find two human ears, apparently quite freshly severed. The box had been sent by parcel post from Belfast upon the morning before. There is no indication as to the sender, and the matter is the more mysterious as Miss Cushing, who is a maiden lady of fifty, has led a most retired life, and has so few acquaintances or correspondents that it is a rare event for her to receive anything through the post. Some years ago, however, when she resided at Penge, she let apartments in her house to three young medical students, whom she was obliged to get rid of on account of their noisy and irregular habits. The police are of opinion that this outrage may have been perpetrated upon Miss Cushing by these youths, who owed her a grudge, and who hoped to frighten her by sending her these relics of the dissecting-rooms. Some probability is lent to the theory by the fact that one of these students came from the north of Ireland, and, to the best of Miss Cushing's belief, from Belfast. In the meantime, the matter is being actively investigated, Mr Lestrade, one of the very smartest of our detective officers, being in charge of the case.

'So much for the *Daily Chronicle*,' said Holmes, as I finished reading. 'Now for our friend Lestrade. I had a note from him this morning, in which he says: "I think that this case is very much in your line. We have every hope of clearing the matter up, but we find a little difficulty in getting anything to work upon. We have, of course, wired to the Belfast post-office, but a large number of parcels were handed in upon that day, and they have no means of identifying this particular one, or of remembering the sender. The box is a half-pound box of honeydew tobacco, and does not help us in any way. The medical student theory still appears to me to be the most feasible, but if you should have a few hours to spare, I should be very happy to see you out here. I shall be either at the house or in the police-station all day." What say you, Watson? Can you rise superior to the heat, and run down to Croydon with me on the off-chance of a case for your annals?'

'I was longing for something to do.'

'You shall have it then. Ring for our boots, and tell them to order a cab. I'll be back in a moment, when I have changed my dressing-gown and filled my cigar-case.'

A shower of rain fell while we were in the train, and the heat was far less oppressive in Croydon than in town. Holmes had sent on a wire, so that Lestrade, as wiry, as dapper, and as ferret-like as ever, was waiting for us at the station. A walk of five minutes took us to Cross Street, where Miss Cushing resided.

It was a very long street of two-storey brick houses, neat and prim, with whitened stone steps and little groups of aproned women gossiping at the doors. Half-way down, Lestrade stopped and tapped at a door, which was opened by a small servant girl. Miss Cushing was sitting in the front room, into which we were ushered. She was a placid-faced woman, with large, gentle eyes, and grizzled hair curving down over her temples on each side. A worked antimacassar lay upon her lap and a basket of coloured silks stood upon a stool beside her.

'They are in the outhouse, those dreadful things,' said she, as Lestrade entered. 'I wish that you would take them away altogether.'

'So I shall, Miss Cushing. I only kept them here until my friend, Mr Holmes, should have seen them in your presence.'

'Why in my presence, sir?'

'In case he wished to ask any questions.'

'What is the use of asking me questions, when I tell you I know nothing whatever about it?'

'Quite so, madam,' said Holmes, in his soothing way. 'I have no doubt that you have been annoyed more than enough already over this business.'

'Indeed, I have, sir. I am a quiet woman and live a retired life. It is something new for me to see my name in the papers and to find the police in my house. I won't have those things in here, Mr Lestrade. If you wish to see them you must go to the outhouse.'

It was a small shed in the narrow garden which ran behind the house. Lestrade went in and brought out a yellow card-board box, with a piece of brown paper and some string. There was a bench at the end of the path, and we all sat down while Holmes examined, one by one, the articles which Lestrade had handed to him.

'The string is exceedingly interesting,' he remarked, holding it up to the light and sniffing at it. 'What do you make of this string, Lestrade?'

'It has been tarred.'

'Precisely. It is a piece of tarred twine. You have also, no doubt, remarked that Miss Cushing has cut the cord with a scissors, as can be seen by the double fray on each side. This is of importance.'

'I cannot see the importance,' said Lestrade.

'The importance lies in the fact that the knot is left intact, and that this knot is of a peculiar character.'

'It is very neatly tied. I had already made a note to that effect,' said Lestrade, complacently.

'So much for the string, then,' said Holmes, smiling; 'now for the box wrapper. Brown paper, with a distinct smell of coffee. What, did not observe it? I think there can be no doubt of it. Address printed in rather straggling characters: "Miss S. Cushing, Cross Street, Croydon." Done with a broad-pointed pen, probably a J, and with very inferior ink. The word Croydon has been originally spelt with an i, which has been changed to y. The parcel was directed then by a man – the printing is distinctly masculine – of limited education and unacquainted with the town of Croydon. So far, so good! The box is a yellow, half-pound honeydew box, with nothing distinctive save two thumb marks at the left bottom corner. It is filled with rough salt of the quality used for preserving hides and other of the coarser commercial purposes. And embedded in it are these very singular enclosures.'

He took out the two ears as he spoke, and laying a board across his knee, he examined them minutely, while Lestrade and I, bending forward on each side of him, glanced alternately at these dreadful relics and at the thoughtful, eager face of our companion. Finally he returned them to the box once more, and sat for a while in deep meditation.

'You have observed, of course,' said he at last, 'that the ears are not a pair.'

'Yes, I have noticed that. But if this were the practical joke of some students from the dissecting-rooms, it would be as easy for them to send two odd ears as a pair.'

'Precisely. But this is not a practical joke.'

'You are sure of it?'

'The presumption is strongly against it. Bodies in the dissecting-rooms are injected with preservative fluid. These ears bear no signs of this. They are fresh too. They have been cut off with a blunt instrument, which would hardly happen if a student had done it. Again, carbolic or rectified spirits would be the preservatives which would suggest themselves to the medical mind, certainly not rough salt. I repeat that there is no practical joke here, but that we are investigating a serious crime.'

A vague thrill ran through me as I listened to my companion's words and saw the stern gravity which had hardened his features. This brutal preliminary seemed to shadow forth some strange and inexplicable horror in the background. Lestrade, however, shook his head like a man who is only half convinced.

'There are objections to the joke theory, no doubt,' said he; 'but there are much stronger reasons against the other. We know that this woman has led a most quiet and respectable life at Penge and here for the last twenty years. She has hardly

been away from her home for a day during that time. Why on
earth, then, should any criminal send her the proofs of
his guilt, especially as, unless she is a most consummate
actress, she understands quite as little of the matter as we
do?'

'That is the problem which we have to solve,' Holmes
answered, 'and for my part I shall set about it by presuming
that my reasoning is correct, and that a double murder has been
committed. One of these ears is a woman's, small, finely formed,
and pierced for an ear-ring. The other is a man's, sun-burned,
discoloured, and also pierced for an ear-ring. These two people
are presumably dead, or we should have heard their story before
now. Today is Friday. The packet was posted on Thursday
morning. The tragedy, then, occurred on Wednesday or Tuesday,
or earlier. If the two people were murdered, who but their
murderer would have sent this sign of his work to Miss Cushing?
We may take it that the sender of the packet is the man whom we
want. But he must have some strong reason for sending Miss
Cushing this packet. What reason, then? It must have been to
tell her that the deed was done; or to pain her, perhaps. But
in that case she knows who it is. Does she know? I doubt it.
If she knew, why should she call the police in? She might
have buried the ears, and no one would have been the wiser.
That is what she would have done if she had wished to shield
the criminal. But if she does not wish to shield him she would
give his name. There is a tangle here which needs straightening
out.' He had been talking in a high, quick voice, staring blankly
up over the garden fence, but now he sprang briskly to his feet
and walked towards the house.

'I have a few questions to ask Miss Cushing,' said he.

'In that case I may leave you here,' said Lestrade, 'for I have
another small business on hand. I think that I have nothing
further to learn from Miss Cushing. You will find me at the
police-station.'

'We shall look in on our way to the train,' answered Holmes.

A moment later he and I were back in the front room, where the impassive lady was still quietly working away at her antimacassar. She put it down on her lap as we entered, and looked at us with her frank, searching blue eyes.

'I am convinced, sir,' she said, 'that this matter is a mistake, and that the parcel was never meant for me at all. I have said this several times to the gentleman from Scotland Yard, but he simply laughs at me. I have not an enemy in the world, as far as I know, so why should anyone play me such a trick?'

'I am coming to be of the same opinion, Miss Cushing,' said Holmes, taking a seat beside her. 'I think that it is more than probable . . . ' he paused, and I was surprised, on glancing round, to see that he was staring with singular intentness at the lady's profile. Surprise and satisfaction were both for an instant to be read upon his eager face, though when she glanced round to find out the cause of his silence he had become as demure as ever. I stared hard myself at her flat, grizzled hair, her trim cap, her little gilt ear-rings, her placid features: but I could see nothing which could account for my companion's evident excitement.

'There were one or two questions——'

'Oh, I am weary of questions!' cried Miss Cushing, impatiently.

'You have two sisters, I believe.'

'How could you know that?'

'I observed the very instant that I entered the room that you have a portrait group of three ladies upon the mantelpiece, one of whom is undoubtedly yourself, while the others are so exceedingly like you that there could be no doubt of the relationship.'

'Yes, you are quite right. Those are my sisters, Sarah and Mary.'

'And here at my elbow is another portrait, taken at Liverpool, of your younger sister, in the company of a man who appears

to be a steward by his uniform. I observe that she was unmarried at the time.'

'You are very quick at observing.'

'That is my trade.'

'Well, you are quite right. But she was married to Mr
Browner a few days afterwards. He was on the South American
line when that was taken, but he was so fond of her that he
couldn't abide to leave her for so long, and he got into the
Liverpool and London boats.'

'Ah, the *Conqueror*, perhaps?'

'No, the *May Day*, when last I heard. Jim came down here
to see me once. That was before he broke the pledge; but afterwards he would always take drink when he was ashore, and a
little drink would send him stark, staring mad. Ah! it was a bad
day that ever he took a glass in his hand again. First he dropped
me, then he quarrelled with Sarah, and now that Mary has
stopped writing we don't know how things are going with
them.'

It was evident that Miss Cushing had come upon a subject
on which she felt very deeply. Like most people who lead a
lonely life, she was shy at first, but ended by becoming extremely communicative. She told us many details about her
brother-in-law the steward, and then wandering off on to the
subject of her former lodgers, the medical students, she gave us
a long account of their delinquencies, with their names and those
of their hospitals. Holmes listened attentively to everything,
throwing in a question from time to time.

'About your second sister, Sarah,' said he. 'I wonder, since
you are both maiden ladies, that you do not keep house together.'

'Ah! you don't know Sarah's temper, or you would wonder
no more. I tried it when I came to Croydon, and we kept on
until about two months ago, when we had to part. I don't want
to say a word against my own sister, but she was always meddle-
some and hard to please, was Sarah.'

'You say that she quarrelled with your Liverpool relations.'

'Yes, and they were the best of friends at one time. Why, she went up there to live in order to be near them. And now she has no word hard enough for Jim Browner. The last six months that she was here she would speak of nothing but his drinking and his ways. He had caught her meddling, I suspect, and given her a bit of his mind, and that was the start of it.'

'Thank you, Miss Cushing,' said Holmes, rising and bowing. 'Your sister Sarah lives, I think you said, at New Street, Wallington? Goodbye, and I am very sorry that you should have been troubled over a case with which, as you say, you have nothing whatever to do.'

There was a cab passing as we came out, and Holmes hailed it.

'How far to Wallington?' he asked.

'Only about a mile, sir.'

'Very good. Jump in, Watson. We must strike while the iron is hot. Simple as the case is, there have been one or two very instructive details in connection with it. Just pull up at a telegraph office as you pass, cabby.'

Holmes sent off a short wire, and for the rest of the drive lay back in the cab with his hat tilted over his nose to keep the sun from his face. Our driver pulled up at a house which was not unlike the one which we had just quitted. My companion ordered him to wait, and had his hand upon the knocker, when the door opened and a grave young gentleman in black, with a very shiny hat, appeared on the step.

'Is Miss Cushing at home?' asked Holmes.

'Miss Sarah Cushing is extremely ill,' said he. 'She has been suffering since yesterday from brain symptoms of great severity. As her medical adviser, I cannot possibly take the responsibility of allowing anyone to see her. I should recommend you to call again in ten days.' He drew on his gloves, closed the door, and marched off down the street.

'Well, if we can't, we can't,' said Holmes, cheerfully.

'Perhaps she could not, or would not have told you much.'

'I did not wish her to tell me anything. I only wanted to look at her. However, I think that I have got all that I want. Drive us to some decent hotel, cabby, where we may have some lunch, and afterwards we shall drop down upon friend Lestrade at the police-station.'

We had a pleasant little meal together, during which Holmes would talk about nothing but violins, narrating with great exultation how he had purchased his own Stradivarius, which was worth at least five hundred guineas, at a Jew broker's in Tottenham Court Road for fifty-five shillings. This led him to Paganini, and we sat for an hour over a bottle of claret while he told me anecdote after anecdote of that extraordinary man. The afternoon was far advanced and the hot glare had softened into a mellow glow before we found ourselves at the police-station. Lestrade was waiting for us at the door.

'A telegram for you, Mr Holmes,' said he.

'Ha! It is the answer!' He tore it open, glanced his eyes over it, and crumpled it into his pocket. 'That's all right,' said he.

'Have you found out anything?'

'I have found out everything!'

'What!' Lestrade stared at him in amazement. 'You are joking.'

'I was never more serious in my life. A shocking crime has been committed, and I think I have now laid bare every detail of it.'

'And the criminal?'

Holmes scribbled a few words upon the back of one of his visiting cards and threw it over to Lestrade.

'That is the name,' he said. 'You cannot effect an arrest until tomorrow night at the earliest. I should prefer that you do not mention my name at all in connection with the case, as I choose to be only associated with those crimes which present some difficulty in their solution. Come on, Watson.' We strode

off together to the station, leaving Lestrade still staring
with a delighted face at the card which Holmes had thrown
him.

'The case,' said Sherlock Holmes, as we chatted over our cigars
that night in our rooms at Baker Street, 'is one where, as in the
investigations which you have chronicled under the names of
the "Study in Scarlet" and of the "Sign of Four", we have been
compelled to reason backward from effects to causes. I have
written to Lestrade asking him to supply us with the details
which are now wanting, and which he will only get after he has
secured his man. That he may be safely trusted to do, for although he is absolutely devoid of reason, he is as tenacious as a
bull-dog when he once understands what he has to do, and indeed
it is just this tenacity which has brought him to the top at
Scotland Yard.'

'Your case is not complete, then?' I asked.

'It is fairly complete in essentials. We know who the author
of the revolting business is, although one of the victims still
escapes us. Of course, you have formed your own conclusions.'

'I presume that this Jim Browner, the steward of a Liverpool
boat, is the man whom you suspect?'

'Oh! it is more than a suspicion.'

'And yet I cannot see anything save very vague indications.'

'On the contrary, to my mind nothing could be more clear.
Let me run over the principal steps. We approached the case,
you remember, with an absolutely blank mind, which is always
an advantage. We had formed no theories. We were simply
there to observe and to draw inferences from our observations.
What did we see first? A very placid and respectable lady, who
seemed quite innocent of any secret, and a portrait which
showed me that she had two younger sisters. It instantly flashed
across my mind that the box might have been meant for one of
these. I set the idea aside as one which could be disproved or
confirmed at our leisure. Then we went to the garden, as you

remember, and we saw the very singular contents of the little
yellow box.

'The string was of the quality which is used by sail-makers
aboard ship, and at once a whiff of the sea was perceptible in our
investigation. When I observed that the knot was one which is
popular with sailors, that the parcel had been posted at a port,
and that the male ear was pierced for an ear-ring which is so
much more common among sailors than landsmen, I was quite
certain that all the actors in the tragedy were to be found
among our seafaring classes.

'When I came to examine the address of the packet I observed
that it was to Miss S. Cushing. Now, the oldest sister would, of
course, be Miss Cushing, and although her initial was "S" it
might belong to one of the others as well. In that case we should
have to commence our investigation from a fresh basis altogether. I therefore went into the house with the intention of
clearing up this point. I was about to assure Miss Cushing that
I was convinced that a mistake had been made, when you may
remember that I came suddenly to a stop. The fact was that I
had just seen something which filled me with surprise, and at the
same time narrowed the field of our inquiry immensely.

'As a medical man, you are aware, Watson, that there is no
part of the body which varies so much as the human ear. Each
ear is as a rule quite distinctive, and differs from all other ones.
In last year's *Anthropological Journal* you will find two short
monographs from my pen upon the subject. I had, therefore,
examined the ears in the box with the eyes of an expert, and had
carefully noted their anatomical peculiarities. Imagine my
surprise then, when, on looking at Miss Cushing, I perceived
that her ear corresponded exactly with the female ear which I
had just inspected. The matter was entirely beyond coincidence.
There was the same shortening of the pinna, the same broad
curve of the upper lobe, the same convolution of the inner
cartilage. In all essentials it was the same ear.

'Of course, I at once saw the enormous importance of the

observation. It was evident that the victim was a blood relation, and probably a very close one. I began to talk to her about her family, and you remember that she at once gave us some exceedingly valuable details.

'In the first place, her sister's name was Sarah, and her address had, until recently, been the same, so that it was quite obvious how the mistake had occurred, and for whom the packet was meant. Then we heard of this steward, married to the third sister, and learned that he had at one time been so intimate with Miss Sarah that she had actually gone up to Liverpool to be near the Browners, but a quarrel had afterwards divided them. This quarrel had put a stop to all communications for some months, so that if Browner had occasion to address a packet to Miss Sarah, he would undoubtedly have done so to her old address.

'And now the matter had begun to straighten itself out wonderfully. We had learned of the existence of this steward, an impulsive man, of strong passions – you remember that he threw up what must have been a very superior berth, in order to be nearer to his wife – subject, too, to occasional fits of hard drinking. We had reason to believe that his wife had been murdered, and that a man – presumably a seafaring man – had been murdered at the same time. Jealousy, of course, at once suggests itself as the motive for the crime. And why should these proofs of the deed be sent to Miss Sarah Cushing? Probably because during her residence in Liverpool she had some hand in bringing about the events which led to the tragedy. You will observe that this line of boats calls at Belfast, Dublin, and Waterford; so that, presuming that Browner had committed the deed, and had embarked at once upon his steamer, the *May Day*, Belfast would be the first place at which he could post his terrible packet.

'A second solution was at this stage obviously possible, and although I thought it exceedingly unlikely, I was determined to elucidate it before going further. An unsuccessful lover might have killed Mr and Mrs Browner, and the male ear might have belonged to the husband. There were many grave objections to this theory, but it was conceivable. I therefore sent off a tele-gram to my friend Algar, of the Liverpool force, and asked him to find out if Mrs Browner were at home, and if Browner had departed in the *May Day*. Then we went on to Wallington to visit Miss Sarah.

'I was curious, in the first place, to see how far the family ear had been reproduced in her. Then, of course, she might give us very important information, but I was not sanguine that she would. She must have heard of the business the day before, since all Croydon was ringing with it, and she alone could have under-stood for whom the packet was meant. If she had been willing to help justice she would probably have communicated with the police already. However, it was clearly our duty to see her, so we went. We found that the news of the arrival of the packet – for her illness dated from that time – had such an effect upon her as to bring on brain fever. It was clearer than ever that she understood its full significance, but equally clear that we should have to wait some time for any assistance from her.

'However, we were really independent of her help. Our answers were waiting for us at the police-station, where I had directed Algar to send them. Nothing could be more conclusive. Mrs Browner's house had been closed for more than three days, and the neighbours were of opinion that she had gone south to see her relatives. It had been ascertained at the shipping offices that Browner had left aboard of the *May Day*, and I calculate that she is due in the Thames tomorrow night. When he arrives he will be met by the obtuse but resolute Lestrade, and I have no doubt that we shall have all our details filled in.'

Sherlock Holmes was not disappointed in his expectations. Two days later he received a bulky envelope, which contained a short note from the detective, and a typewritten document, which covered several pages of foolscap.

'Lestrade has got him all right,' said Holmes, glancing up at me. 'Perhaps it would interest you to hear what he says.'

MY DEAR MR HOLMES, – In accordance with the scheme which we had formed in order to test our theories ('the "we" is rather fine, Watson, is it not?') I went down to the Albert Dock yesterday at 6 p.m., and boarded the s.s. *May Day*, belonging to the Liverpool, Dublin, and London Steam Packet Company. On inquiry, I found that there was a steward on board of the name of James Browner and that he had acted during the voyage in such an extraordinary manner that the captain had been compelled to relieve him of his duties. On descending to his berth, I found him seated upon a chest with his head sunk upon his hands, rocking himself to and fro. He is a big, powerful chap, clean-shaven, and very swarthy – something like Aldridge, who helped us in the bogus laundry affair. He jumped up when he heard my business, and I had my whistle to my lips to call a couple of river police, who were round the corner, but he seemed to have no heart in him, and he held out his hands quietly enough for the darbies. We brought him along to the cells, and his box as well, for we thought there might be something incriminating; but, bar a big sharp knife, such as most sailors have, we got nothing for our trouble. However, we find that we shall want no more evidence, for on being brought before the inspector at the station, he asked leave to make a statement, which was, of course, taken down, just as he made it, by our shorthand man. We had three copies typewritten, one of which I enclose. The affair proves, as I always thought it would, to be an extremely simple one, but I am obliged to you for assisting me in my investigation. With kind regards, yours very truly. – G. LESTRADE.

'Hum! The investigation really was a very simple one,' remarked Holmes; 'but I don't think it struck him in that light

when he first called us in. However, let us see what Jim Browner
has to say for himself. This is his statement, as made before
Inspector Montgomery at the Shadwell Police Station, and it
has the advantage of being verbatim.'

'Have I anything to say? Yes, I have a deal to say. I have
to make a clean breast of it all. You can hang me, or you
can leave me alone. I don't care a plug which you do. I tell
you I've not shut an eye in sleep since I did it, and I don't
believe I ever will again until I get past all waking. Sometimes it's his face, but most generally it's hers. I'm never
without one or the other before me. He looks frowning
and black-like, but she has a kind o' surprise upon her face.
Aye, the white lamb, she might well be surprised when she
read death on a face that had seldom looked anything but
love upon her before.

'But it was Sarah's fault, and may the curse of a broken
man put a blight on her and set the blood rotting in her
veins! It's not that I want to clear myself. I know that I
went back to drink, like the beast that I was. But she would
have forgiven me; she would have stuck as close to me as a
rope to a block if that woman had never darkened our door.
For Sarah Cushing loved me – that's the root of the business – she loved me, until all her love turned to poisonous
hate when she knew that I thought more of my wife's footmark in the mud than I did of her whole body and soul.

'There were three sisters altogether. The old one was
just a good woman, the second was a devil, and the third
was an angel. Sarah was thirty-three, and Mary was
twenty-nine when I married. We were just as happy as the
day was long when we set up house together, and in all
Liverpool there was no better woman than my Mary. And
then we asked Sarah up for a week, and the week grew into
a month, and one thing led to another, until she was just
one of ourselves.

'I was blue ribbon at that time, and we were putting a little money by, and all was as bright as a new dollar. My God, whoever would have thought that it could have come to this? Whoever would have dreamed it?

'I used to be home for the week-ends very often, and sometimes if the ship were held back for cargo I would have a whole week at a time, and in this way I saw a deal of my sister-in-law, Sarah. She was a fine tall woman, black and quick and fierce, with a proud way of carrying her head, and a glint from her eye like a spark from a flint. But when little Mary was there I had never a thought of her, and that I swear as I hope for God's mercy.

'It had seemed to me sometimes that she liked to be alone with me, or to coax me out for a walk with her, but I had never thought anything of that. But one evening my eyes were opened. I had come up from the ship and found my wife out, but Sarah at home. "Where's Mary?" I asked. "Oh, she has gone to pay some accounts." I was impatient and paced up and down the room. "Can't you be happy for five minutes without Mary, Jim?" says she. "It's a bad compliment to me that you can't be contented with my society for so short a time." "That's all right, my lass," said I, putting out my hand towards her in a kindly way, but she had it in both hers in an instant, and they burned as if they were in a fever. I looked into her eyes and I read it all there. There was no need for her to speak, nor for me either. I frowned and drew my hand away. Then she stood by my side in silence for a bit, and then put up her hand and patted me on the shoulder. "Steady, old Jim!" said she; and with a kind of mocking laugh, she ran out of the room.

'Well, from that time Sarah hated me with her whole heart and soul, and she is a woman who can hate, too. I was a fool to let her go on biding with us – a besotted fool – but I never said a word to Mary, for I knew it would grieve

her. Things went on much as before, but after a time I
began to find that there was a bit of a change in Mary herself. She had always been so trusting and so innocent, but
now she became queer and suspicious, wanting to know
where I had been and what I had been doing, and whom my
letters were from, and what I had in my pockets, and a
thousand such follies. Day by day she grew queerer and
more irritable, and we had causeless rows about nothing.
I was fairly puzzled by it all. Sarah avoided me now, but
she and Mary were just inseparable. I can see now how she
was plotting and scheming and poisoning my wife's mind
against me, but I was such a blind beetle that I could not
understand it at the time. Then I broke my blue ribbon
and began to drink again, but I think I should not have
done it if Mary had been the same as ever. She had some
reason to be disgusted with me now, and the gap between
us began to be wider and wider. And then this Alec
Fairbairn chipped in, and things became a thousand times
blacker.

'It was to see Sarah that he came to my house first, but
soon it was to see us, for he was a man with winning ways,
and he made friends wherever he went. He was a dashing,
swaggering chap, smart and curled, who had seen half the
world, and could talk of what he had seen. He was good
company, I won't deny it, and he had wonderful polite
ways with him for a sailor man, so that I think there must
have been a time when he knew more of the poop than the
forecastle. For a month he was in and out of my house, and
never once did it cross my mind that harm might come of
his soft, tricky ways. And then at last something made
me suspect, and from that day my peace was gone for
ever.

'It was only a little thing too. I had come into the parlour
unexpected, and as I walked in at the door I saw a light of
welcome on my wife's face. But as she saw who it was it

faded again, and she turned away with a look of disappointment. That was enough for me. There was no one but Alec Fairbairn whose step she could have mistaken for mine. If I could have seen him then I should have killed him, for I have always been like a madman when my temper gets loose. Mary saw the devil's light in my eyes, and she ran forward with her hands on my sleeve. "Don't, Jim, don't!" says she. "Where's Sarah?" I asked. "In the kitchen," says she. "Sarah," says I, as I went in, "this man Fairbairn is never to darken my door again." "Why not?" says she. "Because I order it." "Oh!" says she, "if my friends are not good enough for this house, then I am not good enough for it either." "You can do what you like," says I, "but if Fairbairn shows his face here again, I'll send you one of his ears for a keepsake." She was frightened by my face, I think, for she never answered a word, and the same evening she left my house.

'Well, I don't know now whether it was pure devilry on the part of this woman, or whether she thought that she could turn me against my wife by encouraging her to misbehave. Anyway, she took a house just two streets off, and let lodgings to sailors. Fairbairn used to stay there, and Mary would go round to have tea with her sister and him. How often she went I don't know, but I followed her one day, and as I broke in at the door, Fairbairn got away over the back garden wall, like the cowardly skunk that he was. I swore to my wife that I would kill her if I found her in his company again, and I led her back with me, sobbing and trembling, and as white as a piece of paper. There was no trace of love between us any longer. I could see that she hated me and feared me, and when the thought of it drove me to drink, then she despised me as well.

'Well, Sarah found that she could not make a living in Liverpool, so she went back, as I understand, to live with her sister in Croydon, and things jogged on much the

same as ever at home. And then came this last week and all
the misery and ruin.

'It was in this way. We had gone on the *May Day* for a
round voyage of seven days, but a hogshead got loose and
started one of our plates, so that we had to put back into
port for twelve hours. I left the ship and came home,
thinking what a surprise it would be for my wife, and hop-
ing that maybe she would be glad to see me so soon. The
thought was in my head as I turned into my own street,
and at that moment a cab passed me, and there she was,
sitting by the side of Fairbairn, the two chatting and
laughing, with never a thought for me as I stood watching
them from the footpath.

'I tell you, that I give you my word for it, that from that
moment I was not my own master, and it is all like a dim
dream when I look back on it. I had been drinking hard of
late, and the two things together fairly turned my brain.
There's something throbbing in my head now, like a
docker's hammer, but that morning I seemed to have all
Niagara whizzing and buzzing in my ears.

'Well, I took to my heels, and I ran after the cab. I had a
heavy oak stick in my hand, and I tell you I saw red from
the first; but as I ran I got cunning, too, and hung back a
little to see them without being seen. They pulled up soon
at the railway station. There was a good crowd round the
booking-office, so I got quite close to them without being
seen. They took tickets for New Brighton. So did I, but I
got in three carriages behind them. When we reached it
it they walked along the Parade, and I was never more than
a hundred yards from them. At last I saw them hire a
boat and start for a row, for it was a very hot day, and
they thought no doubt that it would be cooler on the
water.

'It was just as if they had been given into my hands.
There was a bit of a haze, and you could not see more than

a few hundred yards. I hired a boat for myself, and I pulled after them. I could see the blur of their craft, but they were going nearly as fast as I, and they must have been a long mile from the shore before I caught them up. The haze was like a curtain all round us, and there were we three in the middle of it. My God, shall I ever forget their faces when they saw who was in the boat that was closing in upon them? She screamed out. He swore like a madman, and jabbed at me with an oar, for he must have seen death in my eyes. I got past it and got one in with my stick, that crushed his head like an egg. I would have spared her, perhaps, for all my madness, but she threw her arms round him, crying out to him, and calling him "Alec". I struck again, and she lay stretched beside him. I was like a wild beast then that had tasted blood. If Sarah had been there, by the Lord, she should have joined them. I pulled out my knife, and – well, there! I've said enough. It gave me a kind of savage joy when I thought how Sarah would feel when she had such signs as these of what her meddling had brought about. Then I tied the bodies into the boat, stove a plank, and stood by until they had sunk. I knew very well that the owner would think that they had lost their bearings in the haze, and had drifted off out to sea. I cleaned myself up, got back to land, and joined my ship without a soul having a suspicion of what had passed. That night I made up the packet for Sarah Cushing, and next day I sent it from Belfast.

'There you have the whole truth of it. You can hang me, or do what you like with me, but you cannot punish me as I have been punished already. I cannot shut my eyes but I see those two faces staring at me – staring at me as they stared when my boat broke through the haze. I killed them quick, but they are killing me slow; and if I have another night of it I shall be either mad or dead before morning. You won't put me alone into a cell, sir? For pity's sake don't, and may you be treated in your day of agony as you treat me now.'

'What is the meaning of it, Watson?' said Holmes, solemnly, as he laid down the paper. 'What object is served by this circle of misery and violence and fear? It must tend to some end, or else our universe is ruled by chance, which is unthinkable. But what end? There is the great standing perennial problem to which human reason is as far from an answer as ever.'

The Adventure of the Red Circle

I

'Well, Mrs Warren, I cannot see that you have any particular cause for uneasiness, nor do I understand why I, whose time is of some value, should interfere in the matter. I really have other things to engage me.' So spoke Sherlock Holmes, and turned back to the great scrapbook in which he was arranging and indexing some of his recent material.

But the landlady had the pertinacity, and also the cunning, of her sex. She held her ground firmly.

'You arranged an affair for a lodger of mine last year,' she said – 'Mr Fairdale Hobbs.'

'Ah, yes – a simple matter.'

'But he would never cease talking of it – your kindness, sir, and the way in which you brought light into the darkness. I remembered his words when I was in doubt and darkness myself. I know you could if you only would.'

Holmes was accessible upon the side of flattery, and also, to do him justice, upon the side of kindliness. The two forces made him lay down his gum-brush with a sigh of resignation and push back his chair.

'Well, well, Mrs Warren, let us hear about it, then. You don't object to tobacco, I take it? Thank you, Watson – the matches! You are uneasy, as I understand, because your new lodger remains in his rooms and you cannot see him. Why, bless you, Mrs Warren, if I were your lodger you often would not see me for weeks on end.'

'No doubt, sir; but this is different. It frightens me, Mr Holmes. I can't sleep for fright. To hear his quick step moving here and moving there from early morning to late at night, and yet never to catch so much as a glimpse of him – it's more than I can stand. My husband is as nervous over it as I am, but he is out at his work all day, while I get no rest from it. What is he hiding for? What has he done? Except for the girl, I am all alone in the house with him, and it's more than my nerves can stand.'

Holmes leaned forward and laid his long, thin fingers upon the woman's shoulder. He had an almost hypnotic power of soothing when he wished. The scared look faded from her eyes, and her agitated features smoothed into their usual commonplace. She sat down in the chair which he had indicated.

'If I take it up I must understand every detail,' said he. 'Take time to consider. The smallest point may be the most essential. You say that the man came ten days ago, and paid you for a fortnight's board and lodging?'

'He asked my terms, sir. I said fifty shillings a week. There is a small sitting-room and bedroom, and all complete, at the top of the house.'

'Well?'

'He said, "I'll pay you five pounds a week if I can have it on my own terms." I'm a poor woman, sir, and Mr Warren earns little, and the money meant much to me. He took out a ten-pound note, and he held it out to me then and there. "You can have the same every fortnight for a long time to come if you keep the terms," he said. "If not, I'll have no more to do with you."'

'What were the terms?'

'Well, sir, they were that he was to have a key of the house. That was all right. Lodgers often have them. Also, that he was to be left entirely to himself, and never, upon any excuse, to be disturbed.'

'Nothing wonderful in that, surely?'

'Not in reason, sir. But this is out of all reason. He has been there for ten days, and neither Mr Warren, nor I, nor the girl has once set eyes upon him. We can hear that quick step of his pacing up and down, up and down, night, morning, and noon; but except on that first night he has never once gone out of the house.'

'Oh, he went out the first night, did he?'

'Yes, sir, and returned very late – after we were all in bed. He told me after he had taken the rooms that he would do so, and asked me not to bar the door. I heard him come up the stair after midnight.'

'But his meals?'

'It was his particular direction that we should always, when he rang, leave his meal upon a chair, outside his door. Then he rings again when he has finished, and we take it down from the same chair. If he wants anything else he prints it on a slip of paper and leaves it.'

'Prints it?'

'Yes, sir; prints it in pencil. Just the word, nothing more. Here's one I brought to show you – SOAP. Here's another – MATCH. This is one he left the first morning – DAILY GAZETTE. I leave that paper with his breakfast every morning.'

'Dear me, Watson,' said Holmes, staring with great curiosity at the slips of foolscap which the landlady had handed to him, 'this is certainly a little unusual. Seclusion I can understand; but why print? Printing is a clumsy process. Why not write? What would it suggest, Watson?'

'That he desired to conceal his handwriting.'

'But why? What can it matter to him that his landlady should have a word of his writing? Still, it may be as you say. Then, again, why such laconic messages?'

'I cannot imagine.'

'It opens a pleasing field for intelligent speculation. The words are written with a broad-pointed, violet-tinted pencil of a not unusual pattern. You will observe that the paper is torn away at the side here after the printing was done, so that the

"S" of "SOAP" is partly gone. Suggestive, Watson, is it
not?'

'Of caution?'

'Exactly. There was evidently some mark, some thumbprint,
something which might give a clue to the person's identity.
Now, Mrs Warren, you say that the man was of middle size,
dark, and bearded. What age would he be?'

'Youngish, sir – not over thirty.'

'Well, can you give me no further indications?'

'He spoke good English, sir, and yet I thought he was a
foreigner by his accent.'

'And he was well dressed?'

'Very smartly dressed, sir – quite the gentleman. Dark
clothes – nothing you would note.'

'He gave no name?'

'No, sir.'

'And has had no letters or callers?'

'None.'

'But surely you or the girl enter his room of a morning?'

'No, sir; he looks after himself entirely.'

'Dear me! that is certainly remarkable. What about his
luggage?'

'He had one big brown bag with him – nothing else.'

'Well, we don't seem to have much material to help us.
Do you say nothing has come out of that room – absolutely
nothing?'

The landlady drew an envelope from her bag; from it she
shook out two burnt matches and a cigarette-end upon the table.

'They were on his tray this morning. I brought them because
I had heard that you can read great things out of small ones.'

Holmes shrugged his shoulders.

'There is nothing here,' said he. 'The matches have, of
course, been used to light cigarettes. That is obvious from the
shortness of the burnt end. Half the match is consumed in lighting a pipe or cigar. But, dear me! this cigarette stub is certainly

remarkable. The gentleman was bearded and moustached, you say?'

'Yes, sir.'

'I don't understand that. I should say that only a clean-shaven man could have smoked this. Why, Watson, even your modest moustache would have been singed.'

'A holder?' I suggested.

'No, no; the end is matted. I suppose there could not be two people in your rooms, Mrs Warren?'

'No, sir. He eats so little that I often wonder it can keep life in one.'

'Well, I think we must wait for a little more material. After all, you have nothing to complain of. You have received your rent, and he is not a troublesome lodger, though he is certainly an unusual one. He pays you well, and if he chooses to lie concealed it is no direct business of yours. We have no excuse for an intrusion upon his privacy until we have some reason to think that there is a guilty reason for it. I've taken up the matter, and I won't lose sight of it. Report to me if anything fresh occurs, and rely upon my assistance if it should be needed.

'There are certainly some points of interest in this case, Watson,' he remarked, when the landlady had left us. 'It may, of course, be trivial – individual eccentricity; or it may be very much deeper than appears on the surface. The first thing that strikes one is the obvious possibility that the person now in the rooms may be entirely different from the one who engaged them.'

'Why should you think so?'

'Well, apart from this cigarette-end, was it not suggestive that the only time the lodger went out was immediately after his taking the rooms? He came back – or someone came back – when all witnesses were out of the way. We have no proof that the person who came back was the person who went out. Then, again, the man who took the rooms spoke English well. This other, however, prints "match" when it should have been

"matches". I can imagine that the word was taken out of a
dictionary, which would give the noun but not the plural. The
laconic style may be to conceal the absence of knowledge of
English. Yes, Watson, there are good reasons to suspect that
there has been a substitution of lodgers.'

'But for what possible end?'

'Ah! there lies our problem. There is one rather obvious line
of investigation.' He took down the great book in which, day by
day, he filed the agony columns of the various London journals.
'Dear me!' said he, turning over the pages, 'what a chorus of
groans, cries, and bleatings! What a rag-bag of singular happenings! But surely the most valuable hunting-ground that ever
was given to a student of the unusual! This person is alone, and
cannot be approached by letter without a breach of that absolute
secrecy which is desired. How is any news or any message to
reach him from without? Obviously by advertisement through
a newspaper. There seems no other way, and fortunately we
need concern ourselves with the one paper only. Here are the
Daily Gazette extracts of the last fortnight. "Lady with a black
boa at Prince's Skating Club" – that we may pass. "Surely
Jimmy will not break his mother's heart" – that appears to be
irrelevant. "If the lady who fainted in the Brixton bus" – she
does not interest me. "Every day my heart longs——" Bleat,
Watson – unmitigated bleat! Ah! this is a little more possible.
Listen to this: "Be patient. Will find some sure means of com-
munication. Meanwhile, this column. – G." That is two days
after Mrs Warren's lodger arrived. It sounds plausible, does it
not? The mysterious one could understand English, even if he
could not print it. Let us see if we can pick up the trace again.
Yes, here we are – three days later. "Am making successful
arrangements. Patience and prudence. The clouds will pass.
– G." Nothing for a week after that. Then comes something
much more definite: "The path is clearing. If I find chance
signal message remember code agreed – one A, two B, and so on.
You will hear soon. – G." That was in yesterday's paper, and

there is nothing in today's. It's all very appropriate to Mrs Warren's lodger. If we wait a little, Watson, I don't doubt that the affair will grow more intelligible.'

So it proved; for in the morning I found my friend standing on the hearthrug with his back to the fire, and a smile of complete satisfaction upon his face.

'How's this, Watson?' he cried, picking up the paper from the table. '"High red house with white stone facings. Third floor. Second window left. After dusk. – G." That is definite enough. I think after breakfast we must make a little reconnaissance of Mrs Warren's neighbourhood. Ah, Mrs Warren, what news do you bring us this morning?'

Our client had suddenly burst into the room with an explosive energy which told of some new and momentous development.

'It's a police matter, Mr Holmes!' she cried. 'I'll have no more of it! He shall pack out of that with his baggage. I would have gone straight up and told him so, only I thought it was but fair to you to take your opinion first. But I'm at the end of my patience, and when it comes to knocking my old man about——'

'Knocking Mr Warren about?'

'Using him roughly, anyway.'

'But who used him roughly?'

'Ah! That's what we want to know! It was this morning, sir. Mr Warren is a time-keeper at Morton and Waylight's, in Tottenham Court Road. He has to be out of the house before seven. Well, this morning he had not got ten paces down the road when two men came up behind him, threw a coat over his head, and bundled him into a cab that was beside the kerb. They drove him an hour, and then opened the door and shot him out. He lay in the roadway so shaken in his wits that he never saw what became of the cab. When he picked himself up he found he was on Hampstead Heath; so he took a bus home, and there he lies now on the sofa, while I came straight round to tell you what had happened.'

'Most interesting,' said Holmes. 'Did he observe the appearance of these men – did he hear them talk?'

'No; he is clean dazed. He just knows that he was lifted up as if by magic and dropped as if by magic. Two at least were in it, and maybe three.'

'And you connect this attack with your lodger?'

'Well, we've lived there fifteen years and no such happenings ever came before. I've had enough of him. Money's not everything. I'll have him out of my house before the day is done.'

'Wait a bit, Mrs Warren. Do nothing rash. I begin to think that this affair may be very much more important than appeared at first sight. It is clear now that some danger is threatening your lodger. It is equally clear that his enemies, lying in wait for him near your door, mistook your husband for him in the foggy morning light. On discovering their mistake they released him. What they would have done had it not been a mistake, we can only conjecture.'

'Well, what am I to do, Mr Holmes?'

'I have a great fancy to see this lodger of yours, Mrs Warren.'

'I don't see how that is to be managed, unless you break in the door. I always hear him unlock it as I go down the stair after I leave the tray.'

'He has to take the tray in. Surely we could conceal ourselves and see him do it.'

The landlady thought for a moment.

'Well, sir, there's the box-room opposite. I could arrange a looking-glass, maybe, and if you were behind the door——'

'Excellent!' said Holmes. 'When does he lunch?'

'About one, sir.'

'Then Dr Watson and I will come round in time. For the present, Mrs Warren, goodbye.'

At half-past twelve we found ourselves upon the steps of Mrs Warren's house – a high, thin, yellow-brick edifice in Great Orme Street, a narrow thoroughfare at the north-east side of the British Museum. Standing as it does near the corner of the street, it commands a view down Howe Street, with its more pretentious houses. Holmes pointed with a chuckle to one of these, a row of residential flats, which projected so that they could not fail to catch the eye.

'See, Watson!' said he. '"High red house with stone facings." There is the signal station all right. We know the place, and we know the code; so surely our task should be simple. There's a "To Let" card in that window. It is evidently an empty flat to which the confederate has access. Well, Mrs Warren, what now?'

'I have it all ready for you. If you will both come up and leave your boots below on the landing, I'll put you there now.'

It was an excellent hiding-place which she had arranged. The mirror was so placed that, seated in the dark, we could very plainly see the door opposite. We had hardly settled down in it, and Mrs Warren left us, when a distant tinkle announced that our mysterious neighbour had rung. Presently the landlady appeared with the tray, laid it down upon a chair beside the closed door, and then, treading heavily, departed. Crouching together in the angle of the door, we kept our eyes fixed upon the mirror. Suddenly, as the landlady's footsteps died away, there was the creak of a turning key, the handle revolved, and two thin hands darted out and lifted the tray from the chair. An instant later it was hurriedly replaced, and I caught a glimpse of a dark, beautiful, horrified face glaring at the narrow opening of the box-room. Then the door crashed to, the key turned once more, and all was silence. Holmes twitched my sleeve, and together we stole down the stair.

'I will call again in the evening,' said he to the expectant landlady. 'I think, Watson, we can discuss this business better in our own quarters.'

'My surmise, as you saw, proved to be correct,' said he, speaking from the depths of his easy-chair. 'There has been a substitution of lodgers. What I did not foresee is that we should find a woman, and no ordinary woman, Watson.'

'She saw us.'

'Well, she saw something to alarm her. That is certain. The general sequence of events is pretty clear, is it not? A couple seek refuge in London from a very terrible and instant danger. The measure of that danger is the rigour of their precautions. The man, who has some work which he must do, desires to leave the woman in absolute safety while he does it. It is not an easy problem, but he solved it in an original fashion, and so effectively that her presence was not even known to the landlady who supplies her with food. The printed messages, as is now evident, were to prevent her sex being discovered by her writing. The man cannot come near the woman, or he will guide their enemies to her. Since he cannot communicate with her direct, he has recourse to the agony column of a paper. So far all is clear.'

'But what is at the root of it?'

'Ah, yes, Watson – severely practical, as usual! What is at the root of it all? Mrs Warren's whimsical problem enlarges somewhat and assumes a more sinister aspect as we proceed. This much we can say: that it is no ordinary love escapade. You saw the woman's face at the sign of danger. We have heard, too, of the attack upon the landlord, which was undoubtedly meant for the lodger. These alarms, and the desperate need for secrecy, argue that the matter is one of life or death. The attack upon Mr Warren further shows that the enemy, whoever they are, are themselves not aware of the substitution of the female lodger for the male. It is very curious and complex, Watson.'

'Why should you go further in it? What have you to gain from it?'

'What indeed? It is Art for Art's sake, Watson. I suppose when you doctored you found yourself studying cases without thought of a fee?'

'For my education, Holmes.'

'Education never ends, Watson. It is a series of lessons with the greatest for the last. This is an instructive case. There is neither money nor credit in it, and yet one would wish to tidy it up. When dusk comes we should find ourselves one stage advanced in our investigation.'

When we returned to Mrs Warren's rooms, the gloom of a London winter evening had thickened into one grey curtain, a dead monotone of colour, broken only by the sharp yellow squares of the windows and the blurred haloes of the gas-lamps. As we peered from the darkened sitting-room of the lodging-house, one more dim light glimmered high up through the obscurity.

'Someone is moving in that room,' said Holmes in a whisper, his gaunt and eager face thrust forward to the window-pane. 'Yes, I can see his shadow. There he is again! He has a candle in his hand. Now he is peering across. He wants to be sure that she is on the look-out. Now he begins to flash. Take the message also, Watson, that we may check each other. A single flash – that is "A", surely. Now, then. How many did you make it? Twenty. So did I. That should mean "T". A T – that's intelligible enough! Another "T". Surely this is the beginning of a second word. Now, then – TENTA. Dead stop. That can't be all, Watson? "ATTENTA" gives no sense. Nor is it any better as three words – "AT. TEN. TA", unless "T.A." are a person's initials. There it goes again! What's that? ATTE – why, it is the same message over again. Curious, Watson, very curious! Now he is off once more! AT – why, he is repeating it for the third time. "ATTENTA" three times! How often will he repeat it? No, that seems to be the finish. He has withdrawn from the window. What do you make of it, Watson?'

'A cipher message, Holmes.'

My companion gave a sudden chuckle of comprehension. 'And not a very obscure cipher, Watson,' said he. 'Why, of course, it is Italian! The "A" means that it is addressed to a woman. "Beware! Beware! Beware!" How's that, Watson?'

'I believe you have hit it.'

'Not a doubt of it. It is a very urgent message, thrice repeated

to make it more so. But beware of what? Wait a bit; he is coming
to the window once more.'

Again we saw the dim silhouette of a crouching man and the
whisk of the small flame across the window, as the signals were
renewed. They came more rapidly than before – so rapid that it
was hard to follow them.

'"PERICOLO" – "Pericolo" – Eh, what's that, Watson?
Danger, isn't it? Yes, by Jove, it's a danger signal. There he
goes again! "PERI". Halloa, what on earth——'

The light had suddenly gone out, the glimmering square of
window had disappeared, and the third floor formed a dark
band round the lofty building, with its tiers of shining casements.
That last warning cry had been suddenly cut short. How, and
by whom? The same thought occurred on the instant to us both.
Holmes sprang up from where he crouched by the window.

'This is serious, Watson,' he cried. 'There is some devilry
going forward! Why should such a message stop in such a way?
I should put Scotland Yard in touch with this business – and
yet, it is too pressing for us to leave.'

'Shall I go for the police?'

'We must define the situation a little more clearly. It may
bear some more innocent interpretation. Come, Watson, let us
go across ourselves and see what we can make of it.'

II

As we walked rapidly down Howe Street I glanced back at the
building which we had left. There, dimly outlined at the top
window, I could see the shadow of a head, a woman's head,
gazing tensely, rigidly, out into the night, waiting with breath-
less suspense for the renewal of that interrupted message. At the
doorway of the Howe Street flats a man, muffled in a cravat and
greatcoat, was leaning against the railing. He started as the hall-
light fell upon our faces.

'Holmes!' he cried.

'Why, Gregson!' said my companion, as he shook hands

with the Scotland Yard detective. 'Journey's end with lovers' meetings. What brings you here?'

'The same reasons that bring you, I expect,' said Gregson. 'How you got on to it I can't imagine.'

'Different threads, but leading up to the same tangle. I've been taking the signals.'

'Signals?'

'Yes, from that window. They broke off in the middle. We came over to see the reason. But since it is safe in your hands I see no object in continuing the business.'

'Wait a bit!' cried Gregson, eagerly. 'I'll do you this justice, Mr Holmes, that I was never in a case yet that I didn't feel stronger for having you on my side. There's only the one exit to these flats, so we have him safe.'

'Who is he?'

'Well, well, we score over you for once, Mr Holmes. You must give us best this time.' He struck his stick sharply upon the ground, on which a cabman, his whip in his hand, sauntered over from a four-wheeler which stood on the far side of the street. 'May I introduce you to Mr Sherlock Holmes?' he said to the cabman. 'This is Mr Leverton, of Pinkerton's American Agency.'

'The hero of the Long Island Cave mystery?' said Holmes. 'Sir, I am pleased to meet you.'

The American, a quiet, businesslike young man, with a clean-shaven, hatchet face, flushed up at the words of commendation. 'I am on the trail of my life now, Mr Holmes,' said he. 'If I can get Gorgiano——'

'What! Gorgiano of the Red Circle?'

'Oh, he has a European fame, has he? Well, we've learned all about him in America. We *know* he is at the bottom of fifty murders, and yet we have nothing positive we can take him on. I tracked him over from New York, and I've been close to him for a week in London, waiting for some excuse to get my hand on his collar. Mr Gregson and I ran him to ground in that big

tenement house, and there's only the one door, so he can't slip
us. There's three folk come out since he went in, but I'll swear
he wasn't one of them.'

'Mr Holmes talks of signals,' said Gregson. 'I expect, as
usual, he knows a good deal that we don't.'

In a few clear words Holmes explained the situation as it
had appeared to us. The American struck his hands together
with vexation.

'He's on to us!' he cried.

'Why do you think so?'

'Well, it figures out that way, does it not? Here he is, sending
out messages to an accomplice – there are several of his gang in
London. Then suddenly, just as by your own account he was
telling them that there was danger, he broke off short. What
could it mean except that from the window he had suddenly
either caught sight of us in the street, or in some way come to
understand how close the danger was, and that he must act right
away if he was to avoid it? What do you suggest, Mr Holmes?'

'That we go up at once and see for ourselves.'

'But we have no warrant for his arrest.'

'He is in unoccupied premises under suspicious circumstances,' said Gregson. 'That is good enough for the moment.
When we have him by the heels we can see if New York can't
help us to keep him. I'll take the responsibility of arresting him
now.'

Our official detectives may blunder in the matter of intelligence, but never in that of courage. Gregson climbed the stair
to arrest this desperate murderer with the same absolutely quiet
and businesslike bearing with which he would have ascended the
official staircase of Scotland Yard. The Pinkerton man had tried
to push past him, but Gregson had firmly elbowed him back.
London dangers were the privilege of the London force.

The door of the left-hand flat upon the third landing was
standing ajar. Gregson pushed it open. Within, all was absolute
silence and darkness. I struck a match, and lit the detective's

lantern. As I did so, and as the flicker steadied into a flame, we all gave a gasp of surprise. On the deal boards of the carpetless floor there was outlined a fresh track of blood. The red steps pointed towards us, and led away from an inner room, the door of which was closed. Gregson flung it open and held his light full blaze in front of him, whilst we all peered eagerly over his shoulders.

In the middle of the floor of the empty room was huddled the figure of an enormous man, his clean-shaven, swarthy face grotesquely horrible in its contortion, and his head encircled by a ghastly crimson halo of blood, lying in a broad wet circle upon the white woodwork. His knees were drawn up, his hands thrown out in agony, and from the centre of his broad, brown, upturned throat there projected the white haft of a knife driven blade-deep into his body. Giant as he was, the man must have gone down like a pole-axed ox before that terrific blow. Beside his right hand a most formidable horn-handled, two-edged dagger lay upon the floor, and near it a black kid glove.

'By George! it's Black Gorgiano himself!' cried the American detective. 'Someone has got ahead of us this time.'

'Here is the candle in the window, Mr Holmes,' said Gregson. 'Why, whatever are you doing?'

Holmes had stepped across, had lit the candle, and was passing it backwards and forwards across the window-panes. Then he peered into the darkness, blew the candle out, and threw it on the floor.

'I rather think that will be helpful,' said he. He came over and stood in deep thought while the two professionals were examining the body. 'You say that three people came out from the flat while you were waiting downstairs,' said he, at last. 'Did you observe them closely?'

'Yes, I did.'

'Was there a fellow about thirty, black-bearded, dark, of middle size?'

'Yes; he was the last to pass me.'

'That is your man, I fancy. I can give you his description, and we have a very excellent outline of his footmark. That should be enough for you.'

'Not much, Mr Holmes, among the millions of London.'

'Perhaps not. That is why I thought it best to summon this lady to your aid.'

We all turned round at the words. There, framed in the door-way, was a tall and beautiful woman – the mysterious lodger of Bloomsbury. Slowly she advanced, her face pale and drawn with a frightful apprehension, her eyes fixed and staring, her terrified gaze riveted upon the dark figure on the floor.

'You have killed him!' she muttered. 'Oh, *Dio mio*, you have killed him!' Then I heard a sudden sharp intake of her breath, and she sprang into the air with a cry of joy. Round and round the room she danced, her hands clapping, her dark eyes gleam-ing with delighted wonder, and a thousand pretty Italian exclamations pouring from her lips. It was terrible and amazing to see such a woman so convulsed with joy at such a sight. Suddenly she stopped and gazed at us all with a questioning stare.

'But you! You are police, are you not? You have killed Giuseppe Gorgiano. Is it not so?'

'We are police, madam.'

She looked round into the shadows of the room.

'But where, then, is Gennaro?' she asked. 'He is my husband, Gennaro Lucca. I am Emilia Lucca, and we are both from New York. Where is Gennaro? He called me this moment from this window, and I ran with all my speed.'

'It was I who called,' said Holmes.

'You! How could you call?'

'Your cipher was not difficult, madam. Your presence here was desirable. I knew that I had only to flash "*Vieni*" and you would surely come.'

The beautiful Italian looked with awe at my companion.

'I do not understand how you know these things,' she said.

'Giuseppe Gorgiano – how did he –' She paused, and then suddenly her face lit up with pride and delight. 'Now I see it! My Gennaro! My splendid, beautiful Gennaro, who has guarded me safe from all harm, he did it, with his own strong hand he killed the monster! Oh, Gennaro, how wonderful you are! What woman could ever be worthy of such a man?'

'Well, Mrs Lucca,' said the prosaic Gregson, laying his hand upon the lady's sleeve with as little sentiment as if she were a Notting Hill hooligan, 'I am not very clear yet who you are or what you are; but you've said enough to make it very clear that we shall want you at the Yard.'

'One moment, Gregson,' said Holmes. 'I rather fancy that this lady may be as anxious to give us information as we can be to get it. You understand, madam, that your husband will be arrested and tried for the death of the man who lies before us? What you say may be used in evidence. But if you think that he has acted from motives which are not criminal, and which he would wish to have known, then you cannot serve him better than by telling us the whole story.'

'Now that Gorgiano is dead we fear nothing,' said the lady. 'He was a devil and a monster, and there can be no judge in the world who would punish my husband for having killed him.'

'In that case,' said Holmes, 'my suggestion is that we lock this door, leave things as we found them, go with this lady to her room, and form our opinion after we have heard what it is that she has to say to us.'

Half an hour later we were seated, all four, in the small sitting-room of Signora Lucca, listening to her remarkable narrative of those sinister events, the ending of which we had chanced to witness. She spoke in rapid and fluent but very unconventional English, which, for the sake of clearness, I will make grammatical.

'I was born in Posilippo, near Naples,' said she, 'and was the daughter of Augusto Barelli, who was the chief lawyer and once the deputy of that part. Gennaro was in my father's employment, and I came to love him, as any woman must. He had neither money nor position – nothing but his beauty and strength and energy – so my father forbade the match. We fled together, were married at Bari, and sold my jewels to gain the money which would take us to America. This was four years ago, and we have been in New York ever since.

'Fortune was very good to us at first. Gennaro was able to do a service to an Italian gentleman – he saved him from some ruffians in the place called the Bowery, and so made a powerful friend. His name was Tito Castalotte, and he was the senior partner of the great firm of Castalotte and Zamba, who are the chief fruit importers of New York. Signor Zamba is an invalid, and our new friend Castalotte has all power within the firm, which employs more than three hundred men. He took my husband into his employment, made him head of a department, and showed his goodwill towards him in every way. Signor Castalotte was a bachelor, and I believe that he felt as if Gennaro was his son, and both my husband and I loved him as if he were our father. We had taken and furnished a little house in Brooklyn, and our whole future seemed assured, when that black cloud appeared which was soon to overspread our sky.

'One night, when Gennaro returned from his work, he brought a fellow-countryman back with him. His name was Gorgiano, and he had come also from Posilippo. He was a huge man, as you can testify, for you have looked upon his corpse. Not only was his body that of a giant, but everything about him was grotesque, gigantic, and terrifying. His voice was like thunder in our little house. There was scarce room for the whirl of his great arms as he talked. His thoughts, his emotions, his passions, all were exaggerated and monstrous. He talked, or rather roared, with such energy that others could but sit and listen, cowed with the mighty stream of words. His eyes blazed at you and held you at his mercy. He was a terrible and wonderful man. I thank God that he is dead!

'He came again and again. Yet I was aware that Gennaro was no more happy than I was in his presence. My poor husband would sit pale and listless, listening to the endless raving upon politics and upon social questions which made up our visitor's conversation. Gennaro said nothing, but I who knew him so well could read in his face some emotion which I had never seen there before. At first I thought that it was dislike. And then, gradually, I understood that it was more than dislike. It was fear – a deep, secret, shrinking fear. That night – the night that I read his terror – I put my arms round him and I implored him by his love for me and by all that he held dear to hold nothing from me, and to tell me why this huge man over-shadowed him so.

'He told me, and my own heart grew cold as ice as I listened. My poor Gennaro, in his wild and fiery days, when all the world seemed against him and his mind was driven half mad by the injustices of life, had joined a Neapolitan society, the Red Circle, which was allied to the old Carbonari. The oaths and secrets of this brotherhood were frightful; but once within its rule no escape was possible. When we had fled to America Gennaro thought that he had cast it all off for ever. What was his horror one evening to meet in the streets the very man who had initiated him in Naples, the giant Gorgiano, a man who had earned the name of "Death" in the South of Italy, for he was red to the elbow in murder! He had come to New York to avoid the Italian police, and he had already planted a branch of this dreadful society in his new home. All this Gennaro told me, and showed me a summons which he had received that very day, a Red Circle drawn upon the head of it, telling him that a lodge would be held upon a certain date, and that his presence at it was required and ordered.

'That was bad enough, but worse was to come. I had noticed for some time that when Gorgiano came to us, as he constantly did, in the evening, he spoke much to me; and even when his words were to my husband, those terrible, glaring, wild-beast

eyes of his were always turned upon me. One night his secret
came out. I had awakened what he called "love" within him –
the love of a brute – a savage. Gennaro had not yet returned
when he came. He pushed his way in, seized me in his mighty
arms, hugged me in his bear's embrace, covered me with kisses,
and implored me to come away with him. I was struggling
and screaming when Gennaro entered and attacked him. He
struck Gennaro senseless and fled from the house which he was
never more to enter. It was a deadly enemy that we made that
night.

'A few days later came the meeting. Gennaro returned from
it with a face which told me that something dreadful had
occurred. It was worse than we could have imagined possible.
The funds of the society were raised by blackmailing rich
Italians and threatening them with violence should they refuse
the money. It seems that Castalotte, our dear friend and
benefactor, had been approached. He had refused to yield to
threats, and he had handed the notices to the police. It was
resolved now that such an example should be made of him as
would prevent any other victim from rebelling. At the meeting
it was arranged that he and his house should be blown up with
dynamite. There was a drawing of lots as to who should carry
out the deed. Gennaro saw our enemy's cruel face smiling at
him as he dipped his hand in the bag. No doubt it had been prearranged in some fashion, for it was the fatal disc with the Red
Circle upon it, the mandate for murder, which lay upon his
palm. He was to kill his best friend, or he was to expose himself
and me to the vengeance of his comrades. It was part of their
fiendish system to punish those whom they feared or hated by
injuring not only their own persons, but those whom they loved,
and it was the knowledge of this which hung as a terror over my
poor Gennaro's head and drove him nearly crazy with apprehension.

'All that night we sat together, our arms round each other,
each strengthening each for the troubles that lay before us.

The very next evening had been fixed for the attempt. By mid-day my husband and I were on our way to London, but not before he had given our benefactor full warning of his danger, and had also left such information for the police as would safe-guard his life for the future.

'The rest, gentlemen, you know for yourselves. We were sure that our enemies would be behind us like our own shadows. Gorgiano had his private reasons for vengeance, but in any case we knew how ruthless, cunning, and untiring he could be. Both Italy and America are full of stories of his dreadful powers. If ever they were exerted it would be now. My darling made use of the few clear days which our start had given us in arranging for a refuge for me in such a fashion that no possible danger could reach me. For his own part, he wished to be free that he might communicate both with the American and with the Italian police. I do not myself know where he lived, or how. All that I learned was through the columns of a newspaper. But once, as I looked through my window, I saw two Italians watching the house, and I understood that in some way Gorgiano had found out our retreat. Finally Gennaro told me, through the paper, that he would signal to me from a certain window, but when the signals came they were nothing but warnings, which were suddenly interrupted. It is very clear to me now that he knew Gorgiano to be close upon him, and that, thank God! he was ready for him when he came. And now, gentlemen, I would ask you whether we have anything to fear from the Law, or whether any judge upon earth would condemn my Gennaro for what he has done?'

'Well, Mr Gregson,' said the American, looking across at the official, 'I don't know what your British point of view may be, but I guess that in New York this lady's husband will receive a pretty general vote of thanks.'

'She will have to come with me and see the Chief,' Gregson answered. 'If what she says is corroborated, I do not think she or her husband has much to fear. But what I can't make head or

tail of, Mr Holmes, is how on earth *you* got yourself mixed up
in the matter.'

'Education, Gregson, education. Still seeking knowledge at
the old university. Well, Watson, you have one more specimen
of the tragic and grotesque to add to your collection. By the way,
it is not eight o'clock, and a Wagner night at Covent Garden!
If we hurry, we might be in time for the second act.'

The Adventure of the Bruce-Partington Plans

In the third week of November, in the year 1895, a dense yellow fog settled down upon London. From the Monday to the Thursday I doubt whether it was ever possible from our windows in Baker Street to see the loom of the opposite houses. The first day Holmes had spent in cross-indexing his huge book of references. The second and third had been patiently occupied upon a subject which he had recently made his hobby – the music of the Middle Ages. But when, for the fourth time, after pushing back our chairs from breakfast we saw the greasy, heavy brown swirl still drifting past us and condensing in oily drops upon the window-panes, my comrade's impatient and active nature could endure this drab existence no longer. He paced restlessly about our sitting-room in a fever of suppressed energy, biting his nails, tapping the furniture, and chafing against inaction.

'Nothing of interest in the paper, Watson?' he said.

I was aware that by anything of interest, Holmes meant anything of criminal interest. There was the news of a revolution, of a possible war, and of an impending change of Government; but these did not come within the horizon of my companion. I could see nothing recorded in the shape of crime which was not commonplace and futile. Holmes groaned and resumed his restless meanderings.

'The London criminal is certainly a dull fellow,' said he, in the querulous voice of the sportsman whose game has failed him. 'Look out of this window, Watson. See how the figures loom up, are dimly seen, and then blend once more into the cloud-bank. The thief or the murderer could roam London on such a day as the tiger does the jungle, unseen until he pounces, and then evident only to his victim.'

'There have,' said I, 'been numerous petty thefts.'

Holmes snorted his contempt.

'This great and sombre stage is set for something more worthy than that,' said he. 'It is fortunate for this community that I am not a criminal.'

'It is, indeed!' said I, heartily.

'Suppose that I were Brooks or Woodhouse, or any of the fifty men who have good reason for taking my life, how long could I survive against my own pursuit? A summons, a bogus appointment, and all would be over. It is well they don't have days of fog in the Latin countries – the countries of assassination. By Jove! here comes something at last to break our dead monotony.'

It was the maid with a telegram. Holmes tore it open and burst out laughing.

'Well, well! What next?' said he. 'Brother Mycroft is coming round.'

'Why not?' I asked.

'Why not? It is as if you met a tram-car coming down a country lane. Mycroft has his rails and he runs on them. His Pall Mall lodgings, the Diogenes Club, Whitehall – that is his cycle. Once, and only once, he has been here. What upheaval can possibly have derailed him?'

'Does he not explain?'

Holmes handed me his brother's telegram.

'Must see you over Cadogan West. Coming at once. MYCROFT.'

'Cadogan West? I have heard the name.'

'It recalls nothing to my mind. But that Mycroft should break out in this erratic fashion! A planet might as well leave its orbit. By the way, do you know what Mycroft is?'

I had some vague recollection of an explanation at the time of the Adventure of the Greek Interpreter.

'You told me that he had some small office under the British Government.'

Holmes chuckled.

'I did not know you quite so well in those days. One has to be discreet when one talks of high matters of state. You are right in thinking that he is under the British Government. You would also be right in a sense if you said that occasionally he *is* the British Government.'

'My dear Holmes!'

'I thought I might surprise you. Mycroft draws four hundred and fifty pounds a year, remains a subordinate, has no ambitions of any kind, will receive neither honour nor title, but remains the most indispensable man in the country.'

'But how?'

'Well, his position is unique. He has made it for himself. There has never been anything like it before, nor will be again. He has the tidiest and most orderly brain, with the greatest capacity for storing facts, of any man living. The same great powers which I have turned to the detection of crime he has used for this particular business. The conclusions of every department are passed to him, and he is the central exchange, the clearing-house, which makes out the balance. All other men are specialists, but his specialism is omniscience. We will suppose that a Minister needs information as to a point which involves the Navy, India, Canada and the bimetallic question; he could get his separate advices from various departments upon each, but only Mycroft can focus them all, and say off-hand how each factor would affect the other. They began by using him as a short-cut, a convenience; now he has made himself an essential. In that great brain of his everything is pigeon-holed, and can be handed out in an instant. Again and again his word has decided the national policy. He lives in it. He thinks of nothing else save when, as an intellectual exercise, he unbends if I call upon him and ask him to advise me on one of my little problems. But Jupiter is descending today. What

on earth can it mean? Who is Cadogan West, and what is he to
Mycroft?'

'I have it,' I cried, and plunged among the litter of papers
upon the sofa. 'Yes, yes, here he is, sure enough! Cadogan West
was the young man who was found dead on the Underground
on Tuesday morning.'

Holmes sat up at attention, his pipe half-way to his lips.

'This must be serious, Watson. A death which has caused
my brother to alter his habits can be no ordinary one. What in
the world can he have to do with it? The case was featureless as
I remember it. The young man had apparently fallen out of the
train and killed himself. He had not been robbed, and there was
no particular reason to suspect violence. Is that not so?'

'There has been an inquest,' said I, 'and a good many fresh
facts have come out. Looked at more closely, I should certainly
say that it was a curious case.'

'Judging by its effect upon my brother, I should think it must
be a most extraordinary one.' He snuggled down in his armchair.
'Now, Watson, let us have the facts.'

'The man's name was Arthur Cadogan West. He was twenty-
seven years of age, unmarried, and a clerk at Woolwich Arsenal.'

'Government employ. Behold the link with brother Mycroft!'

'He left Woolwich suddenly on Monday night. Was last seen
by his fiancée, Miss Violet Westbury, whom he left abruptly in
the fog about 7.30 that evening. There was no quarrel between
them and she can give no motive for his action. The next thing
heard of him was when his dead body was discovered by a plate-
layer named Mason, just outside Aldgate Station on the Underground system in London.'

'When?'

'The body was found at six on the Tuesday morning. It was
lying wide of the metals upon the left hand of the track as one
goes eastward, at a point close to the station, where the line
emerges from the tunnel in which it runs. The head was badly
crushed – an injury which might well have been caused by a fall

from the train. The body could only have come on the line in that way. Had it been carried down from any neighbouring street, it must have passed the station barriers, where a collector is always standing. This point seems absolutely certain.'

'Very good. The case was definite enough. The man, dead or alive, either fell or was precipitated from a train. So much is clear to me. Continue.'

'The trains which traverse the lines of rail beside which the body was found are those which run from west to east, some being purely Metropolitan, and some from Willesden and out-lying junctions. It can be stated for certain that this young man, when he met his death, was travelling in this direction at some late hour of the night, but at what point he entered the train it is impossible to state.'

'His ticket, of course, would show that.'

'There was no ticket in his pockets.'

'No ticket! Dear me, Watson, this is really very singular. According to my experience it is not possible to reach the plat-form of a Metropolitan train without exhibiting one's ticket. Presumably, then, the young man had one. Was it taken from him in order to conceal the station from which he came? It is possible. Or did he drop it in the carriage? That also is possible. But the point is of curious interest. I understand that there was no sign of robbery?'

'Apparently not. There is a list here of his possessions. His purse contained two pounds fifteen. He had also a cheque-book on the Woolwich branch of the Capital and Counties Bank. Through this his identity was established. There were also two dress-circle tickets for the Woolwich Theatre, dated for that very evening. Also a small packet of technical papers.'

Holmes gave an exclamation of satisfaction.

'There we have it at last, Watson! British Government – Woolwich Arsenal – Technical papers – Brother Mycroft, the chain is complete. But here he comes, if I am not mistaken, to speak for himself.'

A moment later the tall and portly form of Mycroft Holmes
was ushered into the room. Heavily built and massive, there was
a suggestion of uncouth physical inertia in the figure, but above
this unwieldy frame there was perched a head so masterful in its
brow, so alert in its steel-grey, deep-set eyes, so firm in its lips,
and so subtle in its play of expression, that after the first glance
one forgot the gross body and remembered only the dominant
mind.

At his heels came our old friend Lestrade, of Scotland Yard –
thin and austere. The gravity of both their faces foretold some
weighty quest. The detective shook hands without a word.
Mycroft Holmes struggled out of his overcoat and subsided into
an armchair.

'A most annoying business, Sherlock,' said he. 'I extremely
dislike altering my habits, but the powers that be would take no
denial. In the present state of Siam it is most awkward that I
should be away from the office. But it is a real crisis. I have never
seen the Prime Minister so upset. As to the Admiralty – it is
buzzing like an overturned bee-hive. Have you read up the case ?'

'We have just done so. What were the technical papers ?'

'Ah, there's the point! Fortunately, it has not come out. The
Press would be furious if it did. The papers which this wretched
youth had in his pocket were the plans of the Bruce-Partington
submarine.'

Mycroft Holmes spoke with a solemnity which showed his
sense of the importance of the subject. His brother and I sat
expectant.

'Surely you have heard of it ? I thought everyone had heard
of it.'

'Only as a name.'

'Its importance can hardly be exaggerated. It has been the
most jealously guarded of all Government secrets. You may
take it from me that naval warfare becomes impossible within
the radius of a Bruce-Partington's operation. Two years ago a
very large sum was smuggled through the Estimates and was

expended in acquiring a monopoly of the invention. Every effort has been made to keep the secret. The plans, which are exceedingly intricate, comprising some thirty separate patents, each essential to the working of the whole, are kept in an elaborate safe in a confidential office adjoining the Arsenal, with burglar-proof doors and windows. Under no conceivable circumstances were the plans to be taken from the office. If the Chief Constructor of the Navy desired to consult them, even he was forced to go to the Woolwich office for the purpose. And yet here we find them in the pockets of a dead junior clerk in the heart of London. From an official point of view it's simply awful.'

'But you have recovered them?'

'No, Sherlock, no! That's the pinch. We have not. Ten papers were taken from Woolwich. There were seven in the pockets of Cadogan West. The three most essential are gone – stolen, vanished. You must drop everything, Sherlock. Never mind your usual petty puzzles of the police-court. It's a vital international problem that you have to solve. Why did Cadogan West take the papers, where are the missing ones, how did he die, how came his body where it was found, how can the evil be set right? Find an answer to all these questions, and you will have done good service for your country.'

'Why do you not solve it yourself, Mycroft? You can see as far as I.'

'Possibly, Sherlock. But it is a question of getting details. Give me your details, and from an armchair I will return you an excellent expert opinion. But to run here and run there, to cross-question railway guards, and lie on my face with a lens to my eye – it is not my métier. No, you are the one man who can clear the matter up. If you have a fancy to see your name in the next honours list——'

My friend smiled and shook his head.

'I play the game for the game's own sake,' said he. 'But the problem certainly presents some points of interest, and I shall be very pleased to look into it. Some more facts, please.'

'I have jotted down the more essential ones upon this sheet of paper, together with a few addresses which you will find of service. The actual official guardian of the papers is the famous Government expert, Sir James Walter, whose decorations and sub-titles fill two lines of a book of reference. He has grown grey in the service, is a gentleman, a favoured guest in the most exalted houses, and above all a man whose patriotism is beyond suspicion. He is one of two who have a key of the safe. I may add that the papers were undoubtedly in the office during working hours on Monday, and that Sir James left for London about three o'clock taking his key with him. He was at the house of Admiral Sinclair at Barclay Square during the whole of the evening when this incident occurred.'

'Has the fact been verified?'

'Yes; his brother, Colonel Valentine Walter, has testified to his departure from Woolwich, and Admiral Sinclair to his arrival in London; so Sir James is no longer a direct factor in the problem.'

'Who was the other man with a key?'

'The senior clerk and draughtsman, Mr Sidney Johnson. He is a man of forty, married, with five children. He is a silent, morose man, but he has, on the whole, an excellent record in the public service. He is unpopular with his colleagues, but a hard worker. According to his own account, corroborated only by the word of his wife, he was at home the whole of Monday evening after office hours, and his key has never left the watch-chain upon which it hangs.'

'Tell us about Cadogan West.'

'He has been ten years in the Service, and has done good work. He has the reputation of being hot-headed and impetuous, but a straight, honest man. We have nothing against him. He was next Sidney Johnson in the office. His duties brought him into daily, personal contact with the plans. No one else had the handling of them.'

'Who locked the plans up that night?'

'Mr Sidney Johnson, the senior clerk.'

'Well, it is surely perfectly clear who took them away. They are actually found upon the person of this junior clerk, Cadogan West. That seems final, does it not?'

'It does, Sherlock, and yet it leaves so much unexplained. In the first place, why did he take them?'

'I presume they were of value?'

'He could have got several thousands for them very easily.'

'Can you suggest any possible motive for taking the papers to London except to sell them?'

'No, I cannot.'

'Then we must take that as our working hypothesis. Young West took the papers. Now this could only be done by having a false key——'

'Several false keys. He had to open the building and the room.'

'He had, then, several false keys. He took the papers to London to sell the secret, intending, no doubt, to have the plans themselves back in the safe next morning before they were missed. While in London on this treasonable mission he met his end.'

'How?'

'We will suppose that he was travelling back to Woolwich when he was killed and thrown out of the compartment.'

'Aldgate, where the body was found, is considerably past the station for London Bridge, which would be his route to Woolwich.'

'Many circumstances could be imagined under which he would pass London Bridge. There was someone in the carriage, for example, with whom he was having an absorbing interview. This interview led to a violent scene, in which he lost his life. Possibly he tried to leave the carriage, fell out on the line, and so met his end. The other closed the door. There was a thick fog, and nothing could be seen.'

'No better explanation can be given with our present knowledge; and yet consider, Sherlock, how much you leave untouched. We will suppose, for argument's sake, that young Cadogan West *had* determined to convey these papers to London. He would naturally have made an appointment with the foreign agent and kept his evening clear. Instead of that, he took two tickets for the theatre, escorted his fiancée half way there, and then suddenly disappeared.'

'A blind,' said Lestrade, who had sat listening with some impatience to the conversation.

'A very singular one. That is objection No. 1. Objection No. 2: we will suppose that he reaches London and sees the foreign agent. He must bring back the papers before morning or the loss will be discovered. He took away ten. Only seven were in his pocket. What had become of the other three? He certainly would not leave them of his own free will. Then, again, where is the price of his treason? One would have expected to find a large sum of money in his pocket.'

'It seems to me perfectly clear,' said Lestrade. 'I have no doubt at all as to what occurred. He took the papers to sell them. He saw the agent. They could not agree as to price. He started home again, but the agent went with him. In the train the agent murdered him, took the more essential papers, and threw his body from the carriage. That would account for everything, would it not?'

'Why had he no ticket?'

'The ticket would have shown which station was nearest the agent's house. Therefore he took it from the murdered man's pocket.'

'Good, Lestrade, very good,' said Holmes. 'Your theory holds together. But if this is true, then the case is at an end. On the one hand the traitor is dead. On the other the plans of the Bruce-Partington submarine are presumably already on the Continent. What is there for us to do?'

'To act, Sherlock – to act!' cried Mycroft, springing to his feet. 'All my instincts are against this explanation. Use your powers! Go to the scene of the crime! See the people concerned! Leave no stone unturned! In all your career you have never had so great a chance of serving your country.'

'Well, well!' said Holmes, shrugging his shoulders. 'Come, Watson! And you, Lestrade, could you favour us with your company for an hour or two? We will begin our investigation by a visit to Aldgate Station. Goodbye, Mycroft. I shall let you have a report before evening, but I warn you in advance that you have little to expect.'

An hour later, Holmes, Lestrade and I, stood upon the Underground railroad at the point where it emerges from the tunnel immediately before Aldgate Station. A courteous red-faced old gentleman represented the railway company.

'This is where the young man's body lay,' said he, indicating a spot about three feet from the metals. 'It could not have fallen from above, for these, as you see, are all blank walls. Therefore, it could only have come from a train, and that train, so far as we can trace it, must have passed about midnight on Monday.'

'Have the carriages been examined for any sign of violence?'

'There are no such signs, and no ticket has been found.'

'No record of a door being found open?'

'None.'

'We have had some fresh evidence this morning,' said Lestrade. 'A passenger who passed Aldgate in an ordinary Metropolitan train about 11.40 on Monday night declares that he heard a heavy thud, as of a body striking the line, just before the train reached the station. There was dense fog, however, and nothing could be seen. He made no report of it at the time. Why, whatever is the matter with Mr Holmes?'

My friend was standing with an expression of strained intensity upon his face, staring at the railway metals where they curved out of the tunnel. Aldgate is a junction, and there was a network of points. On these his eager, questioning eyes were fixed, and I saw on his keen, alert face that tightening of the lips, that quiver of the nostrils, and concentration of the heavy tufted brows which I knew so well.

'Points,' he muttered; 'the points.'

'What of it? What do you mean?'

'I suppose there are no great number of points on a system such as this?'

'No; there are very few.'

'And a curve, too. Points, and a curve. By Jove! if it were only so.'

'What is it, Mr Holmes? Have you a clue?'

'An idea – an indication, no more. But the case certainly grows in interest. Unique, perfectly unique, and yet why not? I do not see any indications of bleeding on the line.'

'There were hardly any.'

'But I understand that there was a considerable wound.'

'The bone was crushed, but there was no great external injury.'

'And yet one would have expected some bleeding. Would it be possible for me to inspect the train which contained the passenger who heard the thud of a fall in the fog?'

'I fear not, Mr Holmes. The train has been broken up before now, and the carriages redistributed.'

'I can assure you, Mr Holmes,' said Lestrade, 'that every carriage has been carefully examined. I saw to it myself.'

It was one of my friend's most obvious weaknesses that he was impatient with less alert intelligences than his own.

'Very likely,' said he, turning away. 'As it happens, it was not the carriages which I desired to examine. Watson, we have done all we can here. We need not trouble you any further, Mr Lestrade. I think our investigations must now carry us to Woolwich.'

At London Bridge Holmes wrote a telegram to his brother, which he handed to me before dispatching it. It ran thus:

See some light in the darkness, but it may possibly flicker out. Meanwhile, please send by messenger, to await return at Baker Street, a complete list of all foreign spies or international agents known to be in England, with full address.

SHERLOCK.

'That should be helpful, Watson,' he remarked, as we took our seats in the Woolwich train. 'We certainly owe brother Mycroft a debt for having introduced us to what promises to be a really very remarkable case.'

His eager face still wore that expression of intense and high-strung energy, which showed me that some novel and suggestive circumstance had opened up a stimulating line of thought. See the foxhound with hanging ears and drooping tail as it lolls about the kennels, and compare it with the same hound as, with gleaming eyes and straining muscles, it runs upon a breast-high scent – such was the change in Holmes since the morning. He was a different man to the limp and lounging figure in the mouse-coloured dressing-gown who had prowled so restlessly only a few hours before round the fog-girt room.

'There is material here. There is scope,' said he. 'I am dull indeed not to have understood its possibilities.'

'Even now they are dark to me.'

'The end is dark to me also, but I have hold of one idea which may lead us far. The man met his death elsewhere, and his body was on the *roof* of a carriage.'

'On the roof!'

'Remarkable, is it not? But consider the facts. Is it a coincidence that it is found at the very point where the train pitches and sways as it comes round on the points? Is not that the place where an object upon the roof might be expected to fall off? The points would affect no object inside the train. Either the body fell from the roof, or a very curious coincidence has occurred. But now consider the question of the blood. Of course, there was no bleeding on the line if the body had bled elsewhere. Each fact is suggestive in itself. Together they have a cumulative force.'

'And the ticket, too!' I cried.

'Exactly. We could not explain the absence of a ticket. This would explain it. Everything fits together.'

'But suppose it were so, we are still as far as ever from un-ravelling the mystery of his death. Indeed, it becomes not simpler, but stranger.'

'Perhaps,' said Holmes, thoughtfully; 'perhaps.' He relapsed into a silent reverie, which lasted until the slow train drew up at last in Woolwich Station. There he called a cab and drew Mycroft's paper from his pocket.

'We have quite a little round of afternoon calls to make,' said he. 'I think that Sir James Walter claims our first attention.'

The house of the famous official was a fine villa with green lawns stretching down to the Thames. As we reached it the fog was lifting, and a thin, watery sunshine was breaking through. A butler answered our ring.

'Sir James, sir!' said he, with solemn face. 'Sir James died this morning.'

'Good heavens!' cried Holmes, in amazement. 'How did he die?'

'Perhaps you would care to step in, sir, and see his brother, Colonel Valentine?'

'Yes, we had best do so.'

We were ushered into a dim-lit drawing-room, where an instant later we were joined by a very tall, handsome, light-bearded man of fifty, the younger brother of the dead scientist. His wild eyes, stained cheeks, and unkempt hair all spoke of the sudden blow which had fallen upon the household. He was hardly articulate as he spoke of it.

'It was this horrible scandal,' said he. 'My brother, Sir James, was a man of very sensitive honour, and he could not survive such an affair. It broke his heart. He was always so proud of the efficiency of his department, and this was a crushing blow.'

'We had hoped that he might have given us some indications which would have helped us to clear the matter up.'

'I assure you that it was all a mystery to him as it is to you and to all of us. He had already put all his knowledge at the disposal of the police. Naturally, he had no doubt that Cadogan West was guilty. But all the rest was inconceivable.'

'You cannot throw any new light upon the affair?'

'I know nothing myself save what I have read or heard. I have no desire to be discourteous, but you can understand, Mr Holmes, that we are much disturbed at present, and I must ask you to hasten this interview to an end.'

'This is indeed an unexpected development,' said my friend when we had regained the cab. 'I wonder if the death was natural, or whether the poor old fellow killed himself! If the latter, may it be taken as some sign of self-reproach for duty neglected? We must leave that question to the future. Now we shall turn to the Cadogan Wests.'

A small but well-kept house in the outskirts of the town sheltered the bereaved mother. The old lady was too dazed with grief to be of any use to us, but at her side was a white-faced young lady, who introduced herself as Miss Violet Westbury, the fiancée of the dead man, and the last to see him upon that fatal night.

'I cannot explain it, Mr Holmes,' she said. 'I have not shut an eye since the tragedy, thinking, thinking, thinking, night and day, what the true meaning of it can be. Arthur was the most single-minded, chivalrous, patriotic man upon earth. He would have cut his right hand off before he would sell a State secret confided to his keeping. It is absurd, impossible, preposterous to anyone who knew him.'

'But the facts, Miss Westbury?'

'Yes, yes; I admit I cannot explain them.'

'Was he in any want of money?'

'No; his needs were very simple and his salary ample. He had saved a few hundreds, and we were to marry at the New Year.'

'No signs of any mental excitement? Come, Miss Westbury, be absolutely frank with us.'

The quick eye of my companion had noted some change in her manner. She coloured and hesitated.

'Yes,' she said, at last. 'I had a feeling that there was something on his mind.'

'For long?'

'Only for the last week or so. He was thoughtful and worried. Once I pressed him about it. He admitted that there was something, and that it was concerned with his official life. "It is too serious for me to speak about, even to you," said he. I could get nothing more.'

Holmes looked grave.

'Go on, Miss Westbury. Even if it seems to tell against him, go on. We cannot say what it may lead to.'

'Indeed, I have nothing more to tell. Once or twice it seemed to me that he was on the point of telling me something. He spoke one evening of the importance of the secret, and I have some recollection that he said that no doubt foreign spies would pay a great deal to have it.'

My friend's face grew graver still.

'Anything else?'

'He said that we were slack about such matters – that it would be easy for a traitor to get the plans.'

'Was it only recently that he made such remarks?'

'Yes, quite recently.'

'Now tell us of that last evening.'

'We were to go to the theatre. The fog was so thick that a cab was useless. We walked, and our way took us close to the office. Suddenly he darted away into the fog.'

'Without a word?'

'He gave an exclamation; that was all. I waited but he never returned. Then I walked home. Next morning, after the office opened, they came to inquire. About twelve o'clock we heard the terrible news. Oh, Mr Holmes, if you could only, only save his honour! It was so much to him.'

Holmes shook his head sadly.

'Come, Watson,' said he, 'our ways lie elsewhere. Our next station must be the office from which the papers were taken.

'It was black enough before against this young man, but our inquiries make it blacker,' he remarked, as the cab lumbered off. 'His coming marriage gives a motive for the crime. He naturally wanted money. The idea was in his head, since he spoke about it. He nearly made the girl an accomplice in the treason by telling her his plans. It is all very bad.'

'But surely, Holmes, character goes for something? Then, again, why should he leave the girl in the street and dart away to commit a felony?'

'Exactly! There are certainly objections. But it is a formidable case which they have to meet.'

Mr Sidney Johnson, the senior clerk, met us at the office, and received us with that respect which my companion's card always commanded. He was a thin, gruff, bespectacled man of middle age, his cheeks haggard, and his hands twitching from the nervous strain to which he had been subjected.

'It is bad, Mr Holmes, very bad! Have you heard of the death of the chief?'

'We have just come from his house.'

'The place is disorganized. The chief dead, Cadogan West dead, our papers stolen. And yet, when we closed our door on Monday evening we were as efficient an office as any in the Government service. Good God, it's dreadful to think of! That West, of all men, should have done such a thing!'

'You are sure of his guilt, then?'

'I can see no other way out of it. And yet I would have trusted him as I trust myself.'

'At what hour was the office closed on Monday?'

'At five.'

'Did you close it?'

'I am always the last man out.'

'Where were the plans?'

'In that safe. I put them there myself.'

'Is there no watchman to the building?'

'There is; but he has other departments to look after as well. He is an old soldier and a most trustworthy man. He saw nothing that evening. Of course, the fog was very thick.'

'Suppose that Cadogan West wished to make his way into the building after hours; he would need three keys, would he not, before he could reach the papers?'

'Yes, he would. The key of the outer door, the key of the office, and the key of the safe.'

'Only Sir James Walter and you had those keys?'

'I had no keys of the doors – only of the safe.'

'Was Sir James a man who was orderly in his habits?'

'Yes, I think he was. I know that so far as those three keys are concerned he kept them on the same ring. I have often seen them there.'

'And that ring went with him to London?'

'He said so.'

'And your key never left your possession?'

'Never.'

'Then West, if he is the culprit, must have had a duplicate. And yet none was found upon his body. One other point: if a clerk in this office desired to sell the plans, would it not be simpler to copy the plans for himself than to take the originals, as was actually done?'

'It would take considerable technical knowledge to copy the plans in an effective way.'

'But I suppose either Sir James, or you, or West had that technical knowledge?'

'No doubt we had, but I beg you won't try to drag me into the matter, Mr Holmes. What is the use of our speculating in this way when the original plans were actually found on West?'

'Well, it is certainly singular that he should run the risk of taking originals if he could safely have taken copies, which would have equally served his turn.'

'Singular, no doubt – and yet he did so.'

'Every inquiry in this case reveals something inexplicable. Now there are three papers still missing. They are, as I understand, the vital ones.'

'Yes, that is so.'

'Do you mean to say that anyone holding these three papers, and without the seven others, could construct a Bruce-Partington submarine?'

'I reported to that effect to the Admiralty. But today I have been over the drawings again, and I am not so sure of it. The double valves with the automatic self-adjusting slots are drawn in one of the papers which have been returned. Until the foreigners had invented that for themselves they could not make the boat. Of course, they might soon get over the difficulty.'

'But the three missing drawings are the most important?'

'Undoubtedly.'

'I think, with your permission, I will now take a stroll round the premises. I do not recall any other question which I desired to ask.'

He examined the lock of the safe, the door of the room, and finally the iron shutters of the window. It was only when we were on the lawn outside that his interest was strongly excited. There was a laurel bush outside the window, and several of the branches bore signs of having been twisted or snapped. He examined them carefully with his lens, and then some dim and vague marks upon the earth beneath. Finally he asked the chief clerk to close the iron shutters, and he pointed out to me that they hardly met in the centre, and that it would be possible for anyone outside to see what was going on within the room.

'The indications are ruined by three days' delay. They may mean something or nothing. Well, Watson, I do not think that Woolwich can help us further. It is a small crop which we have gathered. Let us see if we can do better in London.'

Yet we added one more sheaf to our harvest before we left Woolwich Station. The clerk in the ticket office was able to say with confidence that he saw Cadogan West – whom he knew well by sight – upon the Monday night. He was alone, and took a single third-class ticket. The clerk was struck at the time by his excited and nervous manner. So shaky was he that he could hardly pick up his change, and the clerk had helped him with it. A reference to the timetable showed that the 8.15 was the first train which it was possible for West to take after he had left the lady about 7.30.

'Let us reconstruct, Watson,' said Holmes, after half an hour of silence. 'I am not aware that in all our joint researches we have ever had a case which was more difficult to get at. Every fresh advance which we make only reveals a fresh ridge beyond. And yet we have surely made some appreciable progress.

'The effect of our inquiries at Woolwich has in the main been against young Cadogan West; but the indications at the window would lend themselves to a more favourable hypothesis. Let us suppose, for example, that he had been approached by some foreign agent. It might have been done under such pledges as would have prevented him from speaking of it, and yet would have affected his thoughts in the direction indicated by his remarks to his fiancée. Very good. We will now suppose that as he went to the theatre with the young lady he suddenly, in the fog, caught a glimpse of this same agent going in the direction of the office. He was an impetuous man, quick in his decisions. Everything gave way to his duty. He followed the man, reached the window, saw the abstraction of the documents, and pursued the thief. In this way we get over the objection that no one would take originals when he could make copies. This outsider had to take originals. So far it holds together.'

'What is the next step?'

'Then we come into difficulties. One would imagine that under such circumstances the first act of young Cadogan West would be to seize the villain and raise the alarm. Why did he not do so? Could it have been an official superior who took the papers? That would explain West's conduct. Or could the thief have given West the slip in the fog, and West started at once to London to head him off from his own rooms, presuming that he knew where the rooms were? The call must have been very pressing, since he left his girl standing in the fog, and made no effort to communicate with her. Our scent runs cold here, and there is a vast gap between either hypothesis and the laying of West's body, with seven papers in his pocket, on the roof of a Metropolitan train. My instinct now is to work from the other end. If Mycroft has given us the list of addresses we may be able to pick our man, and follow two tracks instead of one.'

Surely enough, a note awaited us at Baker Street. A Government messenger had brought it post-haste. Holmes glanced at it and threw it over to me.

There are numerous small fry, but few who would handle so big an affair. The only men worth considering are Adolph Meyer, of 13, Great George Street, Westminster; Louis La Rothière, of Campden Mansions, Notting Hill: and Hugo Oberstein, 13, Caulfield Gardens, Kensington. The latter was known to be in town on Monday, and is now reported as having left. Glad to hear you have seen some light. The Cabinet awaits your final report with the utmost anxiety. Urgent representations have arrived from the very highest quarter. The whole force of the State is at your back if you should need it.   MYCROFT.

'I'm afraid', said Holmes, smiling, 'that all the Queen's horses and all the Queen's men cannot avail in this matter.' He had spread out his big map of London, and leaned eagerly over it. 'Well, well,' said he presently, with an exclamation of satisfaction, 'things are turning a little in our direction at last. Why, Watson, I do honestly believe that we are going to pull it off after all.' He slapped me on the shoulder with a sudden burst of hilarity. 'I am going out now. It is only a reconnaissance. I will do nothing serious without my trusted comrade and biographer at my elbow. Do you stay here, and the odds are that you will see me again in an hour or two. If time hangs heavy get foolscap and a pen, and begin your narrative of how we saved the State.'

I felt some reflection of his elation in my own mind, for I knew well that he would not depart so far from his usual austerity of demeanour unless there was good cause for exultation. All the long November evening I waited, filled with impatience for his return. At last, shortly after nine o'clock there arrived a messenger with a note:

Am dining at Goldini's Restaurant, Gloucester Road, Kensington. Please come at once and join me there. Bring with you a jemmy, a dark lantern, a chisel, and a revolver.

S.H.

It was a nice equipment for a respectable citizen to carry through the dim, fog-draped streets. I stowed them all discreetly away in my overcoat, and drove straight to the address given. There sat my friend at a little round table near the door of the garish Italian restaurant.

'Have you had something to eat? Then join me in a coffee and curaçao. Try one of the proprietor's cigars. They are less poisonous than one would expect. Have you the tools?'

'They are here, in my overcoat.'

'Excellent. Let me give you a short sketch of what I have done, with some indication of what we are about to do. Now it must be evident to you, Watson, that this young man's body was *placed* on the roof of the train. That was clear from the instant that I determined the fact that it was from the roof, and not from a carriage, that he had fallen.'

'Could it not have been dropped from a bridge?'

'I should say it was impossible. If you examine the roofs you will find that they are slightly rounded, and there is no railing round them. Therefore, we can say for certain that young Cadogan West was placed on it.'

'How could he be placed there?'

'That was the question which we had to answer. There is only one possible way. You are aware that the Underground runs clear of tunnels at some points in the West End. I had a vague memory that as I have travelled by it I have occasionally seen windows just above my head. Now, suppose that a train halted under such a window, would there be any difficulty in laying a body upon the roof?'

'It seems most improbable.'

'We must fall back upon the old axiom that when all other contingencies fail, whatever remains, however improbable, must be the truth. Here all other contingencies *have* failed. When I found that the leading international agent, who had just left London, lived in a row of houses which abutted upon the Underground, I was so pleased that you were a little astonished at my sudden frivolity.'

'Oh, that was it, was it?'

'Yes, that was it. Mr Hugo Oberstein, of 13, Caulfield Gardens, had become my objective. I began my operations at Gloucester Road Station, where a very helpful official walked with me along the track, and allowed me to satisfy myself, not only that the back-stair windows of Caulfield Gardens open on the line, but the even more essential fact that, owing to the intersection of one of the larger railways, the Underground trains are frequently held motionless for some minutes at that very spot.'

'Splendid, Holmes! You have got it!'

'So far – so far, Watson. We advance, but the goal is afar. Well, having seen the back of Caulfield Gardens, I visited the front and satisfied myself that the bird was indeed flown. It is a considerable house, unfurnished, so far as I could judge, in the upper rooms. Oberstein lived there with a single valet, who was probably a confederate entirely in his confidence. We must bear in mind that Oberstein has gone to the Continent to dispose of his booty, but not with any idea of flight; for he had no reason to fear a warrant, and the idea of an amateur domiciliary visit would certainly never occur to him. Yet that is precisely what we are about to make.'

'Could we not get a warrant and legalize it?'

'Hardly on the evidence.'

'What can we hope to do?'

'We cannot tell what correspondence may be there.'

'I don't like it, Holmes.'

'My dear fellow, you shall keep watch in the street. I'll do the criminal part. It's not a time to stick at trifles. Think of Mycroft's note, of the Admiralty, the Cabinet, the exalted person who waits for news. We are bound to go.'

My answer was to rise from the table.

'You are right, Holmes. We are bound to go.'

He sprang up and shook me by the hand.

'I knew you would not shrink at the last,' said he, and for a moment I saw something in his eyes which was nearer to tenderness than I had ever seen. The next instant he was his masterful, practical self once more.

'It is nearly half a mile, but there is no hurry. Let us walk,' said he. 'Don't drop the instruments, I beg. Your arrest as a suspicious character would be a most unfortunate complication.'

Caulfield Gardens was one of those lines of flat-faced, pillared, and porticoed houses which are so prominent a product of the middle Victorian epoch in the West End of London. Next door there appeared to be a children's party, for the merry buzz of young voices and the clatter of a piano resounded through the night. The fog still hung about and screened us with its friendly shade. Holmes had lit his lantern and flashed it upon the massive door.

'This is a serious proposition,' said he. 'It is certainly bolted as well as locked. We would do better in the area. There is an excellent archway down yonder in case a too zealous policeman should intrude. Give me a hand, Watson, and I'll do the same for you.'

A minute later we were both in the area. Hardly had we reached the dark shadows before the step of the policeman was heard in the fog above. As its soft rhythm died away, Holmes set to work upon the lower door. I saw him stoop and strain until with a sharp crash it flew open. We sprang through into the dark passage, closing the area door behind us. Holmes led the way up the curving, uncarpeted stair. His little fan of yellow light shone upon a low window.

'Here we are, Watson – this must be the one.' He threw it open, and as he did so there was a low, harsh murmur, growing steadily into a loud roar as a train dashed past us in the darkness. Holmes swept his light along the window-sill. It was thickly coated with soot from the passing engines, but the black surface was blurred and rubbed in places.

'You can see where they rested the body. Halloa, Watson! what is this? There can be no doubt that it is a blood mark.' He was pointing to faint discolorations along the woodwork of the window. 'Here it is on the stone of the stair also. The demonstration is complete. Let us stay here until a train stops.'

We had not long to wait. The very next train roared from the tunnel as before, but slowed in the open, and then, with a creaking of brakes, pulled up immediately beneath us. It was not four feet from the window-ledge to the roof of the carriages. Holmes softly closed the window.

'So far we are justified,' said he. 'What do you think of it, Watson?'

'A masterpiece. You have never risen to a greater height.'

'I cannot agree with you there. From the moment that I conceived the idea of the body being upon the roof, which surely was not a very abstruse one, all the rest was inevitable. If it were not for the grave interests involved, the affair up to this point would be insignificant. Our difficulties are still before us. But perhaps we may find something here which may help us.'

We had ascended the kitchen stair and entered the suite of rooms upon the first floor. One was a dining-room, severely furnished and containing nothing of interest. A second was a bedroom, which also drew blank. The remaining room appeared more promising, and my companion settled down to a systematic examination. It was littered with books and papers, and was evidently used as a study. Swiftly and methodically Holmes turned over the contents of drawer after drawer and cupboard after cupboard, but no gleam of success came to brighten his austere face. At the end of an hour he was no further than when he started.

'The cunning dog has covered his tracks,' said he. 'He has left nothing to incriminate him. His dangerous correspondence has been destroyed or removed. This is our last chance.'

It was a small tin cash-box which stood upon the writing-desk. Holmes prised it open with his chisel. Several rolls of paper were within, covered with figures and calculations, without any note to show to what they referred. The recurring words, 'Water pressure' and 'Pressure to the square inch' suggested some possible relation to a submarine. Holmes tossed them all impatiently aside. There only remained an envelope with some small newspaper slips inside it. He shook them out on the table, and at once I saw by his eager face that his hopes had been raised.

'What's this, Watson? Eh? What's this? Record of a series of messages in the advertisements of a paper. *Daily Telegraph* agony column by the print and paper. Right-hand top corner of a page. No dates – but messages arrange themselves. This must be the first:

'"Hoped to hear sooner. Terms agreed to. Write fully to address given on card. – Pierrot."

'Next comes: "Too complex for description. Must have full report. Stuff awaits you when goods delivered. – Pierrot."

'Then comes: "Matter presses. Must withdraw offer unless contract completed. Make appointment by letter. Will confirm by advertisement. – Pierrot."

'Finally: "Monday night after nine. Two taps. Only ourselves. Do not be so suspicious. Payment in hard cash when goods delivered. – Pierrot."

'A fairly complete record, Watson! If we could only get at the man at the other end!' He sat lost in thought, tapping his fingers on the table. Finally he sprang to his feet.

'Well, perhaps it won't be so difficult after all. There is nothing more to be done here, Watson. I think we might drive round to the offices of the *Daily Telegraph*, and so bring a good day's work to a conclusion.'

Mycroft Holmes and Lestrade had come round by appointment after breakfast next day, and Sherlock Holmes had recounted to them our proceedings of the day before. The professional shook his head over our confessed burglary.

'We can't do these things in the force, Mr Holmes,' said he. 'No wonder you get results that are beyond us. But some of these days you'll go too far, and you'll find yourself and your friend in trouble.'

'For England, home and beauty – eh, Watson? Martyrs on the altar of our country. But what do you think of it, Mycroft?'

'Excellent, Sherlock! Admirable! But what use will you make of it?'

Holmes picked up the *Daily Telegraph* which lay upon the table.

'Have you seen Pierrot's advertisement today?'

'What! Another one?'

'Yes, here it is: "Tonight. Same hour. Same place. Two taps. Most vitally important. Your own safety at stake. – Pierrot."'

'By George!' cried Lestrade. 'If he answers that we've got him!'

'That was my idea when I put it in. I think if you could both

make it convenient to come with us about eight o'clock to
Caulfield Gardens we might possibly get a little nearer to a
solution.'

One of the most remarkable characteristics of Sherlock Holmes
was his power of throwing his brain out of action and switching
all his thoughts on to lighter things whenever he had convinced himself that he could no longer work to advantage. I
remember that during the whole of that memorable day he lost
himself in a monograph which he had undertaken upon the
Polyphonic Motets of Lassus. For my own part I had none of
this power of detachment, and the day, in consequence, appeared to be interminable. The great national importance of the
issue, the suspense in high quarters, the direct nature of the
experiment which we were trying, all combined to work upon
my nerves. It was a relief to me when at last, after a light dinner,
we set out upon our expedition. Lestrade and Mycroft met us by
appointment at the outside of Gloucester Road Station. The
area door of Oberstein's house had been left open the night
before, and it was necessary for me, as Mycroft Holmes absolutely and indignantly declined to climb the railings, to pass in
and open the hall door. By nine o'clock we were all seated in the
study, waiting patiently for our man.

An hour passed and yet another. When eleven struck, the
measured beat of the great church clock seemed to sound the
dirge of our hopes. Lestrade and Mycroft were fidgeting in their
seats and looking twice a minute at their watches. Holmes sat
silent and composed, his eyelids half shut, but every sense on
the alert. He raised his head with a sudden jerk.

'He is coming,' said he.

There had been a furtive step past the door. Now it returned.
We heard a shuffling sound outside, and then two sharp taps
with the knocker. Holmes rose, motioning to us to remain seated.
The gas in the hall was a mere point of light. He opened the
outer door, and then as a dark figure slipped past him he closed

and fastened it. 'This way!' we heard him say, and a moment later our man stood before us. Holmes had followed him closely, and as the man turned with a cry of surprise and alarm he caught him by the collar and threw him back into the room. Before our prisoner had recovered his balance the door was shut and Holmes standing with his back against it. The man glared round him, staggered, and fell senseless upon the floor. With the shock, his broad-brimmed hat flew from his head, his cravat slipped down from his lips, and there was the long light beard and the soft, handsome delicate features of Colonel Valentine Walter.

Holmes gave a whistle of surprise.

'You can write me down an ass this time, Watson,' said he. 'This was not the bird that I was looking for.'

'Who is he?' asked Mycroft eagerly.

'The younger brother of the late Sir James Walter, the head of the Submarine Department. Yes, yes; I see the fall of the cards. He is coming to. I think that you had best leave his examination to me.'

We had carried the prostrate body to the sofa. Now our prisoner sat up, looked round him with a horror-stricken face, and passed his hand over his forehead, like one who cannot believe his own senses.

'What is this?' he asked. 'I came here to visit Mr Oberstein.'

'Everything is known, Colonel Walter,' said Holmes. 'How an English gentleman could behave in such a manner is beyond my comprehension. But your whole correspondence and relations with Oberstein are within our knowledge. So also are the circumstances connected with the death of young Cadogan West. Let me advise you to gain at least the small credit for repentance and confession, since there are still some details which we can only learn from your lips.'

The man groaned and sank his face in his hands. We waited, but he was silent.

'I can assure you,' said Holmes, 'that every essential is already known. We know that you were pressed for money that you took an impress of the keys which your brother held; and that you entered into a correspondence with Oberstein, who answered your letters through the advertisement columns of the *Daily Telegraph*. We are aware that you went down to the office in the fog on Monday night, but that you were seen and followed by young Cadogan West, who had probably some previous reason to suspect you. He saw your theft, but could not give the alarm, as it was just possible that you were taking the papers to your brother in London. Leaving all his private concerns, like the good citizen that he was, he followed you closely in the fog, and kept at your heels until you reached this very house. There he intervened, and then it was, Colonel Walter, that to treason you added the more terrible crime of murder.'

'I did not! I did not! Before God I swear that I did not!' cried our wretched prisoner.

'Tell us, then, how Cadogan West met his end before you laid him upon the roof of a railway carriage.'

'I will. I swear to you that I will. I did the rest. I confess it. It was just as you say. A Stock Exchange debt had to be paid. I needed the money badly. Oberstein offered me five thousand. It was to save myself from ruin. But as to murder, I am as innocent as you.'

'What happened then?'

'He had his suspicions before, and he followed me as you describe. I never knew it until I was at the very door. It was thick fog, and one could not see three yards. I had given two taps and Oberstein had come to the door. The young man rushed up and demanded to know what we were about to do with the papers. Oberstein had a short life-preserver. He always carried it with him. As West forced his way after us into the house Oberstein struck him on the head. The blow was a fatal one. He was dead within five minutes. There he lay in the hall, and we were at our wits' end what to do. Then Oberstein had this idea about the trains which halted under his back window. But first he examined the papers which I had brought. He said that three of them were essential, and that he must keep them. "You cannot keep them," said I. "There will be a dreadful row at Woolwich if they are not returned." "I must keep them," said he, "for they are so technical that it is impossible in the time to make copies." "Then they must all go back together tonight," said I. He thought for a little, and then he cried out that he had it. "Three I will keep," said he. "The others we will stuff into the pocket of this young man. When he is found the whole business will assuredly be put to his account." I could see no other way out of it, so we did as he suggested. We waited half an hour at the window before a train stopped. It was so thick that nothing could be seen, and we had no difficulty in lowering West's body on to the train. That was the end of the matter so far as I was concerned.'

'And your brother?'

'He said nothing, but he had caught me once with his keys, and I think that he suspected. I read in his eyes that he suspected. As you know, he never held up his head again.'

There was silence in the room. It was broken by Mycroft Holmes.

'Can you not make reparation? It would ease your conscience, and possibly your punishment.'

'What reparation can I make?'

'Where is Oberstein with the papers?'

'I do not know.'

'Did he give you no address?'

'He said that letters to the Hôtel du Louvre, Paris, would eventually reach him.'

'Then reparation is still within your power,' said Sherlock Holmes.

'I will do anything I can. I owe this fellow no particular good-will. He has been my ruin and my downfall.'

'Here are paper and pen. Sit at this desk and write to my dictation. Direct the envelope to the address given. That is right.

Now the letter: "Dear Sir, – With regard to our transaction, you will no doubt have observed by now that one essential detail is missing. I have a tracing which will make it complete. This has involved me in extra trouble, however, and I must ask you for a further advance of five hundred pounds. I will not trust it to the post, nor will I take anything but gold or notes. I would come to you abroad, but it would excite remark if I left the country at present. Therefore I shall expect to meet you in the smoking-room of the Charing Cross Hotel at noon on Saturday. Remember that only English notes, or gold, will be taken." That will do very well. I shall be very much surprised if it does not fetch our man.'

And it did! It is a matter of history – that secret history of a nation which is often so much more intimate and interesting than its public chronicles – that Oberstein, eager to complete the coup of his lifetime, came to the lure and was safely engulfed for fifteen years in a British prison. In his trunk were found the invaluable Bruce-Partington plans, which he had put up for auction in all the naval centres of Europe.

Colonel Walter died in prison towards the end of the second year of his sentence. As to Holmes, he returned refreshed to his monograph upon the Polyphonic Motets of Lassus, which has since been printed for private circulation, and is said by experts to be the last word upon the subject. Some weeks afterwards I learned incidentally that my friend spent a day at Windsor, whence he returned with a remarkably fine emerald tie-pin. When I asked him if he had bought it, he answered that it was a present from a certain gracious lady in whose interests he had once been fortunate enough to carry out a small commission. He said no more; but I fancy that I could guess at that lady's august name, and I have little doubt that the emerald pin will for ever recall to my friend's memory the adventure of the Bruce-Partington plans.

The Adventure of the Dying Detective

Mrs Hudson, the landlady of Sherlock Holmes, was a long-suffering woman. Not only was her first-floor flat invaded at all hours by throngs of singular and often undesirable characters, but her remarkable lodger showed an eccentricity and irregularity in his life which must have sorely tried her patience. His incredible untidiness, his addiction to music at strange hours, his occasional revolver practice within doors, his weird and often malodorous scientific experiments, and the atmosphere of violence and danger which hung around him made him the very worst tenant in London. On the other hand, his payments were princely. I have no doubt that the house might have been purchased at the price which Holmes paid for his rooms during the years that I was with him.

The landlady stood in the deepest awe of him, and never dared to interfere with him, however outrageous his proceedings might seem. She was fond of him, too, for he had a remarkable gentleness and courtesy in his dealings with women. He disliked and distrusted the sex, but he was always a chivalrous opponent. Knowing how genuine was her regard for him, I listened earnestly to her story when she came to my rooms in the second year of my married life and told me of the sad condition to which my poor friend was reduced.

'He's dying, Dr Watson,' said she. 'For three days he has been sinking, and I doubt if he will last the day. He would not let me get a doctor. This morning when I saw his bones sticking out of his face and his great bright eyes looking at me I could stand no more of it. "With your leave or without it, Mr Holmes, I am going for a doctor this very hour," said I. "Let it be

Watson, then," said he. I wouldn't waste an hour in coming to him, sir, or you may not see him alive.'

I was horrified, for I had heard nothing of his illness. I need not say that I rushed for my coat and my hat. As we drove back I asked for the details.

'There is little I can tell you, sir. He has been working at a case down at Rotherhithe, in an alley near the river, and he has brought this illness back with him. He took to his bed on Wednesday afternoon and has never moved since. For these three days neither food nor drink has passed his lips.'

'Good God! Why did you not call in a doctor?'

'He wouldn't have it, sir. You know how masterful he is. I didn't dare to disobey him. But he's not long for this world, as you'll see for yourself the moment that you set eyes on him.'

He was indeed a deplorable spectacle. In the dim light of a foggy November day the sick-room was a gloomy spot, but it was that gaunt, wasted face staring at me from the bed which sent a chill to my heart. His eyes had the brightness of fever, there was a hectic flush upon either cheek, and dark crusts clung to his lips; the thin hands upon the coverlet twitched incessantly, his voice was croaking and spasmodic. He lay listlessly as I entered the room, but the sight of me brought a gleam of recognition to his eyes.

'Well, Watson, we seem to have fallen upon evil days,' said he, in a feeble voice, but with something of his old carelessness of manner.

'My dear fellow!' I cried, approaching him.

'Stand back! Stand right back!' said he, with the sharp imperiousness which I had associated only with moments of crisis. 'If you approach me, Watson, I shall order you out of the house.'

'But why?'

'Because it is my desire. Is that not enough?'

Yes, Mrs Hudson was right. He was more masterful than ever. It was pitiful, however, to see his exhaustion.

'I only wished to help,' I explained.

'Exactly! You will help best by doing what you are told.'

'Certainly, Holmes.'

He relaxed the austerity of his manner.

'You are not angry?' he asked, gasping for breath.

Poor devil, how could I be angry when I saw him lying in such a plight before me?

'It's for your own sake, Watson,' he croaked.

'For *my* sake?'

'I know what is the matter with me. It is a coolie disease from Sumatra – a thing that the Dutch know more about than we, though they have made little of it up to date. One thing only is certain. It is infallibly deadly, and it is horribly contagious.'

He spoke now with a feverish energy, the long hands twitching and jerking as he motioned me away.

'Contagious by touch, Watson – that's it, by touch. Keep your distance and all is well.'

'Good heavens, Holmes! Do you suppose that such a consideration weighs with me for an instant? It would not affect me in the case of a stranger. Do you imagine it would prevent me from doing my duty to so old a friend?'

Again I advanced, but he repulsed me with a look of furious anger.

'If you will stand there I will talk. If you do not you must leave the room.'

I have so deep a respect for the extraordinary qualities of Holmes that I have always deferred to his wishes, even when I least understood them. But now all my professional instincts were aroused. Let him be my master elsewhere, I at least was his in a sick-room.

'Holmes,' said I, 'you are not yourself. A sick man is but a child, and so I will treat you. Whether you like it or not, I will examine your symptoms and treat you for them.'

He looked at me with venomous eyes.

'If I am to have a doctor whether I will or not, let me at least have someone in whom I have confidence,' said he.

'Then you have none in me?'

'In your friendship, certainly. But facts are facts, Watson, and after all you are only a general practitioner with very limited experience and mediocre qualifications. It is painful to have to say these things, but you leave me no choice.'

I was bitterly hurt.

'Such a remark is unworthy of you, Holmes. It shows me very clearly the state of your own nerves. But if you have no confidence in me I would not intrude my services. Let me bring Sir Jasper Meek or Penrose Fisher, or any of the best men in London. But someone you *must* have, and that is final. If you think that I am going to stand here and see you die without either helping you myself or bringing anyone else to help you, then you have mistaken your man.'

'You mean well, Watson,' said the sick man, with something between a sob and a groan. 'Shall I demonstrate your own ignorance? What do you know, pray, of Tapanuli fever? What do you know of the black Formosa corruption?'

'I have never heard of either.'

'There are many problems of disease, many strange pathological possibilities, in the East, Watson.' He paused after each sentence to collect his failing strength. 'I have learned so much during some recent researches which have a medico-criminal aspect. It was in the course of them that I contracted this complaint. You can do nothing.'

'Possibly not. But I happen to know that Dr Ainstree, the greatest living authority upon tropical disease, is now in London. All remonstrance is useless, Holmes. I am going this instant to fetch him.' I turned resolutely to the door.

Never have I had such a shock! In an instant, with a tiger-spring, the dying man had intercepted me. I heard the sharp snap of a twisted key. The next moment he had staggered back to his bed, exhausted and panting after his one tremendous outflame of energy.

'You won't take the key from me by force, Watson. I've got you, my friend. Here you are, and here you will stay until I will otherwise. But I'll humour you.' (All this in little gasps, with terrible struggles for breath between.) 'You've only my own good at heart. Of course I know that very well. You shall have your way, but give me time to get my strength. Not now, Watson, not now. It's four o'clock. At six you can go.'

'This is insanity, Holmes.'

'Only two hours, Watson. I promise you will go at six. Are you content to wait?'

'I seem to have no choice.'

'None in the world, Watson. Thank you, I need no help in arranging the clothes. You will please keep your distance. Now, Watson, there is one other condition that I would make. You will seek help, not from the man you mention, but from the one that I choose.'

'By all means.'

'The first three sensible words that you have uttered since you entered this room, Watson. You will find some books over there. I am somewhat exhausted; I wonder how a battery feels when it pours electricity into a non-conductor? At six, Watson, we resume our conversation.'

But it was destined to be resumed long before that hour, and in circumstances which gave me a shock hardly second to that caused by his spring to the door. I had stood for some minutes looking at the silent figure in the bed. His face was almost covered by the clothes and he appeared to be asleep. Then, unable to settle down to reading, I walked slowly round the room, examining the pictures of celebrated criminals with which every wall was adorned. Finally, in my aimless perambulation, I came to the mantelpiece. A litter of pipes, tobacco-pouches, syringes, penknives, revolver cartridges, and other debris was scattered over it. In the midst of these was a small black and white ivory box with a sliding lid. It was a neat little thing, and I had stretched out my hand to examine it more closely, when——

It was a dreadful cry that he gave – a yell which might have been heard down the street. My skin went cold and my hair bristled at that horrible scream. As I turned I caught a glimpse of a convulsed face and frantic eyes. I stood paralysed, with the little box in my hand.

'Put it down! Down, this instant, Watson – this instant, I say!' His head sank back upon the pillow and he gave a deep sigh of relief as I replaced the box upon the mantelpiece. 'I hate to have my things touched, Watson. You know that I hate it. You fidget me beyond endurance. You, a doctor – you are enough to drive a patient into an asylum. Sit down, man, and let me have my rest!'

The incident left a most unpleasant impression upon my mind. The violent and causeless excitement, followed by this brutality of speech, so far removed from his usual suavity, showed me how deep was the disorganization of his mind. Of all ruins, that of a noble mind is the most deplorable. I sat in silent dejection until the stipulated time had passed. He seemed to have been watching the clock as well as I, for it was hardly six before he began to talk with the same feverish animation as before.

'Now, Watson,' said he. 'Have you any change in your pocket?'

'Yes.'

'Any silver?'

'A good deal.'

'How many half-crowns?'

'I have five.'

'Ah, too few! Too few! How very unfortunate, Watson! However, such as they are you can put them in your watch-pocket. And all the rest of your money in your left trouser-pocket. Thank you. It will balance you so much better like that.'

This was raving insanity. He shuddered, and again made a sound between a cough and a sob.

'You will now light the gas, Watson, but you will be very careful that not for one instant shall it be more than half on. I implore you to be careful, Watson. Thank you, that is excellent. No, you need not draw the blind. Now you will have the kindness to place some letters and papers upon this table within my reach. Thank you. Now some of that litter from the mantelpiece. Excellent, Watson! There is a sugar-tongs there. Kindly raise that small ivory box with its assistance. Place it here among the papers. Good! You can now go and fetch Mr Culverton Smith, of 13, Lower Burke Street.'

To tell the truth, my desire to fetch a doctor had somewhat weakened, for poor Holmes was so obviously delirious that it seemed dangerous to leave him. However, he was as eager now to consult the person named as he had been obstinate in refusing.

'I never heard the name,' said I.

'Possibly not, my good Watson. It may surprise you to know that the man upon earth who is best versed in this disease is not a medical man, but a planter. Mr Culverton Smith is a well-known resident of Sumatra, now visiting London. An outbreak of the disease upon his plantation, which was distant from medical aid, caused him to study it himself, with some rather far-reaching consequences. He is a very methodical person, and I did not desire you to start before six because I was well aware that you would not find him in his study. If you could persuade him to come here and give us the benefit of his unique experience of this disease, the investigation of which has been his dearest hobby, I cannot doubt that he could help me.'

I give Holmes's remarks as a consecutive whole, and will not attempt to indicate how they were interrupted by gaspings for breath and those clutchings of his hands which indicated the pain from which he was suffering. His appearance had changed for the worse during the few hours that I had been with him. Those hectic spots were more pronounced, the eyes shone more

brightly out of darker hollows, and a cold sweat glimmered upon
his brow. He still retained, however, the jaunty gallantry of his
speech. To the last gasp he would always be the master.

'You will tell him exactly how you have left me,' said he.
'You will convey the very impression which is in your own mind
– a dying man – a dying and delirious man. Indeed, I cannot
think why the whole bed of the ocean is not one solid mass of
oysters, so prolific the creatures seem. Ah, I am wandering!
Strange how the brain controls the brain! What was I saying,
Watson?'

'My directions for Mr Culverton Smith.'

'Ah, yes, I remember. My life depends upon it. Plead with
him, Watson. There is no good feeling between us. His nephew,
Watson – I had suspicions of foul play and I allowed him to see
it. The boy died horribly. He has a grudge against me. You will
soften him, Watson. Beg him, pray him, get him here by any
means. He can save me – only he!'

'I will bring him in a cab, if I have to carry him down to it.'

'You will do nothing of the sort. You will persuade him to
come. And then you will return in front of him. Make any
excuse so as not to come with him. Don't forget, Watson. You
won't fail me. You never did fail me. No doubt there are natural
enemies which limit the increase of the creatures. You and I,
Watson, we have done our part. Shall the world, then, be
overrun by oysters? No, no; horrible! You'll convey all that is
in your mind.'

I left him full of the image of this magnificent intellect
babbling like a foolish child. He had handed me the key, and
with a happy thought I took it with me lest he should lock
himself in. Mrs Hudson was waiting, trembling and weeping,
in the passage. Behind me as I passed from the flat I heard
Holmes's high, thin voice in some delirious chant. Below, as
I stood whistling for a cab, a man came on me through the
fog.

'How is Mr Holmes, sir?' he asked.

It was an old acquaintance, Inspector Morton, of Scotland Yard, dressed in unofficial tweeds.

'He is very ill,' I answered.

He looked at me in a most singular fashion. Had it not been too fiendish, I could have imagined that the gleam of the fanlight showed exultation in his face.

'I heard some rumour of it,' said he.

The cab had driven up, and I left him.

Lower Burke Street proved to be a line of fine houses lying in the vague borderland between Notting Hill and Kensington. The particular one at which my cabman pulled up had an air of smug and demure respectability in its old-fashioned iron railings, its massive folding-door, and its shining brasswork. All was in keeping with a solemn butler who appeared framed in the pink radiance of a tinted electric light behind him.

'Yes, Mr Culverton Smith is in. Dr Watson! Very good, sir, I will take up your card.'

My humble name and title did not appear to impress Mr Culverton Smith. Through the half-open door I heard a high, petulant, penetrating voice.

'Who is this person? What does he want? Dear me, Staples, how often have I said that I am not to be disturbed in my hours of study?'

There came a gentle flow of soothing explanation from the butler.

'Well, I won't see him, Staples. I can't have my work interrupted like this. I am not at home. Say so. Tell him to come in the morning if he really must see me.'

Again the gentle murmur.

'Well, well, give him that message. He can come in the morning, or he can stay away. My work must not be hindered.'

I thought of Holmes tossing upon his bed of sickness, and counting the minutes, perhaps, until I could bring help to him. It was not a time to stand upon ceremony. His life depended upon my promptness. Before the apologetic butler had delivered his message I had pushed past him and was in the room.

With a shrill cry of anger a man rose from a reclining chair beside the fire. I saw a great yellow face, coarse-grained and greasy, with heavy, double-chin, and two sullen, menacing grey eyes which glared at me from under tufted and sandy brows. A high bald head had a small velvet smoking-cap poised coquettishly upon one side of its pink curve. The skull was of enormous capacity, and yet, as I looked down, I saw to my amazement that the figure of the man was small and frail, twisted in the shoulders and back like one who has suffered from rickets in his childhood.

'What's this?' he cried, in a high, screaming voice. 'What is the meaning of this intrusion? Didn't I send you word that I would see you tomorrow morning?'

'I am sorry,' said I, 'but the matter cannot be delayed. Mr Sherlock Holmes—'

The mention of my friend's name had an extraordinary effect upon the little man. The look of anger passed in an instant from his face. His features became tense and alert.

'Have you come from Holmes?' he asked.

'I have just left him.'

'What about Holmes? How is he?'

'He is desperately ill. That is why I have come.'

The man motioned me to a chair, and turned to resume his own. As he did so I caught a glimpse of his face in the mirror over the mantelpiece. I could have sworn that it was set in a malicious and abominable smile. Yet I persuaded myself that it must have been some nervous contraction which I had surprised, for he turned to me an instant later with genuine concern upon his features.

'I am sorry to hear this,' said he. 'I only know Mr Holmes through some business dealings which we have had, but I have every respect for his talents and his character. He is an amateur of crime, as I am of disease. For him the villain, for me the microbe. There are my prisons,' he continued, pointing to a row of bottles and jars which stood upon a side table. 'Among those gelatine cultivations some of the very worst offenders in the world are now doing time.'

'It was on account of your special knowledge that Mr Holmes desired to see you. He has a high opinion of you, and thought that you were the one man in London who could help him.'

The little man started, and the jaunty smoking-cap slid to the floor.

'Why? he asked. 'Why should Mr Holmes think that I could help him in his trouble?'

'Because of your knowledge of Eastern diseases.'

'But why should he think that this disease which he has contracted is Eastern?'

'Because, in some professional inquiry, he has been working among Chinese sailors down in the docks.'

Mr Culverton Smith smiled pleasantly and picked up his smoking-cap.

'Oh, that's it – is it?' said he. 'I trust the matter is not so grave as you suppose. How long has he been ill?'

'About three days.'

'Is he delirious?'

'Occasionally.'

'Tut, tut! This sounds serious. It would be inhuman not to answer his call. I very much resent any interruption to my work, Dr Watson, but this case is certainly exceptional. I will come with you at once.'

I remembered Holmes's injunction.

'I have another appointment,' said I.

'Very good. I will go alone. I have a note of Mr Holmes's address. You can rely upon my being there within half an hour at most.'

It was with a sinking heart that I re-entered Holmes's bedroom. For all that I knew the worst might have happened in my absence. To my enormous relief, he had improved greatly in the interval. His appearance was as ghastly as ever, but all trace of delirium had left him and he spoke in a feeble voice, it is true, but with even more than his usual crispness and lucidity.

'Well, did you see him, Watson?'

'Yes; he is coming.'

'Admirable, Watson! Admirable! You are the best of messengers.'

'He wished to return with me.'

'That would never do, Watson. That would be obviously impossible. Did he ask what ailed me?'

'I told him about the Chinese in the East End.'

'Exactly! Well, Watson, you have done all that a good friend could. You can now disappear from the scene.'

'I must wait and hear his opinion, Holmes.'

'Of course you must. But I have reasons to suppose that this opinion would be very much more frank and valuable if he imagines that we are alone. There is just room behind the head of my bed, Watson.'

'My dear Holmes!'

'I fear there is no alternative, Watson. The room does not lend itself to concealment, which is as well, as it is the less likely to arouse suspicion. But just there, Watson, I fancy that it could be done.' Suddenly he sat up with a rigid intentness upon his haggard face. 'There are the wheels, Watson. Quick, man, if you love me! And don't budge, whatever happens – whatever happens, do you hear? Don't speak! Don't move! Just listen with all your ears.' Then in an instant his sudden access of strength departed, and his masterful, purposeful talk droned away into the low, vague murmurings of a semi-delirious man.

From the hiding-place into which I had been so swiftly hustled I heard the footfalls upon the stair, with the opening and the closing of the bedroom door. Then, to my surprise, there came a long silence, broken only by the heavy breathings and gaspings of the sick man. I could imagine that our visitor was standing by the bedside and looking down at the sufferer. At last that strange hush was broken.

'Holmes!' he cried. 'Holmes!' in the insistent tone of one who awakens a sleeper. 'Can't you hear me, Holmes?' There was a rustling, as if he had shaken the sick man roughly by the shoulder.

'Is that you, Mr Smith?' Holmes whispered. 'I hardly dared hope that you would come.'

The other laughed.

'I should imagine not,' he said. 'And yet, you see, I am here. Coals of fire, Holmes – coals of fire!'

'It is very good of you – very noble of you. I appreciate your special knowledge.'

Our visitor sniggered.

'You do. You are, fortunately, the only man in London who does. Do you know what is the matter with you?'

'The same,' said Holmes.

'Ah! You recognize the symptoms?'

'Only too well.'

'Well, I shouldn't be surprised, Holmes. I shouldn't be surprised if it *were* the same. A bad look-out for you if it is. Poor Victor was a dead man on the fourth day – a strong, hearty young fellow. It was certainly, as you said, very surprising that he should have contracted an out-of-the-way Asiatic disease in the heart of London – a disease, too, of which I had made such a very special study. Singular coincidence, Holmes. Very smart of you to notice it, but rather uncharitable to suggest that it was cause and effect.'

'I knew that you did it.'

'Oh, you did, did you? Well, you couldn't prove it, anyhow. But what do you think of yourself spreading reports about me like that, and then crawling to me for help the moment you are in trouble? What sort of a game is that – eh?'

I heard the rasping, laboured breathing of the sick man. 'Give me the water!' he gasped.

'You're precious near your end, my friend, but I don't want you to go till I have had a word with you. That's why I give you water. There, don't slop it about! That's right. Can you understand what I say?'

Holmes groaned.

'Do what you can for me. Let bygones be bygones,' he whispered. 'I'll put the words out of my head – I swear I will. Only cure me, and I'll forget it.'

'Forget what?'

'Well, about Victor Savage's death. You as good as admitted just now that you had done it. I'll forget it.'

'You can forget it or remember it, just as you like. I don't see you in the witness-box. Quite another shaped box, my good Holmes, I assure you. It matters nothing to me that you should know how my nephew died. It's not him we are talking about. It's you.'

'Yes, yes.'

'The fellow who came for me – I've forgotten his name – said that you contracted it down in the East End among the sailors.'

'I could only account for it so.'

'You are proud of your brains, Holmes, are you not? Think yourself smart, don't you? You came across someone who was smarter this time. Now cast your mind back, Holmes. Can you think of no other way you could have got this thing?'

'I can't think. My mind is gone. For Heaven's sake help me!'

'Yes, I will help you. I'll help you to understand just where you are and how you got there. I'd like you to know before you die.'

'Give me something to ease my pain.'

'Painful, is it? Yes, the coolies used to do some squealing towards the end. Takes you as cramp, I fancy.'

'Yes, yes; it is cramp.'

'Well, you can hear what I say, anyhow. Listen now! Can

you remember any unusual incident in your life just about the time your symptoms began?'

'No, no; nothing.'

'Think again.'

'I'm too ill to think.'

'Well, then, I'll help you. Did anything come by post?'

'By post?'

'A box by chance?'

'I'm fainting – I'm gone!'

'Listen, Holmes!' There was a sound as if he was shaking the dying man, and it was all that I could do to hold myself quiet in my hiding-place. 'You must hear me. You *shall* hear me. Do you remember a box – an ivory box? It came on Wednesday. You opened it – do you remember?'

'Yes, yes, I opened it. There was a sharp spring inside it. Some joke——'

'It was no joke, as you will find to your cost. You fool, you would have it and you have got it. Who asked you to cross my path? If you had left me alone I would not have hurt you.'

'I remember,' Holmes gasped. 'The spring! It drew blood. This box – this on the table.'

'The very one, by George! And it may as well leave the room in my pocket. There goes your last shred of evidence. But you have the truth now, Holmes, and you can die with the know-ledge that I killed you. You knew too much of the fate of Victor Savage, so I have sent you to share it. You are very near your end, Holmes. I will sit here and I will watch you die.'

Holmes's voice had sunk to an almost inaudible whisper.

'What is that?' said Smith. 'Turn up the gas? Ah, the shadows begin to fall, do they? Yes, I will turn it up, that I may see you the better.' He crossed the room and the light suddenly bright-ened. 'Is there any other little service that I can do you, my friend?'

'A match and a cigarette.'

I nearly called out in my joy and my amazement. He was

speaking in his natural voice – a little weak, perhaps, but the very voice I knew. There was a long pause, and I felt that Culverton Smith was standing in silent amazement looking down at his companion.

'What's the meaning of this?' I heard him say at last, in a dry, rasping tone.

'The best way of successfully acting a part is to be it,' said Holmes. 'I give you my word that for three days I have tasted neither food nor drink until you were good enough to pour me out that glass of water. But it is the tobacco which I find most irksome. Ah, here *are* some cigarettes.' I heard the striking of a match. 'That is very much better. Halloa! halloa! Do I hear the step of a friend?'

There were footfalls outside, the door opened, and Inspector Morton appeared.

'All is in order and this is your man,' said Holmes.

The officer gave the usual cautions.

'I arrest you on the charge of the murder of one Victor Savage,' he concluded.

'And you might add of the attempted murder of one Sherlock Holmes,' remarked my friend with a chuckle. 'To save an invalid trouble, inspector, Mr Culverton Smith was good enough to give our signal by turning up the gas. By the way, the prisoner has a small box in the right-hand pocket of his coat which it would be as well to remove. Thank you. I would handle it gingerly if I were you. Put it down here. It may play its part in the trial.'

There was a sudden rush and a scuffle, followed by the clash of iron and a cry of pain.

'You'll only get yourself hurt,' said the inspector. 'Stand still, will you?' There was the click of the closing handcuffs.

'A nice trap!' cried the high, snarling voice. 'It will bring *you* into the dock, Holmes, not me. He asked me to come here to cure him. I was sorry for him and I came. Now he will pretend, no poubt, that I have said anything which he may invent which will corroborate his insane suspicions. You can lie as you like, Holmes. My word is always as good as yours.'

'Good heavens!' cried Holmes. 'I had totally forgotten him. My dear Watson, I owe you a thousand apologies. To think that I should have overlooked you! I need not introduce you to Mr Culverton Smith, since I understand that you met somewhat earlier in the evening. Have you the cab below? I will follow you when I am dressed, for I may be of some use at the station.'

'I never needed it more,' said Holmes, as he refreshed himself with a glass of claret and some biscuits in the intervals of his toilet. 'However, as you know, my habits are irregular, and such a feat means less to me than to most men. It was very essential that I should impress Mrs Hudson with the reality of my condition, since she was to convey it to you, and you in turn to him. You won't be offended, Watson? You will realize that among your many talents dissimulation finds no place, and that if you had shared my secret you would never have been able to impress Smith with the urgent necessity of his presence, which was the vital point of the whole scheme. Knowing his vindictive nature, I was perfectly certain that he would come to look upon his handiwork.'

'But your appearance, Holmes – your ghastly face?'

'Three days of absolute fast does not improve one's beauty, Watson. For the rest, there is nothing which a sponge may not cure. With vaseline upon one's forehead, belladonna in one's eyes, rouge over the cheek-bones, and crusts of beeswax round one's lips, a very satisfying effect can be produced. Malingering is a subject upon which I have sometimes thought of writing a monograph. A little occasional talk about half-crowns, oysters, or any other extraneous subject produces a pleasing effect of delirium.'

'But why would you not let me near you, since there was in truth no infection?'

'Can you ask, my dear Watson? Do you imagine that I have no respect for your medical talents? Could I fancy that your astute judgment would pass a dying man who, however weak, had no rise of pulse or temperature? At four yards, I could deceive you. If I failed to do so, who would bring my Smith within my grasp? No, Watson, I would not touch that box. You can just see if you look at it sideways where the sharp spring like a viper's tooth emerges as you open it. I dare say it was by some such device that poor Savage, who stood between this monster and a reversion, was done to death. My correspondence, however, is, as you know, a varied one, and I am somewhat upon my guard against any packages which reach me. It was clear to me, however, that by pretending that he had really succeeded in his design I might surprise a confession. That pretence I have carried out with the thoroughness of the true artist. Thank you, Watson, you must help me on with my coat. When we have finished at the police-station I think that something nutritious at Simpson's would not be out of place.'

The Disappearance of
Lady Frances Carfax

'But why Turkish?' asked Mr Sherlock Holmes, gazing fixedly at my boots. I was reclining in a cane-backed chair at the moment, and my protruded feet had attracted his ever-active attention.

'English,' I answered, in some surprise. 'I got them at Latimer's, in Oxford Street.'

Holmes smiled with an expression of weary patience.

'The bath!' he said; 'the bath! Why the relaxing and expensive Turkish rather than the invigorating home-made article?'

'Because for the last few days I have been feeling rheumatic and old. A Turkish bath is what we call an alterative in medicine – a fresh starting-point, a cleanser of the system.

'By the way, Holmes,' I added, 'I have no doubt the connection between my boots and a Turkish bath is a perfectly self-evident one to a logical mind, and yet I should be obliged to you if you would indicate it.'

'The train of reasoning is not very obscure, Watson,' said Holmes, with a mischievous twinkle. 'It belongs to the same elementary class of deduction which I should illustrate if I were to ask you who shared your cab in your drive this morning.'

'I don't admit that a fresh illustration is an explanation,' said I, with some asperity.

'Bravo, Watson! A very dignified and logical remonstrance. Let me see, what were the points? Take the last one first – the cab. You observe that you have some splashes on the left sleeve and shoulder of your coat. Had you sat in the centre of a hansom you would probably have had no splashes, and if you had they would certainly have been symmetrical. Therefore it is clear that you sat at the side. Therefore it is equally clear that you had a companion.'

'That is very evident.'

'Absurdly commonplace, is it not?'

'But the boots and the bath?'

'Equally childish. You are in the habit of doing up your boots in a certain way. I see them on this occasion fastened with an elaborate double bow, which is not your usual method of tying them. You have, therefore, had them off. Who has tied them? A bootmaker – or the boy at the bath. It is unlikely that it is the bootmaker, since your boots are nearly new. Well, what remains? The bath. Absurd, is it not? But, for all that, the Turkish bath has served a purpose.'

'What is that?'

'You say that you have had it because you need a change. Let me suggest that you take one. How would Lausanne do, my dear Watson – first-class tickets and all expenses paid on a princely scale?'

'Splendid! But why?'

Holmes leaned back in his armchair and took his notebook from his pocket.

'One of the most dangerous classes in the world,' said he, 'is the drifting and friendless woman. She is the most harmless, and often the most useful of mortals, but she is the inevitable inciter of crime in others. She is helpless. She is migratory. She has sufficient means to take her from country to country and from hotel to hotel. She is lost, as often as not, in a maze of obscure *pensions* and boarding-houses. She is a stray chicken in a world of foxes. When she is gobbled up she is hardly missed. I much fear that some evil has come to the Lady Frances Carfax.'

I was relieved at this sudden descent from the general to the particular. Holmes consulted his notes.

'Lady Frances', he continued, 'is the sole survivor of the direct family of the late Earl of Rufton. The estates went, as you

may remember, in the male line. She was left with limited
means, but with some very remarkable old Spanish jewellery of
silver and curiously-cut diamonds to which she was fondly
attached – too attached, for she refused to leave them with her
banker and always carried them about with her. A rather path-
etic figure, the Lady Frances, a beautiful woman, still in fresh
middle age, and yet, by a strange chance, the last derelict of
what only twenty years ago was a goodly fleet.'

'What has happened to her, then?'

'Ah, what has happened to the Lady Frances? Is she alive or
dead? There is our problem. She is a lady of precise habits, and
for four years it has been her invariable custom to write every
second week to Miss Dobney, her old governess, who has long
retired, and lives in Camberwell. It is this Miss Dobney who
consulted me. Nearly five weeks have passed without a word.
The last letter was from the Hôtel National at Lausanne. Lady
Frances seems to have left there and given no address. The
family are anxious, and, as they are exceedingly wealthy, no
sum will be spared if we can clear the matter up.'

'Is Miss Dobney the only source of information? Surely she
had other correspondents?'

'There is one correspondent who is a sure draw, Watson.
That is the bank. Single ladies must live, and their pass-books
are compressed diaries. She banks at Silvester's. I have glanced
over her account. The last cheque but one paid her bill at
Lausanne, but it was a large one and probably left her with cash
in hand. Only one cheque has been drawn since.'

'To whom, and where?'

'To Miss Marie Devine. There is nothing to show where the
cheque was drawn. It was cashed at the Crédit Lyonnais at
Montpelier less than three weeks ago. The sum was fifty pounds.'

'And who is Miss Marie Devine?'

'That also I have been able to discover. Miss Marie Devine
was the maid of Lady Frances Carfax. Why she should have
paid her this cheque we have not yet determined. I have no

doubt, however, that your researches will soon clear the matter up.'

'*My* researches!'

'Hence the health-giving expedition to Lausanne. You know that I cannot possibly leave London while old Abrahams is in such mortal terror of his life. Besides, on general principles it is best that I should not leave the country. Scotland Yard feels lonely without me, and it causes an unhealthy excitement among the criminal classes. Go, then, my dear Watson, and if my humble counsel can ever be valued at so extravagant a rate as twopence a word, it waits your disposal night and day at the end of the Continental wire.'

Two days later found me at the National Hotel at Lausanne, where I received every courtesy at the hands of M. Moser, the well-known manager. Lady Frances, as he informed me, had stayed there for several weeks. She had been much liked by all who met her. Her age was not more than forty. She was still handsome, and bore every sign of having in her youth been a very lovely woman. M. Moser knew nothing of any valuable jewellery, but it had been remarked by the servants that the heavy trunk in the lady's bedroom was always scrupulously locked. Marie Devine, the maid, was as popular as her mistress. She was actually engaged to one of the head waiters in the hotel, and there was no difficulty in getting her address. It was 11, Rue de Trajan, Montpelier. All this I jotted down, and felt that Holmes himself could not have been more adroit in collecting his facts.

Only one corner still remained in the shadow. No light which I possessed could clear up the cause for the lady's sudden departure. She was very happy at Lausanne. There was every reason to believe that she intended to remain for the season in her luxurious rooms overlooking the lake. And yet she had left at a single day's notice, which involved her in the useless payment of a week's rent. Only Jules Vibart, the lover of the maid, had any suggestion to offer. He connected the sudden departure with the visit to the hotel a day or two before of a tall, dark, bearded man. '*Un sauvage – un véritable sauvage!*' cried Jules Vibart. The man had rooms somewhere in the town. He had been seen talking earnestly to madame on the promenade by the lake. Then he had called. She had refused to see him. He was English, but of his name there was no record. Madame had left the place immediately afterwards. Jules Vibart, and, what was of more importance, Jules Vibart's sweetheart, thought that this call and this departure were cause and effect. Only one thing Jules could not discuss. That was the reason why Marie had left her mistress. Of that he could or would say nothing. If I wished to know, I must go to Montpelier and ask her.

So ended the first chapter of my inquiry. The second was devoted to the place which Lady Frances Carfax had sought when she left Lausanne. Concerning this there had been some secrecy, which confirmed the idea that she had gone with the intention of throwing someone off her track. Otherwise why should not her luggage have been openly labelled for Baden? Both she and it reached the Rhenish spa by some circuitous route. Thus much I gathered from the manager of Cook's local office. So to Baden I went, after dispatching to Holmes an account of all my proceedings, and receiving in reply a telegram of half-humorous commendation.

At Baden the track was not difficult to follow. Lady Frances had stayed at the Englischer Hof for a fortnight. Whilst there she had made the acquaintance of a Dr Shlessinger and his wife, a missionary from South America. Like most lonely ladies, Lady Frances found her comfort and occupation in religion. Dr Shlessinger's remarkable personality, his whole-hearted devotion, and the fact that he was recovering from a disease contracted in the exercise of his apostolic duties, affected her deeply. She had helped Mrs Shlessinger in the nursing of the convalescent saint. He spent his day, as the manager described it to me, upon a lounge-chair on the veranda, with an attendant lady upon either side of him. He was preparing a map of the Holy Land, with special reference to the kingdom of the Midianites, upon which he was writing a monograph. Finally, having improved much in health, he and his wife had returned to London, and Lady Frances had started thither in their company. This was just three weeks before, and the manager had heard nothing since. As to the maid, Marie, she had gone off some days beforehand in floods of tears, after informing the other maids that she was leaving service for ever. Dr Shlessinger had paid the bill of the whole party before his departure.

'By the way,' said the landlord, in conclusion, 'you are not the only friend of Lady Frances Carfax who is inquiring after her just now. Only a week or so ago we had a man here upon the same errand.'

'Did he give a name?' I asked.

'None; but he was an Englishman, though of an unusual type.'

'A savage?' said I, linking my facts after the fashion of my illustrious friend.

'Exactly. That describes him very well. He is a bulky, bearded, sunburned fellow, who looks as if he would be more at home in a farmers' inn than in a fashionable hotel. A hard, fierce man, I should think, and one whom I should be sorry to offend.'

Already the mystery began to define itself, as figures grow clearer with the lifting of a fog. Here was this good and pious lady pursued from place to place by a sinister and unrelenting figure. She feared him, or she would not have fled from Lausanne. He had still followed. Sooner or later he would overtake her. Had he already overtaken her? Was *that* the secret of her continued silence? Could the good people who were her companions not screen her from his violence or his blackmail? What horrible purpose, what deep design, lay behind this long pursuit? There was the problem which I had to solve.

To Holmes I wrote showing how rapidly and surely I had

got down to the roots of the matter. In reply I had a telegram asking for a description of Dr Shlessinger's left ear. Holmes's ideas of humour are strange and occasionally offensive, so I took no notice of his ill-timed jest – indeed, I had already reached Montpelier in my pursuit of the maid, Marie, before his message came.

I had no difficulty in finding the ex-servant and in learning all that she could tell me. She was a devoted creature, who had only left her mistress because she was sure that she was in good hands, and because her own approaching marriage made a separation inevitable in any case. Her mistress had, as she confessed with distress, shown some irritability of temper towards her during their stay in Baden, and had even questioned her once as if she had suspicions of her honesty, and this had made the parting easier than it would otherwise have been. Lady Frances had given her fifty pounds as a wedding-present. Like me, Marie viewed with deep distrust the stranger who had driven her mistress from Lausanne. With her own eyes she had seen him seize the lady's wrist with great violence on the public promenade by the lake. He was a fierce and terrible man. She believed that it was out of dread of him that Lady Frances had accepted the escort of the Shlessingers to London. She had never spoken to Marie about it, but many little signs had convinced the maid that her mistress lived in a state of continual nervous apprehension. So far she had got in her narrative, when suddenly she sprang from her chair and her face was convulsed with surprise and fear. 'See!' she cried. 'The miscreant follows still! There is the very man of whom I speak.'

Through the open sitting-room window I saw a huge, swarthy man with a bristling black beard walking slowly down the centre of the street and staring eagerly at the numbers of the houses. It was clear that, like myself, he was on the track of the maid. Acting upon the impulse of the moment, I rushed out and accosted him.

'You are an Englishman,' I said.

'What if I am?' he asked, with a most villainous scowl.

'May I ask what your name is?'

'No, you may not,' said he, with decision.

The situation was awkward, but the most direct way is often the best.

'Where is the Lady Frances Carfax?' I asked.

He stared at me in amazement.

'What have you done with her? Why have you pursued her? I insist upon an answer!' said I.

The fellow gave a bellow of anger and sprang upon me like a tiger. I have held my own in many a struggle, but the man had a grip of iron and the fury of a fiend. His hand was on my throat and my senses were nearly gone before an unshaven French *ouvrier*, in a blue blouse, darted out from a *cabaret* opposite, with a cudgel in his hand, and struck my assailant a sharp crack over the forearm, which made him leave go his hold. He stood for an instant fuming with rage and uncertain whether he should not renew his attack. Then, with a snarl of anger, he left me and entered the cottage from which I had just come. I turned to thank my preserver, who stood beside me in the roadway.

'Well, Watson,' said he, 'a very pretty hash you have made of it! I rather think you had better come back with me to London by the night express.'

An hour afterwards Sherlock Holmes, in his usual garb and style, was seated in my private room at the hotel. His explanation of his sudden and opportune appearance was simplicity itself, for, finding that he could get away from London, he determined to head me off at the next obvious point of my travels. In the disguise of a working-man he had sat in the *cabaret* waiting for my appearance.

'And a singularly consistent investigation you have made, my dear Watson,' said he. 'I cannot at the moment recall any possible blunder which you have omitted. The total effect of your proceedings has been to give the alarm everywhere and yet to discover nothing.'

'Perhaps you would have done no better,' I answered, bitterly.

'There is no "perhaps" about it. I *have* done better. Here is the Hon. Philip Green, who is a fellow-lodger with you in this hotel, and we may find in him the starting-point for a more successful investigation.'

A card had come up on a salver, and it was followed by the same bearded ruffian who had attacked me in the street. He started when he saw me.

'What is this, Mr Holmes?' he asked. 'I had your note and I have come. But what has this man to do with the matter?'

'This is my old friend and associate, Dr Watson, who is helping us in this affair.'

The stranger held out a huge, sunburned hand, with a few words of apology.

' I hope I didn't harm you. When you accused me of hurting her I lost my grip of myself. Indeed, I'm not responsible in these days. My nerves are like live wires. But this situation is beyond me. What I want to know, in the first place, Mr Holmes, is, how in the world you came to hear of my existence at all.'

'I am in touch with Miss Dobney, Lady Frances's governess.'

'Old Susan Dobney with the mob cap! I remember her well.'

'And she remembers you. It was in the days before – before you found it better to go to South Africa.'

'Ah, I see you know my whole story. I need hide nothing from you. I swear to you, Mr Holmes, that there never was in this world a man who loved a woman with a more wholehearted love than I had for Frances. I was a wild youngster, I know – not worse than others of my class. But her mind was pure as snow. She could not bear a shadow of coarseness. So, when she came to hear of things that I had done, she would have no more to say to me. And yet she loved me – that is the wonder of it! – loved me well enough to remain single all her sainted days just for my sake alone. When the years had passed and I had made my money at Barberton I thought perhaps I could seek her out and soften her. I had heard that she was still unmarried. I found her at Lausanne, and tried all I knew. She weakened, I think, but her will was strong, and when next I called she had left the town. I traced her to Baden, and then after a time heard that her maid was here. I'm a rough fellow, fresh from a rough life, and when Dr Watson spoke to me as he did I lost hold of myself for a moment. But for God's sake tell me what has become of the Lady Frances.'

'That is for us to find out,' said Sherlock Holmes, with peculiar gravity. 'What is your London address, Mr Green?'

'The Langham Hotel will find me.'

'Then may I recommend that you return there and be on hand in case I should want you? I have no desire to encourage false hopes, but you may rest assured that all that can be done will be done for the safety of Lady Frances. I can say no more for the instant. I will leave you this card so that you may be able to keep in touch with us. Now, Watson, if you will pack your bag I will cable to Mrs Hudson to make one of her best efforts for two hungry travellers at seven-thirty tomorrow.'

A telegram was awaiting us when we reached our Baker Street rooms, which Holmes read with an exclamation of interest and threw across to me. 'Jagged or torn,' was the message, and the place of origin Baden.

'What is this?' I asked.

'It is everything,' Holmes answered. 'You may remember my seemingly irrelevant question as to this clerical gentleman's left ear. You did not answer it.'

'I had left Baden, and could not inquire.'

'Exactly. For this reason I sent a duplicate to the manager of the Englischer Hof, whose answer lies here.'

'What does it show?'

'It shows, my dear Watson, that we are dealing with an exceptionally astute and dangerous man. The Rev. Dr Shlessinger, missionary from South America, is none other than Holy

Peters, one of the most unscrupulous rascals that Australia has ever evolved – and for a young country it has turned out some very finished types. His particular speciality is the beguiling of lonely ladies by playing upon their religious feelings, and his so-called wife, an Englishwoman named Fraser, is a worthy helpmate. The nature of his tactics suggested his identity to me, and this physical peculiarity – he was badly bitten in a saloon-fight at Adelaide in '89 – confirmed my suspicion. This poor lady is in the hands of a most infernal couple, who will stick at nothing, Watson. That she is already dead is a very likely supposition. If not, she is undoubtedly in some sort of confinement, and unable to write to Miss Dobney or her other friends. It is always possible that she never reached London, or that she has passed through it, but the former is improbable, as, with their system of registration, it is not easy for foreigners to play tricks with the Continental police; and the latter is also unlikely, as these rogues could not hope to find any other place where it would be as easy to keep a person under restraint. All my instincts tell me that she is in London, but, as we have at present no possible means of telling where, we can only take the obvious steps, eat our dinner, and possess our souls in patience. Later in the evening I will stroll down and have a word with friend Lestrade at Scotland Yard.'

But neither the official police nor Holmes's own small, but very efficient, organization sufficed to clear away the mystery. Amid the crowded millions of London the three persons we sought were as completely obliterated as if they had never lived. Advertisements were tried, and failed. Clues were followed, and led to nothing. Every criminal resort which Shlessinger might frequent was drawn in vain. His old associates were watched, but they kept clear of him. And then suddenly, after a week of helpless suspense, there came a flash of light. A silver-and-brilliant pendant of old Spanish design had been pawned at Bevington's, in Westminster Road. The pawner was a large, clean-shaven man of clerical appearance. His name and address were demonstrably false. The ear had escaped notice, but the description was surely that of Shlessinger.

Three times had our bearded friend from the Langham called for news – the third time within an hour of this fresh development. His clothes were getting looser on his great body. He seemed to be wilting away in his anxiety. 'If you will only give me something to do!' was his constant wail. At last Holmes could oblige him.

'He has begun to pawn the jewels. We should get him now.'

'But does this mean that any harm has befallen the Lady Frances?'

Holmes shook his head very gravely.

'Supposing that they have held her prisoner up to now, it is clear that they cannot let her loose without their own destruction. We must prepare for the worst.'

'What can I do?'

'These people do not know you by sight?'

'No.'

'It is possible that he will go to some other pawnbroker in the future. In that case, we must begin again. On the other hand, he has had a fair price and no questions asked, so if he is in need of ready money he will probably come back to Bevington's. I will give you a note to them, and they will let you wait in the shop. If the fellow comes you will follow him home. But no indiscretion, and, above all, no violence. I put you on your honour that you will take no step without my knowledge and consent.'

For two days the Hon. Philip Green (he was, I may mention, the son of the famous admiral of that name who commanded the Sea of Azof fleet in the Crimean War) brought us no news. On the evening of the third he rushed into our sitting-room, pale, trembling, with every muscle of his powerful frame quivering with excitement.

'We have him! We have him!' he cried.

He was incoherent in his agitation. Holmes soothed him with a few words, and thrust him into an armchair.

'Come, now, give us the order of events,' said he.

'She came only an hour ago. It was the wife, this time, but the pendant she brought was the fellow of the other. She is a tall, pale woman, with ferret eyes.'

'That is the lady,' said Holmes.

'She left the office and I followed her. She walked up the Kennington Road, and I kept behind her. Presently she went into a shop. Mr Holmes, it was an undertaker's.'

My companion started. 'Well?' he asked, in that vibrant voice which told of the fiery soul behind the cold, grey face.

'She was talking to the woman behind the counter. I entered as well. "It is late," I heard her say, or words to that effect. The woman was excusing herself. "It should be there before now," she answered. "It took longer, being out of the ordinary." They both stopped and looked at me, so I asked some question and then left the shop.'

'You did excellently well. What happened next?'

'The woman came out, but I had hid myself in a doorway. Her suspicions had been aroused, I think, for she looked round her. Then she called a cab and got in. I was lucky enough to get another and so to follow her. She got down at last at No. 36, Poultney Square, Brixton. I drove past, left my cab at the corner of the square, and watched the house.'

'Did you see anyone?'

'The windows were all in darkness save one on the lower floor. The blind was down, and I could not see in. I was standing there, wondering what I should do next, when a covered van drove up with two men in it. They descended, took something out of the van, and carried it up the steps to the hall door. Mr Holmes, it was a coffin.'

'Ah!'

'For an instant I was on the point of rushing in. The door had been opened to admit the men and their burden. It was the woman who had opened it. But as I stood there she caught a glimpse of me, and I think that she recognized me. I saw her start, and she hastily closed the door. I remembered my promise to you, and here I am.'

'You have done excellent work,' said Holmes scribbling a few words upon a half-sheet of paper. 'We can do nothing legal without a warrant, and you can serve the cause best by taking this note down to the authorities and getting one. There may be some difficulty, but I should think that the sale of the jewellery should be sufficient. Lestrade will see to all details.'

'But they may murder her in the meanwhile. What could the coffin mean, and for whom could it be but for her?'

'We will do all that can be done, Mr Green. Not a moment will be lost. Leave it in our hands. Now, Watson,' he added, as our client hurried away, 'he will set the regular forces on the move. We are, as usual, the irregulars, and we must take our own line of action. The situation strikes me as so desperate that the most extreme measures are justified. Not a moment is to be lost in getting to Poultney Square.

'Let us try to reconstruct the situation,' said he, as we drove swiftly past the Houses of Parliament and over Westminster Bridge. 'These villains have coaxed this unhappy lady to London, after first alienating her from her faithful maid. If she has written any letters they have been intercepted. Through some confederate they have engaged a furnished house. Once inside it, they have made her a prisoner, and they have become possessed of the valuable jewellery which has been their object from the first. Already they have begun to sell part of it, which seems safe enough to them, since they have no reason to think that anyone is interested in the lady's fate. When she is released she will, of course, denounce them. Therefore, she must not be released. But they cannot keep her under lock and key for ever. So murder is their only solution.'

'That seems very clear.'

'Now we will take another line of reasoning. When you follow two separate chains of thought, Watson, you will find some point of intersection which should approximate to the truth. We will start now, not from the lady, but from the coffin, and argue backwards. That incident proves, I fear, beyond all doubt that the lady is dead. It points also to an orthodox burial with proper accompaniment of medical certificate and official sanction. Had the lady been obviously murdered, they would have buried her in a hole in the back garden. But here all is open and regular. What does that mean? Surely that they have done her to death in some way which has deceived the doctor, and simulated a natural end – poisoning, perhaps. And yet how strange that they should ever let a doctor approach her unless he were a confederate, which is hardly a credible proposition.'

'Could they have forged a medical certificate?'

'Dangerous, Watson, very dangerous. No, I hardly see them doing that. Pull up, cabby! This is evidently the undertaker's, for we have just passed the pawnbroker's. Would you go in, Watson? Your appearance inspires confidence. Ask what hour the Poultney Square funeral takes place tomorrow.'

The woman in the shop answered me without hesitation that it was to be at eight o'clock in the morning.

'You see, Watson, no mystery; everything above board! In some way the legal forms have undoubtedly been complied with, and they think that they have little to fear. Well, there's nothing for it now but a direct frontal attack. Are you armed?'

'My stick!'

'Well, well, we shall be strong enough. "Thrice is he armed who hath his quarrel just." We simply can't afford to wait for the police, or to keep within the four corners of the law. You can drive off, cabby. Now, Watson, we'll just take our luck together, as we have occasionally done in the past.'

He had rung loudly at the door of a great dark house in the centre of Poultney Square. It was opened immediately, and the figure of a tall woman was outlined against the dim-lit hall.

'Well, what do you want?' she asked, sharply, peering at us through the darkness.

'I want to speak to Dr Shlessinger,' said Holmes.

'There is no such person here,' she answered, and tried to close the door, but Holmes had jammed it with his foot.

'Well, I want to see the man who lives here, whatever he may call himself,' said Holmes firmly.

She hesitated. Then she threw open the door. 'Well, come in!' said she. 'My husband is not afraid to face any man in the world.' She closed the door behind us, and showed us into a sitting-room on the right side of the hall, turning up the gas as she left us. 'Mr Peters will be with you in an instant,' she said.

Her words were literally true, for we had hardly time to look round the dusty and moth-eaten apartment in which we found ourselves before the door opened and a big, clean-shaven, bald-headed man stepped lightly into the room. He had a large red face, with pendulous cheeks, and a general air of superficial benevolence which was marred by a cruel, vicious mouth.

'There is surely some mistake here, gentlemen,' he said, in an unctuous, make-everything-easy voice. 'I fancy that you have been misdirected. Possibly if you tried farther down the street—'

'That will do; we have no time to waste,' said my companion, firmly. 'You are Henry Peters, of Adelaide, late the Rev. Dr Shlessinger, of Baden and South America. I am as sure of that as that my own name is Sherlock Holmes.'

Peters, as I will now call him, started and stared hard at his formidable pursuer. 'I guess your name does not frighten me, Mr Holmes,' said he, coolly. 'When a man's conscience is easy, you can't rattle him. What is your business in my house?'

'I want to know what you have done with the Lady Frances Carfax, whom you brought away with you from Baden.'

'I'd be very glad if you could tell me where that lady may be,' Peters answered, coolly. 'I've a bill against her for nearly a hundred pounds, and nothing to show for it but a couple of trumpery pendants that the dealer would hardly look at. She attached herself to Mrs Peters and me at Baden (it is a fact that

I was using another name at the time), and she stuck on to us until we came to London. I paid her bill and her ticket. Once in London, she gave us the slip, and, as I say, left these out-of-date jewels to pay her bills. You find her, Mr Holmes, and I'm your debtor.'

'I *mean* to find her,' said Sherlock Holmes. 'I'm going through this house till I do find her.'

'Where is your warrant?'

Holmes half drew a revolver from his pocket. 'This will have to serve till a better one comes.'

'Why, you are a common burglar.'

'So you might describe me,' said Holmes cheerfully. 'My companion is also a dangerous ruffian. And together we are going through your house.'

Our opponent opened the door.

'Fetch a policeman, Annie!' said he. There was a whisk of feminine skirts down the passage, and the hall door was opened and shut.

'Our time is limited, Watson,' said Holmes. 'If you try to stop us, Peters, you will most certainly get hurt. Where is that coffin which was brought into your house?'

'What do you want with the coffin? It is in use. There is a body in it.'

'I must see that body.'

'Never with my consent.'

'Then without it.' With a quick movement Holmes pushed the fellow to one side and passed into the hall. A door half open stood immediately before us. We entered. It was the dining-room. On the table, under a half-lit chandelier, the coffin was lying. Holmes turned up the gas and raised the lid. Deep down in the recesses of the coffin lay an emaciated figure. The glare from the lights above beat down upon an aged and withered face. By no possible process of cruelty, starvation, or disease could this worn-out wreck be the still beautiful Lady Frances. Holmes's face showed his amazement, and also his relief.

'Thank God!' he muttered. 'It's someone else.'

'Ah, you've blundered badly for once, Mr Sherlock Holmes,' said Peters, who had followed us into the room.

'Who is this dead woman?'

'Well, if you really must know, she is an old nurse of my wife's, Rose Spender her name, whom we found in the Brixton Workhouse Infirmary. We brought her round here, called in Dr Horsom, of 13, Firbank Villas – mind you take the address, Mr Holmes – and had her carefully tended, as Christian folk should. On the third day she died – certificate says senile decay – but that's only the doctor's opinion, and, of course, you know better. We ordered her funeral to be carried out by Stimson and Co., of the Kennington Road, who will bury her at eight o'clock tomorrow morning. Can you pick any hole in that, Mr Holmes? You've made a silly blunder, and you may as well own up to it. I'd give something for a photograph of your gaping, staring face when you pulled aside that lid expecting to see the Lady Frances Carfax, and only found a poor old woman of ninety.'

Holmes's expression was as impassive as ever under the jeers of his antagonist, but his clenched hands betrayed his acute annoyance.

'I am going through your house,' said he.

'Are you, though!' cried Peters, as a woman's voice and heavy steps sounded in the passage. 'We'll soon see about that. This way, officers, if you please. These men have forced their way into my house, and I cannot get rid of them. Help me to put them out.'

A sergeant and a constable stood in the doorway. Holmes drew his card from his case.

'This is my name and address. This is my friend, Dr Watson.'

'Bless you, sir, we know you very well,' said the sergeant, 'but you can't stay here without a warrant.'

'Of course not. I quite understand that.'

'Arrest him!' cried Peters.

'We know where to lay our hands on this gentleman if he is

wanted,' said the sergeant, majestically, 'but you'll have to go, Mr Holmes.'

'Yes, Watson, we shall have to go.'

A minute later we were in the street once more. Holmes was as cool as ever, but I was hot with anger and humiliation. The sergeant had followed us.

'Sorry, Mr Holmes, but that's the law.'

'Exactly, sergeant; you could not do otherwise.'

'I expect there was good reason for your presence there. If there is anything I can do——'

'It's a missing lady, sergeant, and we think she is in that house. I expect a warrant presently.'

'Then I'll keep my eye on the parties, Mr Holmes. If anything comes along, I will surely let you know.'

It was only nine o'clock, and we were off full cry upon the trail at once. First we drove to Brixton Workhouse Infirmary, where we found that it was indeed the truth that a charitable couple had called some days before, that they had claimed an imbecile old woman as a former servant, and that they had obtained permission to take her away with them. No surprise was expressed at the news that she had since died.

The doctor was our next goal. He had been called in, had found the woman dying of pure senility, had actually seen her pass away, and had signed the certificate in due form. 'I assure you that everything was perfectly normal and there was no room for foul play in the matter,' said he. Nothing in the house had struck him as suspicious, save that for people of their class it was remarkable that they should have no servant. So far and no farther went the doctor.

Finally, we found our way to Scotland Yard. There had been difficulties of procedure in regard to the warrant. Some delay was inevitable. The magistrate's signature might not be obtained until next morning. If Holmes would call about nine he could go down with Lestrade and see it acted upon. So ended the day, save that near midnight our friend, the sergeant, called to say that he had seen flickering lights here and there in the windows of the great dark house, but that no one had left it and none had entered. We could but pray for patience, and wait for the morrow.

Sherlock Holmes was too irritable for conversation and too restless for sleep. I left him smoking hard, with his heavy, dark brows knotted together, and his long, nervous fingers tapping upon the arms of his chair, as he turned over in his mind every possible solution of the mystery. Several times in the course of the night I heard him prowling about the house. Finally, just after I had been called in the morning, he rushed into my room. He was in his dressing-gown, but his pale, hollow-eyed face told me that his night had been a sleepless one.

'What time was the funeral? Eight, was it not?' he asked, eagerly. 'Well, it is seven-twenty now. Good heavens, Watson, what has become of any brains that God has given me? Quick, man, quick! It's life or death – a hundred chances on death to one on life. I'll never forgive myself, never, if we are too late!'

Five minutes had not passed before we were flying in a hansom down Baker Street. But even so it was twenty-five to eight as we passed Big Ben, and eight struck as we tore down the Brixton Road. But others were late as well as we. Ten minutes after the hour the hearse was still standing at the door of the house, and even as our foaming horse came to a halt the coffin, supported by three men, appeared on the threshold. Holmes darted forward and barred their way.

'Take it back!' he cried, laying his hand on the breast of the foremost. 'Take it back this instant!'

'What the devil do you mean? Once again I ask you, where is your warrant?' shouted the furious Peters, his big red face glaring over the farther end of the coffin.

'The warrant is on its way. This coffin shall remain in the house until it comes.'

The authority in Holmes's voice had its effect upon the bearers. Peters had suddenly vanished into the house, and they obeyed these new orders. 'Quick, Watson, quick! Here is a screw-driver!' he shouted as the coffin was replaced upon the table. 'Here's one for you, my man! A sovereign if the lid comes off in a minute! Ask no questions – work away! That's good! Another! And another! Now pull all together! It's giving! It's giving! Ah, that does it at last!'

With a united effort we tore off the coffin-lid. As we did so there came from the inside a stupefying and overpowering smell of chloroform. A body lay within, its head all wreathed in cotton-wool, which had been soaked in the narcotic. Holmes plucked it off and disclosed the statuesque face of a handsome and spiritual woman of middle age. In an instant he had passed his arm round the figure and raised her to a sitting position.

'Is she gone, Watson? Is there a spark left? Surely we are not too late!'

For half an hour it seemed that we were. What with actual suffocation, and what with the poisonous fumes of the chloroform, the Lady Frances seemed to have passed the last point of recall. And then, at last, with artificial respiration, with injected ether, with every device that science could suggest, some flutter of life, some quiver of the eyelids, some dimming of a mirror, spoke of the slowly returning life. A cab had driven up, and Holmes, parting the blind, looked out at it. 'Here is Lestrade with his warrant,' said he. 'He will find that his birds have flown. And here,' he added, as a heavy step hurried along the passage, 'is someone who has a better right to nurse this lady than we have. Good morning, Mr Green; I think that the sooner we can move the Lady Frances the better. Meanwhile, the funeral may proceed, and the poor old woman who still lies in that coffin may go to her last resting-place alone.'

'Should you care to add the case to your annals, my dear Watson,' said Holmes that evening, 'it can only be as an example of that temporary eclipse to which even the best-balanced mind may be exposed. Such slips are common to all mortals, and the greatest is he who can recognize and repair them. To this modified credit I may, perhaps, make some claim. My night was haunted by the thought that somewhere a clue, a strange sentence, a curious observation, had come under my notice and had been too easily dismissed. Then, suddenly, in the grey of the morning, the words came back to me. It was the remark of the undertaker's wife, as reported by Philip Green. She had said, "It should be there before now. It took longer, being out of the ordinary." It was the coffin of which she spoke. It had been out of the ordinary. That could only mean that it had been made to some special measurement. But why? Why? Then in an instant I remembered the deep sides, and the little wasted figure at the bottom. Why so large a coffin for so small a body? To leave room for another body. Both would be buried under the one certificate. It had all been so clear, if only my own sight had not been dimmed. At eight the Lady Frances would be buried. Our one chance was to stop the coffin before it left the house.

'It was a desperate chance that we might find her alive, but it *was* a chance, as the result showed. These people had never, to my knowledge, done a murder. They might shrink from actual violence at the last. They could bury her with no sign of how she met her end, and even if she were exhumed there was a chance for them. I hoped that such considerations might prevail with them. You can reconstruct the scene well enough. You saw the horrible den upstairs, where the poor lady had been kept so long. They rushed in and overpowered her with their chloroform, carried her down, poured more into the coffin to insure against her waking, and then screwed down the lid. A clever device, Watson. It is new to me in the annals of crime. If our ex-missionary friends escape the clutches of Lestrade, I shall expect to hear of some brilliant incidents in their future career.'

The Adventure of the Devil's Foot

In recording from time to time some of the curious experiences and interesting recollections which I associate with my long and intimate friendship with Mr Sherlock Holmes, I have continually been faced by difficulties caused by his own aversion to publicity. To his sombre and cynical spirit all popular applause was always abhorrent, and nothing amused him more at the end of a successful case than to hand over the actual exposure to some orthodox official, and to listen with a mocking smile to the general chorus of misplaced congratulation. It was indeed this attitude upon the part of my friend, and certainly not any lack of interesting material, which has caused me of late years to lay very few of my records before the public. My participation in some of his adventures was always a privilege which entailed discretion and reticence upon me.

It was, then, with considerable surprise that I received a telegram from Holmes last Tuesday – he has never been known to write where a telegram would serve – in the following terms: 'Why not tell them of the Cornish horror – strangest case I have handled.' I have no idea what backward sweep of memory had brought the matter fresh to his mind, or what freak had caused him to desire that I should recount it; but I hasten, before another cancelling telegram may arrive, to hunt out the notes which give me the exact details of the case, and to lay the narrative before my readers.

It was, then, in the spring of the year 1897 that Holmes's iron constitution showed some symptoms of giving way in the face of constant hard work of a most exacting kind, aggravated, perhaps, by occasional indiscretions of his own. In March of that year Dr Moore Agar, of Harley Street, whose dramatic introduction to Holmes I may some day recount, gave positive injunctions that the famous private agent would lay aside all his cases and surrender himself to complete rest if he wished to avert an absolute breakdown. The state of his health was not a matter in which he himself took the faintest interest, for his mental detachment was absolute, but he was induced at last, on the threat of being permanently disqualified from work, to give himself a complete change of scene and air. Thus it was that in the early spring of that year we found ourselves together in a small cottage near Poldhu Bay, at the further extremity of the Cornish peninsula.

It was a singular spot, and one peculiarly well suited to the grim humour of my patient. From the windows of our little whitewashed house, which stood high upon a grassy headland, we looked down upon the whole sinister semicircle of Mounts Bay, that old death-trap of sailing vessels, with its fringe of black cliffs and surge-swept reefs on which innumerable seamen have met their end. With a northerly breeze it lies placid and sheltered, inviting the storm-tossed craft to tack into it for rest and protection.

Then comes the sudden swirl round of the wind, the blustering gale from the south-west, the dragging anchor, the lee shore, and the last battle in the creaming breakers. The wise mariner stands far out from that evil place.

On the land side our surroundings were as sombre as on the sea. It was a country of rolling moors, lonely and dun-coloured, with an occasional church tower to mark the site of some old-world village. In every direction upon these moors there were traces of some vanished race which had passed utterly away, and left as its sole record strange monuments of stone, irregular mounds which contained the burned ashes of the dead, and curious earth-works which hinted at prehistoric strife. The glamour and mystery of the place, with its sinister atmosphere of forgotten nations, appealed to the imagination of my friend, and he spent much of his time in long walks and solitary meditations upon the moor. The ancient Cornish language had also arrested his attention, and he had, I remember, conceived the idea that it was akin to the Chaldean, and had been largely derived from the Phoenician traders in tin. He had received a consignment of books upon philology and was settling down to develop this thesis, when suddenly, to my sorrow and to his unfeigned delight, we found ourselves, even in that land of dreams, plunged into a problem at our very doors which was more intense, more engrossing, and infinitely more mysterious than any of those which had driven us from London. Our simple life and peaceful, healthy routine were violently interrupted, and we were precipitated into the midst of a series of events which caused the utmost excitement not only in Cornwall, but throughout the whole West of England. Many of my readers may retain some recollection of what was called at the time 'The Cornish Horror', though a most imperfect account of the matter reached the London press. Now, after thirteen years, I will give the true details of this inconceivable affair to the public.

I have said that scattered towers marked the villages which dotted this part of Cornwall. The nearest of these was the hamlet of Tredannick Wollas, where the cottages of a couple of hundred inhabitants clustered round an ancient, moss-grown church. The vicar of the parish, Mr Roundhay, was something of an archaeologist, and as such Holmes had made his acquaintance. He was a middle-aged man, portly and affable, with a considerable fund of local lore. At his invitation we had taken tea at the vicarage, and had come to know, also, Mr Mortimer Tregennis, an independent gentleman, who increased the clergyman's scanty resources by taking rooms in his large, straggling house. The vicar, being a bachelor, was glad to come to such an arrangement, though he had little in common with his lodger, who was a thin, dark, spectacled man, with a stoop which gave the impression of actual, physical deformity. I remember that during our short visit we found the vicar garrulous, but his lodger strangely reticent, a sad-faced, introspective man, sitting with averted eyes, brooding apparently upon his own affairs.

These were the two men who entered abruptly into our little sitting-room on Tuesday, March the 16th, shortly after our breakfast hour, as we were smoking together, preparatory to our daily excursion upon the moors.

'Mr Holmes,' said the vicar, in an agitated voice, 'the most extraordinary and tragic affair has occurred during the night. It is the most unheard-of business. We can only regard it as a special Providence that you should chance to be here at the time, for in all England you are the one man we need.'

I glared at the intrusive vicar with no very friendly eyes; but Holmes took his pipe from his lips and sat up in his chair like an old hound who hears the view-holloa. He waved his hand to the sofa, and our palpitating visitor with his agitated companion sat side by side upon it. Mr Mortimer Tregennis was more self-contained than the clergyman, but the twitching of his thin hands and the brightness of his dark eyes showed that they shared a common emotion.

'Shall I speak or you?' he asked of the vicar.

'Well, as you seem to have made the discovery, whatever it may be, and the vicar to have had it second-hand, perhaps you had better do the speaking,' said Holmes.

I glanced at the hastily-clad clergyman, with the formally-dressed lodger seated beside him, and was amused at the surprise which Holmes's simple deduction had brought to their faces.

'Perhaps I had best say a few words first,' said the vicar, 'and then you can judge if you will listen to the details from Mr Tregennis, or whether we should not hasten at once to the scene of this mysterious affair. I may explain, then, that our friend here spent last evening in the company of his two brothers, Owen and George, and of his sister Brenda, at their house of

Tredannick Wartha, which is near the old stone cross upon the
moor. He left them shortly after ten o'clock, playing cards round
the dining-room table, in excellent health and spirits. This
morning, being an early riser, he walked in that direction
before breakfast, and was overtaken by the carriage of Dr
Richards, who explained that he had just been sent for on a most
urgent call to Tredannick Wartha. Mr Mortimer Tregennis
naturally went with him. When he arrived at Tredannick
Wartha he found an extraordinary state of things. His two
brothers and his sister were seated round the table exactly as he
had left them, the cards still spread in front of them and the
candles burned down to their sockets. The sister lay back stone-
dead in her chair, while the two brothers sat on each side of her
laughing, shouting, and singing, the senses stricken clean out of
them. All three of them, the dead woman and the two demented
men, retained upon their faces an expression of the utmost
horror – a convulsion of terror which was dreadful to look
upon. There was no sign of the presence of anyone in the house,
except Mrs Porter, the old cook and housekeeper, who declared
that she had slept deeply and heard no sound during the night.
Nothing had been stolen or disarranged, and there is absolutely
no explanation of what the horror can be which has frightened
a woman to death and two strong men out of their senses.
There is the situation, Mr Holmes, in a nutshell, and if you can
help us to clear it up you will have done a great work.'

I had hoped that in some way I could coax my companion
back into the quiet which had been the object of our journey; but
one glance at his intense face and contracted eyebrows told me
how vain was now the expectation. He sat for some little time in
silence, absorbed in the strange drama which had broken in upon
our peace.

'I will look into this matter,' he said at last. 'On the face of it,
it would appear to be a case of a very exceptional nature. Have
you been there yourself, Mr Roundhay?'

'No, Mr Holmes. Mr Tregennis brought back the account

to the vicarage, and I at once hurried over with him to consult you.'

'How far is it to the house where this singular tragedy occurred?'

'About a mile inland.'

'Then we shall walk over together. But, before we start, I must ask you a few questions, Mr Mortimer Tregennis.'

The other had been silent all this time, but I had observed that his more controlled excitement was even greater than the obtrusive emotion of the clergyman. He sat with a pale, drawn face, his anxious gaze fixed upon Holmes, and his thin hands clasped convulsively together. His pale lips quivered as he listened to the dreadful experience which had befallen his family, and his dark eyes seemed to reflect something of the horror of the scene.

'Ask what you like, Mr Holmes,' said he eagerly. 'It is a bad thing to speak of, but I will answer you the truth.'

'Tell me about last night.'

'Well, Mr Holmes, I supped there, as the vicar has said, and my elder brother George proposed a game of whist afterwards. We sat down about nine o'clock. It was a quarter past ten when I moved to go. I left them all round the table, as merry as could be.'

'Who let you out?'

'Mrs Porter had gone to bed, so I let myself out. I shut the hall door behind me. The window of the room in which they sat was closed, but the blind was not drawn down. There was no change in door or window this morning, nor any reason to think that any stranger had been to the house. Yet there they sat, driven clean mad with terror, and Brenda lying dead of fright, with her head hanging over the arm of the chair. I'll never get the sight of that room out of my mind so long as I live.'

'The facts, as you state them, are certainly most remarkable,' said Holmes. 'I take it that you have no theory yourself which can in any way account for them?'

'It's devilish, Mr Holmes; devilish!' cried Mortimer Tregennis. 'It is not of this world. Something has come into that room which has dashed the light of reason from their minds. What human contrivance could do that?'

'I fear,' said Holmes, 'that if the matter is beyond humanity it is certainly beyond me. Yet we must exhaust all natural explanations before we fall back upon such a theory as this. As to yourself, Mr Tregennis, I take it you were divided in some way from your family, since they lived together and you had rooms apart?'

'That is so, Mr Holmes, though the matter is past and done with. We were a family of tin-miners at Redruth, but we sold out our venture to a company, and so retired with enough to keep us. I won't deny that there was some feeling about the division of the money and it stood between us for a time, but it was all forgiven and forgotten, and we were the best of friends together.'

'Looking back at the evening which you spent together, does anything stand out in your memory as throwing any possible light upon the tragedy? Think carefully, Mr Tregennis, for any clue which can help me.'

'There is nothing at all, sir.'

'Your people were in their usual spirits?'

'Never better.'

'Were they nervous people? Did they ever show any apprehension of coming danger?'

'Nothing of the kind.'

'You have nothing to add then, which could assist me?'

Mortimer Tregennis considered earnestly for a moment.

'There is one thing occurs to me,' said he at last. 'As we sat at the table my back was to the window, and my brother George, he being my partner at cards, was facing it. I saw him once look hard over my shoulder, so I turned round and looked also. The blind was up and the window shut, but I could just make out the bushes on the lawn, and it seemed to me for a moment that I saw something moving among them. I couldn't even say if it were man or animal, but I just thought there was something

there. When I asked him what he was looking at, he told me that
he had the same feeling. That is all that I can say.'

'Did you not investigate?'

'No; the matter passed as unimportant.'

'You left them, then, without any premonition of evil?'

'None at all.'

'I am not clear how you came to hear the news so early this
morning.'

'I am an early riser, and generally take a walk before breakfast. This morning I had hardly started when the doctor in his
carriage overtook me. He told me that old Mrs Porter had sent
a boy down with an urgent message. I sprang in beside him and
we drove on. When we got there we looked into that dreadful
room. The candles and the fire must have burned out hours
before, and they had been sitting there in the dark until dawn
had broken. The doctor said Brenda must have been dead at
least six hours. There were no signs of violence. She just lay
across the arm of the chair with that look on her face. George
and Owen were singing snatches of songs and gibbering like two
great apes. Oh, it was awful to see! I couldn't stand it, and the
doctor was as white as a sheet. Indeed, he fell into a chair in a
sort of faint, and we nearly had him on our hands as well.'

'Remarkable – most remarkable!' said Holmes, rising and
taking his hat. 'I think, perhaps, we had better go down to
Tredannick Wartha without further delay. I confess that I have
seldom known a case which at first sight presented a more
singular problem.'

Our proceedings of that first morning did little to advance the
investigation. It was marked, however, at the outset by an
incident which left the most sinister impression upon my mind.
The approach to the spot at which the tragedy occurred is down
a narrow, winding, country lane. While we made our way along
it we heard the rattle of a carriage coming towards us, and stood
aside to let it pass. As it drove by us I caught a glimpse through

the closed window of a horribly contorted, grinning face glaring out at us. Those staring eyes and gnashing teeth flashed past us like a dreadful vision.

'My brothers!' cried Mortimer Tregennis, white to the lips. 'They are taking them to Helston.'

We looked with horror after the black carriage, lumbering upon its way. Then we turned our steps towards this ill-omened house in which they had met their strange fate.

It was a large and bright dwelling, rather a villa than a cottage, with a considerable garden which was already, in that Cornish air, well filled with spring flowers. Towards this garden the window of the sitting-room fronted, and from it, according to Mortimer Tregennis, must have come that thing of evil which had by sheer horror in a single instant blasted their minds. Holmes walked slowly and thoughtfully among the flower-pots and along the path before we entered the porch. So absorbed was he in his thoughts, I remember, that he stumbled over the watering-pot, upset its contents, and deluged both our feet and the garden path. Inside the house we were met by the elderly Cornish housekeeper, Mrs Porter, who, with the aid of a young girl, looked after the wants of the family. She readily answered all Holmes's questions. She had heard nothing in the night. Her employers had all been in excellent spirits lately, and she had never known them more cheerful and prosperous. She had fainted with horror upon entering the room in the morning and seeing that dreadful company round the table. She had, when she recovered, thrown open the window to let the morning air in, and had run down to the lane, whence she sent a farm-lad for the doctor. The lady was on her bed upstairs, if we cared to see her. It took four strong men to get the brothers into the asylum carriage. She would not herself stay in the house another day, and was starting that very afternoon to rejoin her family at St Ives.

We ascended the stairs and viewed the body. Miss Brenda Tregennis had been a very beautiful girl, though now verging upon middle age. Her dark, clear-cut face was handsome, even in death, but there still lingered upon it something of that convulsion of horror which had been her last human emotion. From her bedroom we descended to the sitting-room where this strange tragedy had actually occurred. The charred ashes of the overnight fire lay in the grate. On the table were the four guttered and burned-out candles, with the cards scattered over its surface. The chairs had been moved back against the walls, but all else was as it had been the night before. Holmes paced with light, swift steps about the room; he sat in the various chairs, drawing them up and reconstructing their positions. He tested how much of the garden was visible; he examined the floor, the ceiling, and the fireplace; but never once did I see that sudden brightening of his eyes and tightening of his lips which would have told me that he saw some gleam of light in this utter darkness.

'Why a fire?' he asked once. 'Had they always a fire in this small room on a spring evening?'

Mortimer Tregennis explained that the night was cold and damp. For that reason, after his arrival, the fire was lit. 'What are you going to do now, Mr Holmes?' he asked.

My friend smiled and laid his hand upon my arm. 'I think, Watson, that I shall resume that course of tobacco-poisoning which you have so often and so justly condemned,' said he. 'With your permission, gentlemen, we will now return to our cottage, for I am not aware that any new factor is likely to come to our notice here. I will turn the facts over in my mind, Mr Tregennis, and should anything occur to me I will certainly communicate with you and the vicar. In the meantime I wish you both good morning.'

It was not until long after we were back in Poldhu Cottage that Holmes broke his complete and absorbed silence. He sat coiled in his armchair, his haggard and ascetic face hardly visible amid the blue swirl of his tobacco smoke, his black brows drawn down, his forehead contracted, his eyes vacant and far away. Finally, he laid down his pipe and sprang to his feet.

'It won't do, Watson!' said he, with a laugh. 'Let us walk along the cliffs together and search for flint arrows. We are more likely to find them than clues to this problem. To let the brain work without sufficient material is like racing an engine. It racks itself to pieces. The sea air, sunshine, and patience, Watson – all else will come.

'Now, let us calmly define our position, Watson,' he continued, as we skirted the cliffs together. 'Let us get a firm grip of the very little which we *do* know, so that when fresh facts arise we may be ready to fit them into their places. I take it, in the first place, that neither of us is prepared to admit diabolical intrusions into the affairs of men. Let us begin by ruling that entirely out of our minds. Very good. There remain three persons who have been grievously stricken by some conscious or unconscious human agency. That is firm ground. Now, when did this occur? Evidently, assuming his narrative to be true, it was immediately after Mr Mortimer Tregennis had left the room. That is a very important point. The presumption is that it was within a few minutes afterwards. The cards still lay upon the table. It was already past their usual hour for bed. Yet they had not changed their position or pushed back their chairs. I repeat, then, that the occurrence was immediately after his departure, and not later than eleven o'clock last night.

'Our next obvious step is to check, so far as we can, the movements of Mortimer Tregennis after he left the room. In this there is no difficulty, and they seem to be above suspicion. Knowing my methods as you do, you were, of course, conscious of the somewhat clumsy water-pot expedient by which I obtained a clearer impress of his foot than might otherwise have been possible. The wet, sandy path took it admirably. Last night was also wet, you will remember, and it was not difficult – having obtained a sample print – to pick out his track among others and to follow his movements. He appears to have walked away swiftly in the direction of the vicarage.

'If, then, Mortimer Tregennis disappeared from the scene,

and yet some outside person affected the card-players, how can we reconstruct that person, and how was such an impression of horror conveyed? Mrs Porter may be eliminated. She is evidently harmless. Is there any evidence that someone crept up to the garden window and in some manner produced so terrific an effect that he drove those who saw it out of their senses? The only suggestion in this direction comes from Mortimer Tregennis himself, who says that his brother spoke about some movement in the garden. That is certainly remarkable, as the night was rainy, cloudy, and dark. Anyone who had the design to alarm these people would be compelled to place his very face against the glass before he could be seen. There is a three-foot flower-border outside this window, but no indication of a footmark. It is difficult to imagine, then, how an outsider could have made so terrible an impression upon the company, nor have we found any possible motive for so strange and elaborate an attempt. You perceive our difficulties, Watson?'

'They are only too clear,' I answered, with conviction.

'And yet, with a little more material, we may prove that they are not insurmountable,' said Holmes. 'I fancy that among your extensive archives, Watson, you may find some which were nearly as obscure. Meanwhile, we shall put the case aside until more accurate date are available, and devote the rest of our morning to the pursuit of neolithic man.'

I may have commented upon my friend's power of mental detachment, but never have I wondered at it more than upon that spring morning in Cornwall when for two hours he discoursed upon Celts, arrowheads, and shards, as lightly as if no sinister mystery was waiting for his solution. It was not until we had returned in the afternoon to our cottage that we found a visitor awaiting us, who soon brought our minds back to the matter in hand. Neither of us needed to be told who that visitor was. The huge body, the craggy and deeply-seamed face with the fierce eyes and hawk-like nose, the grizzled hair which nearly brushed our cottage ceiling, the beard – golden at the fringes and white near the lips, save for the nicotine stain from his perpetual cigar – all these were as well known in London as in Africa, and could only be associated with the tremendous personality of Dr Leon Sterndale, the great lion-hunter and explorer.

We had heard of his presence in the district, and had once or twice caught sight of his tall figure upon the moorland paths. He made no advances to us, however, nor would we have dreamed of doing so to him, as it was well known that it was his love of seclusion which caused him to spend the greater part of the intervals between his journeys in a small bungalow buried in the lonely wood of Beauchamp Arriance. Here, amid his books and his maps, he lived an absolutely lonely life, attending to his own simple wants, and paying little apparent heed to the affairs of his neighbours. It was a surprise to me, therefore, to hear him asking Holmes in an eager voice, whether he had made any advance in his reconstruction of this mysterious episode. 'The county police are utterly at fault,' said he; 'but perhaps your wider experience has suggested some conceivable explanation. My only claim to being taken into your confidence is that during my many residences here I have come to know this family of Tregennis very well – indeed, upon my Cornish mother's side I could call them cousins – and their strange fate has naturally been a great shock to me. I may tell you that I had got as far as Plymouth upon my way to Africa, but the news reached me this morning, and I came straight back again to help in the inquiry.'

Holmes raised his eyebrows.

'Did you lose your boat through it?'

'I will take the next.'

'Dear me! that is friendship indeed.'

'I tell you they were relatives.'

'Quite so – cousins of your mother. Was your baggage aboard the ship?'

'Some of it, but the main part at the hotel.'

'I see. But surely this event could not have found its way into the Plymouth morning papers?'

'No, sir; I had a telegram.'

'Might I ask from whom?'

A shadow passed over the gaunt face of the explorer.

'You are very inquisitive, Mr Holmes.'

'It is my business.'

With an effort, Dr Sterndale recovered his ruffled composure.

'I have no objection to telling you,' he asid. 'It was Mr Roundhay, the vicar, who sent me the telegram which recalled me.'

'Thank you,' said Holmes. 'I may say in answer to your original question, that I have not cleared my mind entirely on the subject of this case, but that I have every hope of reaching some conclusion. It would be premature to say more.'

'Perhaps you would not mind telling me if your suspicions point in any particular direction?'

'No, I can hardly answer that.'

'Then I have wasted my time, and need not prolong my visit.' The famous doctor strode out of our cottage in considerable ill-humour, and within five minutes Holmes had followed him. I saw him no more until the evening, when he returned with a slow step and haggard face which assured me that he had made no great progress with his investigation. He glanced at a telegram which awaited him, and threw it into the grate.

'From the Plymouth hotel, Watson,' he said. 'I learned the name of it from the vicar, and I wired to make certain that Dr Leon Sterndale's account was true. It appears that he did indeed spend last night there, and that he has actually allowed some of his baggage to go on to Africa, while he returned to be present at this investigation. What do you make of that, Watson?'

'He is deeply interested.'

'Deeply interested – yes. There is a thread here which we have not yet grasped, and which might lead us through the tangle. Cheer up, Watson, for I am very sure that our material has not yet all come to hand. When it does, we may soon leave our difficulties behind us.'

Little did I think how soon the words of Holmes would be realized, or how strange and sinister would be that new development which opened up an entirely fresh line of investigation. I was shaving at my window in the morning when I heard the rattle of hoofs, and, looking up, saw a dogcart coming at a gallop down the road. It pulled up at our door, and our friend the vicar sprang from it and rushed up our garden path. Holmes was already dressed, and we hastened down to meet him.

Our visitor was so excited that he could hardly articulate, but at last in gasps and bursts his tragic story came out of him.

'We are devil-ridden, Mr Holmes! My poor parish is devil-ridden!' he cried. 'Satan himself is loose in it! We are given over into his hands!' He danced about in his agitation, a ludicrous object if it were not for his ashy face and startled eyes. Finally he shot out his terrible news.

'Mr Mortimer Tregennis died during the night, and with exactly the same symptoms as the rest of his family.'

Holmes sprang to his feet, all energy in an instant.

'Can you fit us both into your dogcart?'

'Yes, I can.'

'Then, Watson, we will postpone our breakfast. Mr Roundhay, we are entirely at your disposal. Hurry – hurry, before things get disarranged.'

The lodger occupied two rooms at the vicarage, which were in an angle by themselves, the one above the other. Below was a large sitting-room; above, his bedroom. They looked out upon a croquet lawn which came up to the windows. We had arrived before the doctor or the police, so that everything was absolutely undisturbed. Let me describe exactly the scene as we saw it upon that misty March morning. It has left an impression which can never be effaced from my mind.

The atmosphere of the room was of a horrible and depressing stuffiness. The servant who had first entered had thrown up the window, or it would have been even more intolerable. This might partly be due to the fact that a lamp stood flaring and smoking on the centre table. Beside it sat the dead man, leaning back in his chair, his thin beard projecting, his spectacles pushed up on to his forehead, and his lean, dark face turned towards the window and twisted into the same distortion of terror which had marked the features of his dead sister. His limbs were convulsed and his fingers contorted as though he had died in a very paroxysm of fear. He was fully clothed, though there were signs that his dressing had been done in a hurry. We had already learned that his bed had been slept in, and that the tragic end had come to him in the early morning.

One realized the red-hot energy which underlay Holmes's phlegmatic exterior when one saw the sudden change which came over him from the moment that he entered the fatal apartment. In an instant he was tense and alert, his eyes shining, his face set, his limbs quivering with eager activity. He was out on the lawn, in through the window, round the room, and up into the bedroom, for all the world like a dashing foxhound drawing a cover. In the bedroom he made a rapid cast around, and ended by throwing open the window, which appeared to give him some fresh cause for excitement, for he leaned out of it with loud ejaculations of interest and delight. Then he rushed down the stair, out through the open window, threw himself upon his face on the lawn, sprang up and into the room once more, all with the energy of the hunter who is at the very heels of his quarry. The lamp, which was an ordinary standard, he examined with minute care, making certain measurements upon its bowl. He carefully scrutinized with his lens the talc shield which covered the top of the chimney, and scraped off some ashes which adhered to its upper surface, putting some of them into an envelope, which he placed in his pocket-book. Finally, just as the doctor and the official police put in an appearance, he beckoned to the vicar and we all three went out upon the lawn.

'I am glad to say that my investigation has not been entirely barren,' he remarked. 'I cannot remain to discuss the matter with the police, but I should be exceedingly obliged, Mr Roundhay, if you would give the inspector my compliments and direct his attention to the bedroom window and to the sitting-room lamp. Each is suggestive, and together they are almost conclusive. If the police would desire further information I shall be happy to see any of them at the cottage. And now, Watson, I think that, perhaps, we shall be better employed elsewhere.'

It may be that the police resented the intrusion of an amateur, or that they imagined themselves to be upon some hopeful line of investigation; but it is certain that we heard nothing from them for the next two days. During this time Holmes spent some of his time smoking and dreaming in the cottage; but a greater portion in country walks which he undertook alone, returning after many hours without remark as to where he had been. One experiment served to show me the line of his investigation. He had bought a lamp which was the duplicate of the one which had burned in the room of Mortimer Tregennis on the morning of the tragedy. This he filled with the same oil as that used at the vicarage, and he carefully timed the period which it would take to be exhausted. Another experiment which he made was of a more unpleasant nature, and one which I am not likely ever to forget.

'You will remember, Watson,' he remarked one afternoon, 'that there is a single common point of resemblance in the varying reports which have reached us. This concerns the effect of the atmosphere of the room in each case upon those who had first entered it. You will recollect that Mortimer Tregennis, in describing the episode of his last visit to his brother's house, remarked that the doctor on entering the room fell into a chair? You had forgotten? Well, I can answer for it that it was so. Now, you will remember also that Mrs Porter, the housekeeper, told

us that she herself fainted upon entering the room and had afterwards opened the window. In the second case – that of Mortimer
Tregennis himself – you cannot have forgotten the horrible
stuffiness of the room when we arrived, though the servant had
thrown open the window. That servant, I found upon inquiry,
was so ill that she had gone to her bed. You will admit, Watson,
that these facts are very suggestive. In each case there is evidence of a poisonous atmosphere. In each case, also, there is
combustion going on in the room – in the one case a fire, in the
other a lamp. The fire was needed, but the lamp was lit – as a
comparison of the oil consumed will show – long after it was
broad daylight. Why? Surely because there is some connection
between three things – the burning, the stuffy atmosphere, and,
finally, the madness or death of those unfortunate people. That
is clear, is it not?'

'It would appear so.'

'At least we may accept it as a working hypothesis. We will
suppose, then, that something was burned in each case which
produced an atmosphere causing strange toxic effects. Very
good. In the first instance – that of the Tregennis family – this
substance was placed in the fire. Now the window was shut, but
the fire would naturally carry fumes to some extent up the
chimney. Hence one would expect the effects of the poison to be
less than in the second case, where there was less escape for the
vapour. The result seems to indicate that it was so, since in the
first case only the woman, who had presumably the more sensitive organism, was killed, the others exhibiting that temporary
or permanent lunacy which is evidently the first effect of the
drug. In the second case the result was complete. The facts,
therefore, seem to bear out the theory of a poison which worked
by combustion.

'With this train of reasoning in my head I naturally looked
about in Mortimer Tregennis's room to find some remains of
this substance. The obvious place to look was the talc shield or
smoke-guard of the lamp. There, sure enough, I perceived a

number of flaky ashes, and round the edges a fringe of brownish powder, which had not yet been consumed. Half of this I took, as you saw, and I placed it in an envelope.'

'Why half, Holmes?'

'It is not for me, my dear Watson, to stand in the way of the official police force. I leave them all the evidence which I found. The poison still remained upon the talc, had they the wit to find it. Now, Watson, we will light our lamp; we will, however, take the precaution to open our window to avoid the premature decease of two deserving members of society, and you will seat yourself near that open window in an armchair, unless, like a sensible man, you determine to have nothing to do with the affair. Oh, you will see it out, will you? I thought I knew my Watson. This chair I will place opposite yours, so that we may be the same distance from the poison, and face to face. The door we will leave ajar. Each is now in a position to watch the other and to bring the experiment to an end should the symptoms seem alarming. Is that all clear? Well, then, I take our powder – or what remains of it – from the envelope, and I lay it above the burning lamp. So! Now, Watson, let us sit down and await developments.'

They were not long in coming. I had hardly settled in my chair before I was conscious of a thick, musky odour, subtle and nauseous. At the very first whiff of it my brain and my imagination were beyond all control. A thick, black cloud swirled before my eyes, and my mind told me that in this cloud, unseen as yet, but about to spring out upon my appalled senses, lurked all that was vaguely horrible, all that was monstrous and inconceivably wicked in the universe. Vague shapes swirled and swam amid the dark cloud-bank, each a menace and a warning of something coming, the advent of some unspeakable dweller upon the threshold, whose very shadow would blast my soul. A freezing horror took possession of me. I felt that my hair was rising, that my eyes were protruding, that my mouth was opened, and my tongue like leather. The turmoil within my brain was such that something must surely snap. I tried to scream, and was vaguely aware of some hoarse croak which was my own voice, but distant and detached from myself. At the same moment, in some effort of escape, I broke through that cloud of despair, and had a glimpse of Holmes's face, white, rigid, and drawn with horror – the very look which I had seen upon the features of the dead. It was that vision which gave me an instant of sanity and of strength. I dashed from my chair, threw my arms round Holmes, and together we lurched through the door, and an instant afterwards had thrown ourselves down upon the grass plot and were lying side by side, conscious only of the glorious sunshine which was bursting its way through the hellish cloud of terror which had girt us in. Slowly it rose from our souls like the mists from a landscape, until peace and reason had returned, and we were sitting upon the grass, wiping our clammy fore-heads, and looking with apprehension at each other to mark the last traces of that terrific experience which we had undergone.

'Upon my word, Watson!' said Holmes at last, with an unsteady voice, 'I owe you both my thanks and an apology. It was an unjustifiable experiment even for oneself, and doubly so for a friend. I am really very sorry.'

'You know', I answered, with some emotion, for I had never seen so much of Holmes's heart before, 'that it is my greatest joy and privilege to help you.'

He relapsed at once into the half-humorous, half-cynical vein which was his habitual attitude to those about him. 'It would be superfluous to drive us mad, my dear Watson,' said he. 'A candid observer would certainly declare that we were so already before we embarked upon so wild an experiment. I confess that I never imagined that the effect could be so sudden and so severe.' He dashed into the cottage, and reappearing with the burning lamp held at full arm's length, he threw it among a bank of brambles. 'We must give the room a little time to clear. I take it, Watson, that you have no longer a shadow of a doubt as to how these tragedies were produced?'

'None whatever.'

'But the cause remains as obscure as before. Come into the arbour here, and let us discuss it together. That villainous stuff seems still to linger round my throat. I think we must admit that all the evidence points to this man, Mortimer Tregennis, having been the criminal in the first tragedy, though he was the victim in the second one. We must remember, in the first place, that there is some story of a family quarrel, followed by a reconciliation. How bitter that quarrel may have been, or how hollow the reconciliation we cannot tell. When I think of Mortimer Tregennis, with the foxy face and the small, shrewd, beady eyes, behind the spectacles, he is not a man whom I should judge to be of a particularly forgiving disposition. Well, in the next place, you will remember that this idea of someone moving in the garden, which took our attention for a moment from the real cause of the tragedy, emanated from him. He had a motive in misleading us. Finally, if he did not throw this substance into the fire at the moment of leaving the room, who did do so? The affair happened immediately after his departure. Had anyone else come in, the family would certainly have risen from the table. Besides, in peaceful Cornwall, visitors do not arrive after ten o'clock at night. We may take it, then, that all the evidence points to Mortimer Tregennis as the culprit.'

'Then his own death was suicide!'

'Well, Watson, it is on the face of it a not impossible supposition. The man who had the guilt upon his soul of having brought such a fate upon his own family might well be driven by remorse to inflict it upon himself. There are, however, some cogent reasons against it. Fortunately, there is one man in England who knows all about it, and I have made arrangements by which we shall hear the facts this afternoon from his own lips. Ah! he is a little before his time. Perhaps you would kindly step this way, Dr Leon Sterndale. We have been conducting a chemical experiment indoors which has left our little room hardly fit for the reception of so distinguished a visitor.'

I had heard the click of the garden gate, and now the majestic figure of the great African explorer appeared upon the path. He turned in some surprise towards the rustic arbour in which we sat.

'You sent for me, Mr Holmes. I had your note about an hour ago, and I have come, though I really do not know why I should obey your summons.'

'Perhaps we can clear the point up before we separate,' said Holmes. 'Meanwhile, I am much obliged to you for your courteous acquiescence. You will excuse this informal reception in the open air, but my friend Watson and I have nearly furnished an additional chapter to what the papers call the Cornish Horror, and we prefer a clear atmosphere for the present. Perhaps, since the matters which we have to discuss will affect you personally in a very intimate fashion, it is as well that we should talk where there can be no eavesdropping.'

The explorer took his cigar from his lips and gazed sternly at my companion.

'I am at a loss to know, sir,' he said, 'what you can have to speak about which affects me personally in a very intimate fashion.'

'The killing of Mortimer Tregennis,' said Holmes.

For a moment I wished that I were armed. Sterndale's fierce face turned to a dusky red, his eyes glared, and the knotted, passionate veins started out in his forehead, while he sprang forward with clenched hands towards my companion. Then he stopped, and with a violent effort he resumed a cold, rigid calmness which was, perhaps, more suggestive of danger than his hot-headed outburst.

'I have lived so long among savages and beyond the law,' said he, 'that I have got into the way of being a law to myself. You would do well, Mr Holmes, not to forget it, for I have no desire to do you an injury.'

'Nor have I any desire to do you an injury, Dr Sterndale. Surely the clearest proof of it is that, knowing what I know, I have sent for you and not for the police.'

Sterndale sat down with a gasp, overawed for, perhaps, the first time in his adventurous life. There was a calm assurance of power in Holmes's manner which could not be withstood. Our visitor stammered for a moment, his great hands opening and shutting in his agitation.

'What do you mean?' he asked, at last. 'If this is bluff upon your part, Mr Holmes, you have chosen a bad man for your experiment. Let us have no more beating about the bush. What *do* you mean?'

'I will tell you,' said Holmes, 'and the reason why I tell you is that I hope frankness may beget frankness. What my next step may be will depend entirely upon the nature of your own defence.'

'My defence?'

'Yes, sir.'

'My defence against what?'

'Against the charge of killing Mortimer Tregennis.'

Sterndale mopped his forehead with his handkerchief. 'Upon my word, you are getting on,' said he. 'Do all your successes depend upon this prodigious power of bluff?'

'The bluff', said Holmes, sternly, 'is upon your side, Dr Leon Sterndale, and not upon mine. As a proof I will tell you some of the facts upon which my conclusions are based. Of your return from Plymouth, allowing much of your property to go on to Africa, I will say nothing save that it first informed me that you were one of the factors which had to be taken into account in reconstructing this drama——'

'I came back——'

'I have heard your reasons and regard them as unconvincing and inadequate. We will pass that. You came down here to ask me whom I suspected. I refused to answer you. You then went to the vicarage, waited outside it for some time, and finally returned to your cottage.'

'How do you know that?'

'I followed you.'

'I saw no one.'

'That is what you may expect to see when I follow you. You spent a restless night at your cottage, and you formed certain plans, which in the early morning you proceeded to put into execution. Leaving your door just as day was breaking, you filled your pocket with some reddish gravel that was lying heaped beside your gate.'

Sterndale gave a violent start and looked at Holmes in amazement.

'You then walked swiftly for the mile which separated you from the vicarage. You were wearing, I may remark, the same pair of ribbed tennis shoes which are at the present moment upon your feet. At the vicarage you passed through the orchard and the side hedge, coming out under the window of the lodger Tregennis. It was now daylight, but the household was not yet stirring. You drew some of the gravel from your pocket, and you threw it up at the window above you.'

Sterndale sprang to his feet.

'I believe that you are the devil himself!' he cried.

Holmes smiled at the compliment. 'It took two, or possibly three, handfuls before the lodger came to the window. You beckoned him to come down. He dressed hurriedly and descended to his sitting-room. You entered by the window. There was an interview – a short one – during which you walked up and down the room. Then you passed out and closed the window, standing on the lawn outside smoking a cigar and watching what occurred. Finally, after the death of Tregennis, you withdrew as you had come. Now, Dr Sterndale, how do you justify such conduct, and what were the motives for your actions? If you prevaricate or trifle with me, I give you my assurance that the matter will pass out of my hands for ever.'

Our visitor's face had turned ashen grey as he listened to the words of his accuser. Now he sat for some time in thought with his face sunk in his hands. Then with a sudden impulsive gesture he plucked a photograph from his breast-pocket and threw it on the rustic table before us.

'That is why I have done it,' he said.

It showed the bust and face of a very beautiful woman. Holmes stooped over it.

'Brenda Tregennis,' said he.

'Yes, Brenda Tregennis,' repeated our visitor. 'For years I have loved her. For years she has loved me. There is the secret of that Cornish seclusion which people have marvelled at. It has brought me close to the one thing on earth that was dear to me. I could not marry her, for I have a wife who has left me for years and yet whom, by the deplorable laws of England, I could not divorce. For years Brenda waited. For years I waited. And this is what we have waited for.' A terrible sob shook his great frame, and he clutched his throat under his brindled beard. Then with an effort he mastered himself and spoke on.

'The vicar knew. He was in our confidence. He would tell you that she was an angel upon earth. That was why he tele-graphed to me and I returned. What was my baggage or Africa to me when I learned that such a fate had come upon my darling? There you have the missing clue to my action, Mr Holmes.'

'Proceed,' said my friend.

Dr Sterndale drew from his pocket a paper packet and laid it upon the table. On the outside was written, *'Radix pedis diaboli'* with a red poison label beneath it. He pushed it towards me. 'I understand that you are a doctor, sir. Have you ever heard of this preparation?'

'Devil's-foot root! No, I have never heard of it.'

'It is no reflection upon your professional knowledge,' said he, 'for I believe that, save for one sample in a laboratory at Buda, there is no other specimen in Europe. It has not yet found its way either into the pharmacopoeia or into the literature of toxicology. The root is shaped like a foot, half human, half

goat-like; hence the fanciful name given by a botanical missionary. It is used as an ordeal poison by the medicine-men in
certain districts of West Africa, and is kept as a secret among
them. This particular specimen I obtained under very extraordinary circumstances in the Ubanghi country.' He opened
the paper as he spoke, and disclosed a heap of reddish-brown,
snuff-like powder.

'Well, sir?' asked Holmes sternly.

'I am about to tell you, Mr Holmes, all that actually occurred,
for you already know so much that it is clearly to my interest
that you should know all. I have already explained the relationship in which I stood to the Tregennis family. For the sake of
the sister I was friendly with the brothers. There was a family
quarrel about money which estranged this man Mortimer, but
it was supposed to be made up, and I afterwards met him as I
did the others. He was a sly, subtle, scheming man, and several
things arose which gave me a suspicion of him, but I had no
cause for any positive quarrel.

'One day, only a couple of weeks ago, he came down to my
cottage and I showed him some of my African curiosities.
Among other things I exhibited this powder, and I told him of
its strange properties, how it stimulates those brain centres
which control the emotion of fear, and how either madness or
death is the fate of the unhappy native who is subjected to the
ordeal by the priest of his tribe. I told him also how powerless
European science would be to detect it. How he took it I cannot
say, for I never left the room, but there is no doubt that it was
then, while I was opening cabinets and stooping to boxes, that
he managed to abstract some of the devil's-foot root. I well
remember how he plied me with questions as to the amount and
the time that was needed for its effect, but I little dreamed that
he could have a personal reason for asking.

'I thought no more of the matter until the vicar's telegram
reached me at Plymouth. This villain had thought that I would
be at sea before the news could reach me, and that I should be

lost for years in Africa. But I returned at once. Of course, I
could not listen to the details without feeling assured that my
poison had been used. I came round to see you on the chance
that some other explanation had suggested itself to you. But
there could be none. I was convinced that Mortimer Tregennis
was the murderer; that for the sake of money, and with the idea,
perhaps, that if the other members of his family were all insane
he would be the sole guardian of their joint property, he had
used the devil's-foot powder upon them, driven two of them out
of their senses, and killed his sister Brenda, the one human
being whom I have ever loved or who has ever loved me. There
was his crime; what was to be his punishment?

'Should I appeal to the law? Where were my proofs? I knew
that the facts were true, but could I hope to make a jury of
countrymen believe so fantastic a story? I might or I might not.
But I could not afford to fail. My soul cried out for revenge. I
have said to you once before, Mr Holmes, that I have spent
much of my life outside the law, and that I have come at last to
be a law to myself. So it was now. I determined that the fate
which he had given to others should be shared by himself.
Either that or I would do justice upon him with my own hand.
In all England there can be no man who sets less value upon
his own life than I do at the present moment.

'Now I have told you all. You have yourself supplied the
rest. I did, as you say, after a restless night, set off early from
my cottage. I foresaw the difficulty of arousing him, so I
gathered some gravel from the pile which you have mentioned,
and I used it to throw up to his window. He came down and
admitted me through the window of the sitting-room. I laid
his offence before him. I told him that I had come both as judge
and executioner. The wretch sank into a chair paralysed at the
sight of my revolver. I lit the lamp, put the powder above it, and
stood outside the window, ready to carry out my threat to shoot
him should he try to leave the room. In five minutes he died.
My God! how he died! But my heart was flint, for he endured

nothing which my innocent darling had not felt before him. There is my story, Mr Holmes. Perhaps, if you loved a woman, you would have done as much yourself. At any rate, I am in your hands. You can take what steps you like. As I have already said, there is no man living who can fear death less than I do.'

Holmes sat for some little time in silence.

'What were your plans?' he asked, at last.

'I had intended to bury myself in Central Africa. My work there is but half finished.'

'Go and do the other half,' said Holmes. 'I, at least, am not prepared to prevent you.'

Dr Sterndale raised his giant figure, bowed gravely, and walked from the arbour. Holmes lit his pipe and handed me his pouch.

'Some fumes which are not poisonous would be a welcome change,' said he. 'I think you must agree, Watson, that it is not a case in which we are called upon to interfere. Our investigation has been independent, and our action shall be so also. You would not denounce the man?'

'Certainly not,' I answered.

'I have never loved, Watson, but if I did and if the woman I loved had met such an end, I might act even as our lawless lion-hunter has done. Who knows? Well, Watson, I will not offend your intelligence by explaining what is obvious. The gravel upon the window-sill was, of course, the starting-point of my research. It was unlike anything in the vicarage garden. Only when my attention had been drawn to Dr Sterndale and his cottage did I find its counterpart. The lamp shining in broad daylight and the remains of powder upon the shield were successive links in a fairly obvious chain. And now, my dear Watson, I think we may dismiss the matter from our mind, and go back with a clear conscience to the study of those Chaldean roots which are surely to be traced in the Cornish branch of the great Celtic speech.'

His Last Bow

An Epilogue of Sherlock Holmes

It was nine o'clock at night upon the second of August – the most terrible August in the history of the world. One might have thought already that God's curse hung heavy over a degenerate world, for there was an awesome hush and a feeling of vague expectancy in the sultry and stagnant air. The sun had long set, but one blood-red gash like an open wound lay low in the distant west. Above, the stars were shining brightly; and below, the lights of the shipping glimmered in the bay. The two famous Germans stood beside the stone parapet of the garden walk, with the long, low, heavily gabled house behind them, and they looked down upon the broad sweep of the beach at the foot of the great chalk cliff on which Von Bork, like some wandering eagle, had perched himself four years before. They stood with their heads close together, talking in low, confidential tones. From below, the two glowing ends of their cigars might have been the smouldering eyes of some malignant fiend looking down in the darkness.

A remarkable man this Von Bork – a man who could hardly be matched among all the devoted agents of the Kaiser. It was his talents which had first recommended him for the English mission, the most important mission of all, but since he had taken it over, those talents had become more and more manifest to the half-dozen people in the world who were really in touch with the truth. One of these was his present companion, Baron Von Herling, the chief secretary of the legation, whose huge

100-horse-power Benz car was blocking the country lane as it
waited to waft its owner back to London.

'So far as I can judge the trend of events, you will probably
be back in Berlin within the week,' the secretary was saying.
'When you get there, my dear Von Bork, I think you will be
surprised at the welcome you will receive. I happen to know
what is thought in the highest quarters of your work in this
country.' He was a huge man, the secretary, deep, broad, and
tall, with a slow, heavy fashion of speech which had been his
main asset in his political career.

Von Bork laughed.

'They are not very hard to deceive,' he remarked. 'A more
docile, simple folk could not be imagined.'

'I don't know about that,' said the other thoughtfully. 'They
have strange limits and one must learn to observe them. It is
that surface simplicity of theirs which makes a trap for the
stranger. One's first impression is that they are entirely soft.
Then one comes suddenly upon something very hard, and you
know that you have reached the limit, and must adapt yourself
to the fact. They have, for example, their insular conventions
which simply *must* be observed.'

'Meaning "good form" and that sort of thing?' Von Bork
sighed, as one who had suffered much.

'Meaning British prejudice in all its queer manifestations.
As an example I may quote one of my own worst blunders – I
can afford to talk of my blunders, for you know my work
well enough to be aware of my successes. It was on my first
arrival. I was invited to a weekend gathering at the country
house of a cabinet minister. The conversation was amazingly
indiscreet.'

Von Bork nodded. 'I've been there,' said he dryly.

'Exactly. Well, I naturally sent a résumé of the information
to Berlin. Unfortunately our good Chancellor is a little heavy-
handed in these matters, and he transmitted a remark which
showed that he was aware of what had been said. This, of course,

took the trail straight up to me. You've no idea the harm that it did me. There was nothing soft about our British hosts on that occasion, I can assure you. I was two years living it down. Now you, with this sporting pose of yours.'

'No, no, don't call it a pose. A pose is an artificial thing. This is quite natural. I am a born sportsman. I enjoy it.'

'Well, that makes it the more effective. You yacht against them, you hunt with them, you play polo, you match them in every game, your four-in-hand takes the prize at Olympia. I have even heard that you go to the length of boxing with the young officers. What is the result? Nobody takes you seriously. You are a "good old sport", "quite a decent fellow for a German", hard-drinking, night-club, knock-about-town, devil-may-care young fellow. And all the time this quiet country house of yours is the centre of half the mischief in England, and the sporting squire the most astute secret-service man in Europe. Genius, my dear Von Bork – genius!'

'You flatter me, Baron. But certainly I may claim that my four years in this country have not been unproductive. I've never shown you my little store. Would you mind stepping in for a moment.'

The door of the study opened straight on to the terrace. Von Bork pushed it back, and, leading the way, he clicked the switch of the electric light. He then closed the door behind the bulky form which followed him, and carefully adjusted the heavy curtain over the latticed window. Only when all these precautions had been taken and tested did he turn his sunburned aquiline face to his guest.

'Some of my papers have gone,' said he; 'when my wife and the household left yesterday for Flushing they took the less important with them. I must, of course, claim the protection of the Embassy for the others.'

'Your name has already been filed as one of the personal suite. There will be no difficulties for you or your baggage. Of course, it is just possible that we may not have to go. England may leave France to her fate. We are sure that there is no binding treaty between them.'

'And Belgium?'

'Yes, and Belgium, too.'

Von Bork shook his head. 'I don't see how that could be. There is a definite treaty there. She could never recover from such a humiliation.'

'She would at least have peace for the moment.'

'But her honour?'

'Tut, my dear sir, we live in a utilitarian age. Honour is a mediaeval conception. Besides England is not ready. It is an inconceivable thing, but even our special war tax of fifty million, which one would think made our purpose as clear as if we had advertised it on the front page of *The Times*, has not roused these people from their slumbers. Here and there one hears a question. It is my business to find an answer. Here and there also there is an irritation. It is my business to soothe it. But I can assure you that so far as the essentials go – the storage of munitions, the preparation for submarine attack, the arrangements for making high explosives – nothing is prepared. How then can England come in, especially when we have stirred her up such a devil's brew of Irish civil war, window-breaking Furies, and God knows what to keep her thoughts at home?'

'She must think of her future.'

'Ah, that is another matter. I fancy that in the future, we have our own very definite plans about England, and that your information will be very vital to us. It is today or tomorrow with Mr John Bull. If he prefers today we are perfectly ready. If it is tomorrow we shall be more ready still. I should think they would be wiser to fight with allies than without them, but that is their own affair. This week is their week of destiny. But you were speaking of your papers.' He sat in the armchair with the light shining upon his broad bald head, while he puffed sedately at his cigar.

The large oak-panelled, book-lined room had a curtain hung

in the further corner. When this was drawn it disclosed a large brass-bound safe. Von Bork detached a small key from his watch-chain, and after some considerable manipulation of the lock he swung open the heavy door.

'Look!' said he, standing clear, with a wave of his hand.

The light shone vividly into the opened safe, and the secretary of the Embassy gazed with an absorbed interest at the rows of stuffed pigeon-holes with which it was furnished. Each pigeon-hole had its label, and his eyes as he glanced along them read a long series of such titles as 'Fords', 'Harbour-defences', 'Aeroplanes', 'Ireland', 'Egypt', 'Portsmouth forts', 'The Channel', 'Rosyth', and a score of others. Each compartment was bristling with papers and plans.

'Colossal!' said the secretary. Putting down his cigar he softly clapped his fat hands.

'And all in four years, Baron. Not such a bad show for the hard-drinking, hard-riding country squire. But the gem of my collection is coming and there is the setting all ready for it.' He pointed to a space over which 'Naval Signals' was printed.

'But you have a good dossier there already.'

'Out of date and waste paper. The Admiralty in some way got the alarm and every code has been changed. It was a blow, Baron – the worst set-back in my whole campaign. But thanks to my cheque-book and the good Altamont all will be well tonight.'

The Baron looked at his watch, and gave a guttural exclamation of disappointment.

'Well, I really can wait no longer. You can imagine that things are moving at present in Carlton Terrace and that we have all to be at our posts. I had hoped to be able to bring news of your great coup. Did Altamont name no hour?'

Von Bork pushed over a telegram.

'Will come without fail tonight and bring new sparking plugs. Altamont.'

'Sparking plugs, eh?'

'You see he poses as a motor expert and I keep a full garage. In our code everything likely to come up is named after some spare part. If he talks of a radiator it is a battleship, of an oil pump a cruiser, and so on. Sparking plugs are naval signals.'

'From Portsmouth at midday,' said the secretary, examining the superscription. 'By the way, what do you give him?'

'Five hundred pounds for this particular job. Of course he has a salary as well.'

'The greedy rogue. They are useful, these traitors, but I grudge them their blood money.'

'I grudge Altamont nothing. He is a wonderful worker. If I pay him well, at least he delivers the goods, to use his own phrase. Besides he is not a traitor. I assure you that our most pan-Germanic Junker is a sucking dove in his feelings towards England as compared with a real bitter Irish-American.'

'Oh, an Irish-American?'

'If you heard him talk you would not doubt it. Sometimes I assure you I can hardly understand him. He seems to have declared war on the King's English as well as on the English King. Must you really go? He may be here any moment.'

'No. I'm sorry but I have already over-stayed my time. We shall expect you early tomorrow, and when you get that signal book through the little door on the Duke of York's steps you can put a triumphant Finis to your record in England. What! Tokay!' He indicated a heavily sealed dust-covered bottle which stood with two high glasses upon a salver.

'May I offer you a glass before your journey?'

'No, thanks. But it looks like revelry.'

'Altamont has a nice taste in wines, and he took a fancy to my Tokay. He is a touchy fellow and needs humouring in small things. I have to study him, I assure you.' They had strolled out on to the terrace again, and along it to the further end where at a touch from the Baron's chauffeur the great car shivered and chuckled. 'Those are the lights of Harwich, I suppose,' said the secretary, pulling on his dust coat. 'How still and peaceful it all seems. There may be other lights within the week, and the English coast a less tranquil place! The heavens, too, may not be quite so peaceful if all that the good Zeppelin promises us comes true. By the way, who is that?'

Only one window showed a light behind them; in it there stood a lamp, and beside it, seated at a table, was a dear old ruddy-faced woman in a country cap. She was bending over her knitting and stopping occasionally to stroke a large black cat upon a stool beside her.

'That is Martha, the only servant I have left.'

The secretary chuckled.

'She might almost personify Britannia,' said he, 'with her complete self-absorption and general air of comfortable somnolence. Well, au revoir, Von Bork!' – with a final wave of his hand he sprang into the car, and a moment later the two golden cones from the headlights shot forward through the darkness. The secretary lay back in the cushions of the luxurious limousine, with his thoughts so full of the impending European tragedy that he hardly observed that as his car swung round the village street it nearly passed over a little Ford coming in the opposite direction.

Von Bork walked slowly back to the study when the last gleams of the motor lamps had faded into the distance. As he passed he observed that his old housekeeper had put out her lamp and retired. It was a new experience for him, the silence and darkness of his widespread house, for his family and household had been a large one. It was a relief to him, however, to think that they were all in safety and that, but for that one old woman who had lingered in the kitchen, he had the whole place to himself. There was a good deal of tidying up to do inside his study and he set himself to do it, until his keen, handsome face was flushed with the heat of the burning papers. A leather valise stood beside his table, and into this he began to pack very neatly and systematically the precious contents of his safe. He had hardly got started with the work, however, when his quick ears

caught the sound of a distant car. Instantly he gave an exclamation of satisfaction, strapped up the valise, shut the safe, locked
it, and hurried out on to the terrace. He was just in time to see
the lights of a small car come to a halt at the gate. A passenger
sprang out of it and advanced swiftly towards him, while the
chauffeur, a heavily built, elderly man, with a grey moustache,
settled down, like one who resigns himself to a long vigil.

'Well?' asked Von Bork eagerly, running forward to meet
his visitor.

For answer the man waved a small brown-paper parcel
triumphantly above his head.

'You can give me the glad hand tonight, Mister,' he cried.
'I'm bringing home the bacon at last.'

'The signals?'

'Same as I said in my cable. Every last one of them, sema-
phore, lamp code, Marconi – a copy, mind you, not the original.
That was too dangerous. But it's the real goods, and you can lay
to that.' He slapped the German upon the shoulder with a rough
familiarity from which the other winced.

'Come in,' he said. 'I'm all alone in the house. I was only
waiting for this. Of course a copy is better than the original. If
an original were missing they would change the whole thing.
You think it's all safe about the copy?'

The Irish-American had entered the study and stretched
his long limbs from the armchair. He was a tall, gaunt man of
sixty, with clear-cut features and a small goatee beard which
gave him a general resemblance to the caricatures of Uncle Sam.
A half-smoked, sodden cigar hung from the corner of his mouth,
and as he sat down he struck a match and relit it. 'Making ready
for a move?' he remarked as he looked round him. 'Say, Mister,'
he added, as his eyes fell upon the safe from which the curtain
was now removed, 'you don't tell me you keep your papers in
that?'

'Why not?'

'Gosh, in a wide-open contraption like that! And they

reckon you to be some spy. Why, a Yankee crook would be into that with a can-opener. If I'd known that any letter of mine was goin' to lie loose in a thing like that I'd have been a mug to write to you at all.'

'It would puzzle any crook to force that safe,' Von Bork answered. 'You won't cut that metal with any tool.'

'But the lock?'

'No, it's a double combination lock. You know what that is?'

'Search me,' said the American.

'Well, you need a word as well as a set of figures before you can get the lock to work.' He rose and showed a double-radiating disc round the keyhole. 'This outer one is for the letters, the inner one for the figures.'

'Well, well, that's fine.'

'So it's not quite as simple as you thought. It was four years ago that I had it made, and what do you think I chose for the word and figures?'

'It's beyond me.'

'Well, I chose August for the word, and 1914 for the figures, and here we are.'

The American's face showed his surprise and admiration.

'My, but that was smart! You had it down to a fine thing.'

'Yes, a few of us even then could have guessed the date. Here it is, and I'm shutting down tomorrow morning.'

'Well, I guess you'll have to fix me up also. I'm not staying in this goldarned country all on my lonesome. In a week or less, from what I see, John Bull will be on his hind legs and fair ramping. I'd rather watch him from over the water.'

'But you're an American citizen?'

'Well, so was Jack James an American citizen, but he's doing time in Portland all the same. It cuts no ice with a British copper to tell him you're an American citizen. "It's British law and order over here," says he. By the way, Mister, talking of Jack James it seems to me you don't do much to cover your men.'

'What do you mean?' Von Bork asked sharply.

'Well, you are their employer, ain't you? It's up to you to see
that they don't fall down. But they do fall down, and when did
you ever pick them up? There's James——'

'It was James's own fault. You know that yourself. He was
too self-willed for the job.'

'James was a bonehead – I give you that. Then there was
Hollis.'

'The man was mad.'

'Well, he went a bit woozy towards the end. It's enough to
make a man bughouse when he has to play a part from morning
to night with a hundred guys all ready to set the coppers wise
to him. But now there is Steiner——'

Von Bork started violently, and his ruddy face turned a shade
paler.

'What about Steiner?'

'Well, they've got him, that's all. They raided his store last
night, and he and his papers are all in Portsmouth gaol. You'll
go off and he, poor devil, will have to stand the racket, and lucky
if he gets off with his life. That's why I want to get over the
water as soon as you do.'

Von Bork was a strong, self-contained man, but it was easy
to see that the news had shaken him.

'How could they have got on to Steiner?' he muttered.
'That's the worst blow yet.'

'Well, you nearly had a worse one, for I believe they are not
far off me.'

'You don't mean that!'

'Sure thing. My landlady down Fratton way had some
inquiries, and when I heard of it I guessed it was time for me to
hustle. But what I want to know, Mister, is how the coppers
know these things? Steiner is the fifth man you've lost since I
signed on with you, and I know the name of the sixth if I don't
get a move on. How do you explain it, and ain't you ashamed
to see your men go down like this?'

Von Bork flushed crimson.

'How dare you speak in such a way!'

'If I didn't dare things, Mister, I wouldn't be in your service. But I'll tell you straight what is in my mind. I've heard that with you German politicians, when an agent has done his work you are not sorry to see him put away.'

Von Bork sprang to his feet.

'Do you dare to suggest that I have given away my own agents!'

'I don't stand for that, Mister, but there's a stool pigeon or a cross somewhere, and it's up to you to find out where it is. Anyhow I am taking no more chances. It's me for little Holland, and the sooner the better.'

Von Bork had mastered his anger.

'We have been allies too long to quarrel now at the very hour of victory,' he said. 'You've done splendid work, and taken risks and I can't forget it. By all means go to Holland, and you can get a boat from Rotterdam to New York. No other line will be safe a week from now. I'll take that book and pack it with the rest.'

The American held the small parcel in his hand, but made no motion to give it up.

'What about the dough?' he asked.

'The what?'

'The boodle. The reward. The £500. The gunner turned damned nasty at the last, and I had to square him with an extra hundred dollars or it would have been nitsky for you and me. "Nothin' doin'!" says he, and he meant it too, but the last hundred did it. It's cost me two hundred pound from first to last, so it isn't likely I'd give it up without gettin' my wad.'

Von Bork smiled with some bitterness. 'You don't seem to have a very high opinion of my honour,' said he, 'you want the money before you give up the book.'

'Well, Mister, it is a business proposition.'

'All right. Have your way.' He sat down at the table and scribbled a cheque, which he tore from the book, but he refrained from handing it to his companion. 'After all, since we are to be on such terms, Mr Altamont,' said he, 'I don't see why I should trust you any more than you trust me. Do you understand?' he added, looking back over his shoulder at the American. 'There's the cheque upon the table. I claim the right to examine that parcel before you pick the money up.'

The American passed it over without a word. Von Bork undid a winding of string and two wrappers of paper. Then he sat gazing for a moment in silent amazement at a small blue book which lay before him. Across the cover was printed in golden letters *Practical Handbook of Bee Culture*. Only for one instant did the master spy glare at this strangely irrelevant inscription. The next he was gripped at the back of his neck by a grasp of iron, and a chloroformed sponge was held in front of his writhing face.

'Another glass, Watson!' said Mr Sherlock Holmes, as he extended the bottle of Imperial Tokay.

The thickset chauffeur, who had seated himself by the table, pushed forward his glass with some eagerness.

'It is a good wine, Holmes.'

'A remarkable wine, Watson. Our friend upon the sofa has assured me that it is from Franz Joseph's special cellar at the Schoenbrunn Palace. Might I trouble you to open the window, for chloroform vapour does not help the palate.'

The safe was ajar, and Holmes standing in front of it was removing dossier after dossier, swiftly examining each, and then packing it neatly in Von Bork's valise. The German lay upon the sofa sleeping stertorously with a strap round his upper arms and another round his legs.

'We need not hurry ourselves, Watson. We are safe from interruption. Would you mind touching the bell. There is no one in the house except old Martha, who has played her part to admiration. I got her the situation here when first I took the matter up. Ah, Martha, you will be glad to hear that all is well.'

The pleasant old lady had appeared in the doorway. She

curtseyed with a smile to Mr Holmes, but glanced with some apprehension at the figure upon the sofa.

'It is all right, Martha. He has not been hurt at all.'

'I am glad of that, Mr Holmes. According to his lights he has been a kind master. He wanted me to go with his wife to Germany yesterday, but that would hardly have suited your plans, would it, sir?'

'No, indeed, Martha. So long as you were here I was easy in my mind. We waited some time for your signal tonight.'

'It was the secretary, sir.'

'I know. His car passed ours.'

'I thought he would never go. I knew that it would not suit your plans, sir, to find him here.'

'No, indeed. Well, it only meant that we waited half an hour or so until I saw your lamp go out and knew that the coast was clear. You can report to me tomorrow in London, Martha, at Claridge's Hotel.'

'Very good, sir.'

'I suppose you have everything ready to leave.'

'Yes, sir. He posted seven letters today. I have the addresses as usual.'

'Very good, Martha. I will look into them tomorrow. Goodnight. These papers,' he continued, as the old lady vanished, 'are not of very great importance for, of course, the information which they represent has been sent off long ago to the German Government. These are the originals which could not safely be got out of the country.'

'Then they are of no use.'

'I should not go so far as to say that, Watson. They will at least show our people what is known and what is not. I may say that a good many of these papers have come through me, and I need not add are thoroughly untrustworthy. It would brighten my declining years to see a German cruiser navigating the Solent according to the minefield plans which I have furnished. But you, Watson,' he stopped his work and took his old friend by the shoulders, 'I've hardly seen you in the light yet. How have the years used you? You look the same blithe boy as ever.'

'I feel twenty years younger, Holmes. I have seldom felt so happy as when I got your wire asking me to meet you at Harwich with the car. But you, Holmes – you have changed very little – save for that horrible goatee.'

'These are the sacrifices one makes for one's country, Watson,' said Holmes, pulling at his little tuft. 'Tomorrow it will be but a dreadful memory. With my hair cut and a few other superficial changes I shall no doubt reappear at Claridge's tomorrow as I was before this American stunt – I beg your pardon, Watson, my well of English seems to be permanently defiled – before this American job came my way.'

'But you had retired, Holmes. We heard of you as living the life of a hermit among your bees and your books in a small farm upon the South Downs.'

'Exactly, Watson. Here is the fruit of my leisured ease, the magnum opus of my latter years!' He picked up the volume from the table and read out the whole title, *Practical Handbook of Bee Culture, with some Observations upon the Segregation of the Queen*. Alone I did it. Behold the fruit of pensive nights and laborious days, when I watched the little working gangs as once I watched the criminal world of London.'

'But how did you get to work again?'

'Ah, I have often marvelled at it myself. The Foreign Minister alone I could have withstood, but when the Premier also deigned to visit my humble roof——! The fact is, Watson, that this gentleman upon the sofa was a bit too good for our people. He was in a class by himself. Things were going wrong, and no one could understand why they were going wrong. Agents were suspected or even caught, but there was evidence of some strong and secret central force. It was absolutely necessary to expose it. Strong pressure was brought upon me to look into the matter. It has cost me two years, Watson, but they have not been devoid of excitement. When I say that I started my pilgrimage at Chicago, graduated in an Irish secret society at Buffalo, gave serious trouble to the constabulary at Skibbereen and so eventually caught the eye of a subordinate agent of Von Bork, who recommended me as a likely man, you will realize that the matter was complex. Since then I have been honoured by his confidence, which has not prevented most of his plans going subtly wrong and five of his best agents being in prison. I watched them, Watson, and I picked them as they ripened. Well, sir, I hope that you are none the worse!'

The last remark was addressed to Von Bork himself, who after much gasping and blinking had lain quietly listening to Holmes's statement. He broke out now into a furious stream of German invective, his face convulsed with passion. Holmes continued his swift investigation of documents while his prisoner cursed and swore.

'Though unmusical, German is the most expressive of all languages,' he observed, when Von Bork had stopped from pure exhaustion. 'Hullo! Hullo!' he added, as he looked hard at the corner of a tracing before putting it in the box. 'This should put another bird in the cage. I had no idea that the paymaster was such a rascal, though I have long had an eye upon him. Mister Von Bork, you have a great deal to answer for.'

The prisoner had raised himself with some difficulty upon the sofa and was staring with a strange mixture of amazement and hatred at his captor.

'I shall get level with you, Altamont,' he said, speaking with slow deliberation, 'if it takes me all my life I shall get level with you!'

'The old sweet song,' said Holmes. 'How often have I heard it in days gone by. It was a favourite ditty of the late lamented Professor Moriarty. Colonel Sebastian Moran has also been known to warble it. And yet I live and keep bees upon the South Downs.'

'Curse you, you double traitor!' cried the German, straining against his bonds and glaring murder from his furious eyes.

'No, no, it is not so bad as that,' said Holmes, smiling. 'As my speech surely shows you, Mr Altamont of Chicago had no existence in fact. I used him and he is gone.'

'Then who are you?'

'It is really immaterial who I am, but since the matter seems to interest you, Mr Von Bork, I may say that this is not my first acquaintance with the members of your family. I have done a good deal of business in Germany in the past and my name is probably familiar to you.'

'I would wish to know it,' said the Prussian grimly.

'It was I who brought about the separation between Irene Adler and the late King of Bohemia when your cousin Heinrich was the Imperial Envoy. It was I also who saved from murder, by the Nihilist Klopman, Count Von und Zu Grafenstein, who was your mother's elder brother. It was I——'

Von Bork sat up in amazement.

'There is only one man,' he cried.

'Exactly,' said Holmes.

Von Bork groaned and sank back on the sofa. 'And most of that information came through you,' he cried. 'What is it worth? What have I done? It is my ruin for ever!'

'It is certainly a little untrustworthy,' said Holmes. 'It will require some checking and you have little time to check it. Your admiral may find the new guns rather larger than he expects, and the cruisers perhaps a trifle faster.'

Von Bork clutched at his own throat in despair.

'There are a good many other points of detail which will, no doubt, come to light in good time. But you have one quality which is very rare in a German, Mr Von Bork; you are a sports-man and you will bear me no ill-will when you realize that you, who have outwitted so many other people, have at last been outwitted yourself. After all, you have done your best for your country, and I have done my best for mine, and what could be more natural? Besides,' he added, not unkindly, as he laid his hand upon the shoulder of the prostrate man, 'it is better than

to fall before some more ignoble foe. These papers are now
ready, Watson. If you will help me with our prisoner, I think
that we may get started for London at once.'

It was no easy task to move Von Bork, for he was a strong
and a desperate man. Finally, holding either arm, the two friends
walked him very slowly down the garden walk which he had
trod with such proud confidence when he received the con-
gratulations of the famous diplomatist only a few hours before.
After a short, final struggle he was hoisted, still bound hand and
foot, into the spare seat of the little car. His precious valise was
wedged in beside him.

'I trust that you are as comfortable as circumstances permit,'
said Holmes, when the final arrangements were made. 'Should I
be guilty of a liberty if I lit a cigar and placed it between your
lips?'

But all amenities were wasted upon the angry German.

'I suppose you realize, Mr Sherlock Holmes,' said he, 'that
if your Government bears you out in this treatment it becomes
an act of war.'

'What about your Government and all this treatment?' said
Holmes, tapping the valise.

'You are a private individual. You have no warrant for my
arrest. The whole proceeding is absolutely illegal and outrageous.'

'Absolutely,' said Holmes.

'Kidnapping a German subject.'

'And stealing his private papers.'

'Well, you realize your position, you and your accomplice
here. If I were to shout for help as we pass through the village——'

'My dear sir, if you did anything so foolish you would
probably enlarge the too limited titles of our village inns by
giving us "The Dangling Prussian" as a sign-post. The Englishman is a patient creature, but at present his temper is a little
inflamed and it would be as well not to try him too far. No, Mr

Von Bork, you will go with us in a quiet, sensible fashion to Scotland Yard, whence you can send for your friend Baron Von Herling and see if even now you may not fill that place which he has reserved for you in the ambassadorial suite. As to you, Watson, you are joining up with your old service, as I understand, so London won't be out of your way. Stand with me here upon the terrace for it may be the last quiet talk that we shall ever have.'

The two friends chatted in intimate converse for a few minutes, recalling once again the days of the past whilst their prisoner vainly wriggled to undo the bonds that held him. As they turned to the car, Holmes pointed back to the moonlit sea, and shook a thoughtful head.

'There's an east wind coming, Watson.'

'I think not, Holmes. It is very warm.'

'Good old Watson! You are the one fixed point in a changing age. There's an east wind coming all the same, such a wind as never blew on England yet. It will be cold and bitter, Watson, and a good many of us may wither before its blast. But it's God's own wind none the less, and a cleaner, better, stronger land will lie in the sunshine when the storm has cleared. Start her up, Watson, for it's time that we were on our way. I have a cheque for five hundred pounds which should be cashed early, for the drawer is quite capable of stopping it, if he can.'